BROKEN TEETH

CHRISTIAN WALLIS

Published by arrangement with the author.

YOU'RE READING ANOTHER TERRIFYING COLLECTION FROM

**FOLLOW VELOX TO KEEP
THE NIGHTMARES COMING:**

CONTENTS

IMMOLATION

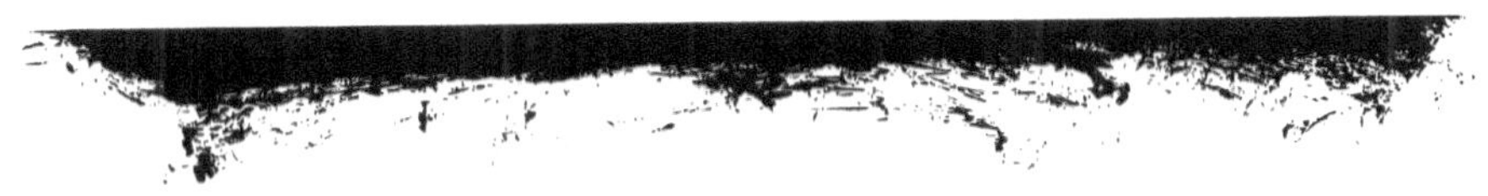

When Ben died, he made very little noise. It was the computers that alerted me. Shrill alarms and flashing lights. I hadn't even gotten out of my sleeping bag before my smart watch had lit up with half a dozen messages about system failures.

Astronaut 1—Heart rate monitor failure

Astronaut 1—Skin conductance monitor failure

Astronaut 1—VO2 monitor failure

The situation didn't sink in until I was shaking an unresponsive Ben. White eyes rolling back into his skull. Blood pooling in his ears like red jelly. Viscosity. Mass. No gravity. It made me nauseous to look at. HQ would later say Ben died from an aneurysm. One in a million. A freak death that just happened to occur in low Earth orbit.

So what now? I asked after all the panic had died down and the reality of my situation finally settled in.

HQ sent me a rarely used or discussed document that outlined what I'd have to do. Bodies pose a unique threat in microgravity, it explained. All that order becomes disordered. What is solid turns to liquid. What is liquid turns to gas. First thing I needed to do was to put Ben's body somewhere that had no oxygen and was freezing cold. Somewhere he would pose no danger to himself or me. Isolated, but easily retrievable. The conclusion was obvious.

I knew what they'd suggest before I even reached that part of the booklet. It happened so fast that Ben was still warm when I put him in the special bag designed to endure the vacuum of space. I kept expecting him to protest as I pulled at stiffening limbs and manipulated swelling joints. Every step of the process. Every zip. Every bit of velcro. I had to remind myself he wasn't going to complain. It felt intimate, but it wasn't. Intimacy requires two people. By that point, Ben was just meat.

The space walk itself was something else. The bag that surrounded Ben's body inflated in the vacuum and I instinctively felt the urge to undo what I'd done. There was a body in there, and bodies aren't meant to have so little between them and outer space. When I touched the bag, I could still feel him beneath the paper-thin material. The crease of an elbow. The bump of his nose. By the time I reached my destination, his body already felt brittle. Attaching him to the station was easy enough, on a technical level. Leaving him there went against every instinct I had.

After that, there was no pretending he was coming back. A day later and I began to pack his things away. There was a catharsis in it that I found calming. I catalogued his belongings with thin detachment. Most of his things were dry and uninteresting. Photos of him with a dog. A copy of a Michael Shea book. A certificate of excellence from NASA that he received when he was ten. He discovered a comet; he'd told me during our first meeting. Backyard with a telescope. NASA let him name it and everything. That was how he knew he wanted to be an astronaut. Described it as a calling. Ben was like that. A real life boy scout. In life he'd had no edges.

You'd think given our history, we'd be close. Two men selected based on extensive psychological profiling. Together, we had simulated multiple missions to Mars. Two on the ground. One in space. All of them highly secretive. An official mission to Mars was meant to be next, at which point the whole project would be made public. But the key to having two people work together, alone, for nearly an entire year isn't to find two guys who are best friends forever.

It's finding people who won't grate on one another. Neither hate nor love. Two men who enjoy their own company, but don't mind one another. Ben and I had become acquainted over all that time together, but it wasn't like we were brothers in arms. We worked so well precisely because there was no meat to the friendship. No stakes. Nothing to argue over. To me, Ben was a nice guy, but that was all. I figured he was plain and simple all the way down. No dark secrets. No real problems to speak of.

The journal changed that.

It was taped to the inside of a panel of a computer at his workstation. He must have hidden it close to his things, somewhere out of sight but easily retrievable. Frayed leaves and yellowed pages, like some ancient artefact. Last thing I expected to find in a space station. I almost mistook its leather cover for some sort of personal bible, the sort of well-worn tome held up by a preacher making exclamations about the devil, but its insides were handwritten, and hardly in keeping with a bible.

Scribbles. Shapes. Phrases repeated and dissected. Some of it was even in binary. It seemed like the ravings of a child or a lunatic. I thought it was maybe a mindfulness exercise. Empty-headed doodling to help him get his head straight during stressful moments. But that didn't explain why he'd hidden it, and why the numbers and pages seemed strangely organised. I don't know how to describe it, exactly. Except to say there was the vague impression that it meant *something* to the person who'd made it. Every last gram on a shuttle is accounted for. What you bring up with you, it can't be some random crap you want last minute. Ben would have had to clear the journal. I'm assuming he kept the contents secret. One look at what he'd been writing, and NASA would have had him in psych eval before the end of the day. But the book's size and weight would have had to be logged and accounted for. It could not have gotten on the station by accident, so I knew immediately that Ben had wanted it for something. I studied it for over an hour, trying to figure out what that was. Flicking from one page to the next, glaring at rows of numbers, strange fractals, something that looked like a cross between an eye and a textbook drawing of an atom. Given the way his writing and art skills developed throughout the book, I began to suspect he'd been adding to it since his childhood, which was just another layer to the growing mystery.

I thought I was never going to get any insight into the book until, about three-quarters of the way through, I came across yet another page filled with rows and rows of numbers. Only this time, one of the strings was underlined and a single word had been scratched ragged and angry next to it. The only bit of English, or any human language, in all those pages. The only thing written in a way that could make sense to a living human. The word itself made me stop dead in my tracks. Made my blood run cold.

170318042636 Aneurysm.

The suspicion that came over me felt like a kind of madness. I told myself I had to be nuts when I checked the data from Ben's biomonitor, that I had to be crazy to even entertain the notion, but the information recorded by several different machines confirmed it. Ben's exact time of death was the 17th March 2018 0426 hours and 36 seconds.

I don't think I moved for a good fifteen minutes after that. Just stared at the data as my mind worked its way around a giant, impossible, realisation.

Ben knew he was going to die.

Of course I tried to rationalise this. Anyone would. I came up with half-a-dozen reasons he'd written what he'd written. None of them were comforting, although they at least fit in with a more rational worldview. Take, for example, the idea that Ben had killed himself at that exact moment in time to meet some sort of prophecy he'd scrawled days or even hours before. Was that a good thing? What did it mean for me? Ignore the logistical issues (what poison can be timed to the second?). Let's just say that's what he did. That left the hair-raising question of *why?* And there was no comfortable answer that I could see. Of course I went through that book with a fine-tooth comb looking for any more clues. I wish I hadn't. I eventually found another word, this one closer to the very end of the journal. Another date and timestamp, one that lay six weeks in the future, and another word scratched painfully into the paper by a clumsy fist.

Immolation.

Permission denied.

I bit my lip and took a deep breath.

What about the station's integrity? I asked.

No sign of any issue from external cameras, they replied.

I can hear something banging on the hull, I told them.

Nothing is visible on the cameras.

That's why I need to go take a look, I wrote.

It's hard to argue with a computer. You can't shoot it a death-glare. HQ could have easily arranged video calls. But really they wanted the distance. Made it easier to say no.

Solo space walk is incredibly dangerous, they quickly wrote back. *Microphones in station hull are reporting nothing of concern. Usual impact from debris. Nothing that corroborates reports of external tapping. Permission for space walk is denied.*

I made no further response but instead closed the screen and wondered if they were being entirely truthful. The tapping sound, coming and going over the last few days, was unmistakable even over all those whirring machines and motors. Space stations are loud. They even give us ear plugs to handle it. But whatever was out there was somehow louder. Or perhaps, given the circumstances, I was just sensitive to the thought of something, *anything*, out there. There was no denying it annoyed me. Just one of those sounds I found impossible to block out, like water dripping in a bathtub at 3am. *Tap tap. Tap tap tap. Tap. Tap tap. Tap.* No sense of order, not on the surface level, but something, maybe. Underneath. Some sense or reason. Some kind of regularity that the brain detects and can't let go of.

How could the microphones possibly miss it?

Sleep was getting progressively difficult. At times I thought the station was under some kind of hidden stress. Materials freezing and warming in irregular ways. No atmosphere, no conduction of heat. Things get *hot* in the sun's rays. Objects warm and cool to both extremes. This is routine stuff for anything up in space, of course. But it didn't stop me thinking about all the ways the station was just a pile of metal that could come undone. Could break and tear. Bend and stretch. Like watching the wing of your plane wobble during turbulence, it's an uncomfortable reminder that you're just a monkey in a fancy toy.

And what if something had come loose? *Something*. Oh haha! At first I stuck to this notion strictly, asking myself what if some antenna or strap or bit of metal had gotten loose and was banging against the hull? That would be bad. But of course, that wasn't really what I was thinking. It's what I wrote to HQ about. Over and over and over. But what was really on my mind was the thought that maybe, somehow, *he* had gotten loose. And of course that's not so silly, right? The specially designed bag he was in, the one that would vent any gases produced by decomposition while maintaining his body's integrity, was brand-spanking new. Know how many times it had been tested? Never. Never ever. Ben was the first. So of course it might come loose. Just because its space age technology doesn't mean it's sophisticated. He was strapped to the outside like a Christmas tree to the family sedan. Maybe, I wondered, one of the straps had broken and now he was thumping against the side every now and again. Never mind that there wasn't anything out there to prompt that kind of buffeting. No air. No wind. If he'd come loose, he'd just float a little farther away. But *something* was making that noise, and I worried almost constantly that it was him.

Only problem was I had cameras. Lots. And all of them, every single time, showed the same thing. The bag, barely changed from when I last saw it in person, strapped firmly and securely to the station's hull. This should have reassured me. Should have, but it didn't. Something was out there, tapping at the hull. On and off. No pattern. No reason. No correlation. It came and it went, seemingly choosing its moments to bother me the most.

Sleep was difficult for multiple reasons. The tapping was bad enough, but lately my nightmares had taken a strange turn. Black. Cold. In them I was trapped in a suffocating film. Freezing cold. Non-stop agony, fighting furiously to free myself from this black void of a nightmare. Like all deeply terrible dreams, it coloured my thoughts for the rest of the day, and each time I had it, it got harder to shake. I tried to endure. Compartmentalise. Take my mental turmoil and put it in a box, write *unhinged* across the lid, and sit rocking back and forth, waiting for my rescue. And that *was* an option. A good one. But there was one little word that stopped me going the route of hunkering down and ignoring my own madness.

Immolation.

When HQ told me the date of the shuttle would reach me, I spent quite a bit of time wondering if this wasn't just some big experiment. The sheer coincidence of it all. The magnitude of it. They'd sent me the message and the subject line had three exclamation points, like the communications officer on the other side couldn't wait to deliver good news for once. Let their professionalism slip. They'd finally arranged a shuttle to retrieve me after it was done dropping some guys off at the ISS. It was lucky it'd come so soon. A stroke of logistical genius allowed them to sneak Ben and me back without it being too conspicuous. I should be very thankful, they told me.

But I was just stunned. The date matched the one Ben had written out. Factoring in travel time, I'd be entering Earth's atmosphere at the exact time the prophesied moment would come and go. Ripe for an error, a misplaced heat pad, a mistimed thruster... something, anything, to go wrong and leave me plunging to my death in a burning metal tube.

Ripe for immolation.

If it wasn't Ben out there tapping away, I wanted to know. I needed to know. I was a rational man. A sceptic. I did not believe the natural world would produce a man that could predict his death down to the minute, or the second. Nor did I believe he could predict mine. But I am only an animal. I am made of meat. Vulnerable. A raw nerve in a world of jagged rocks. And I am risk averse. That word. Immolation. Not random. Not chance. Up in the void surrounded by pure oxygen, fire was a constant risk. Ben's little numbers loomed large in my mind. I had to make sure everything was in place. Had to make sure there were no errors. If it was a prediction, which I refused to accept at face value, then maybe I could take heart from it. What could Ben do in the face of an aneurysm? Nothing! But immolation. Fire. An accident. That sort of thing could be avoided. Just so long as everything was in working order. Just so long as everything was where it was meant to be.

What did HQ know? Cameras and remote operators. Not enough. No one else was in that tin can except me. Why even have humans in space if you wouldn't trust their instincts and judgements?

I needed to know what was making that noise.

I needed to get out there.

HQ caught on too late. I was inside the suit, the airlock cycling by the time they realised. I chose my timing well. Halfway through my maintenance shift. Told them I was taking a look at the suit, make sure everything was in order. Meant they were slow to catch on to what I was doing. Technically they could stop the process at any stage. They could do anything from their side. But I threatened to force a manual override that would shut them out from that part of the system. They told me they'd court martial on return, but that was a piss-weak threat. For me, the stakes were higher than a court martial. In the end they backed down. Know how hard it is to build a space station in secret? It came first. If the space walk went wrong and I died, the station would still be there. A billion dollar asset awaiting the next top secret mission.

It was my neck on the line, not theirs. I accepted it. Under time pressure HQ accepted it too. By the time the door finally opened and I was able to gently guide myself out and around the rim so that I was clinging onto the station's exterior, they'd already tapped into the cameras and were guiding me along to my destination. But it was background noise to me at that point. Their voices and little pings. Constant readouts of suit temperatures and the distance to the station hull. Meaningless. All of it. What mattered was the sound. *Tap tap tap.*

I was anxious by this point. Or perhaps, if I'm honest, scared. Space is all extremes. Not just heat, but light too. The shadows cast are vast and strange. You move in and out of the Earth's shadow like it's a hand in front of a projector. And the ones cast by yourself and your surroundings are a special kind of black. The station, with its myriad of pipes and cables, was covered in abyssal shadows. Long warped things with ambiguous origins. Sometimes I looked at the darkness and wondered if there was anything there at all, or if the station was simply bisected by some kind of strange cosmic force. Like I might fall into it, somehow. Forever lost.

Normally I'd think it was beautiful. Space walks had for me, in the past, been an almost religious experience. This carried the same sense of weight, but for very different reasons. I felt watched. Something I tried to ignore, but it got harder and harder. Kept looking over my shoulder. Kept overthinking every little bump and vibration I felt on the station's hull. By the time I reached the place where I had strapped Ben's body I was close to a panic attack. That whole part of the station was covered in darkness. The kind where I couldn't see a damn thing. It was only HQ's voice telling me I'd reached my destination that let me know Ben was lying just a few feet from me. Under their direction I found him, and when my light fell upon the bag itself, I saw the metallic fabric glitter with ice. Touching it, I felt Ben's frozen body inside. Hard as rock. I gave him a nudge, and he didn't move an inch. The straps holding him in place were still there, firm as ever.

"What else could be causing the sound?" I asked.

"There is one option."

The nameless voice on the other end sounded reticent, but that had been the default since Ben died. HQ always sounded like they were holding something back.

"What's that?"

"We are not a hundred percent certain how corpses would respond to the changing temperatures in vacuum. Obviously, parts of the body will freeze and expand. Fluids, in particular. Right now the bag has a lot of surface contact with the metallic hull. One theory is that blood may be freezing and sublimating as the surface beneath changes temperature."

I looked at the bag and grimaced.

"How much... blood, exactly?"

"We cannot possibly say for certain how much would have left the body. Only that the bag's job is to contain it until return. We *are* able to confirm using instruments in the station that the panel you are standing on is well below freezing. Everything should be in a... *manageable* state, so to speak. Solid, likely one large clump." They replied, and then after a moment they added, "You wanted this. It would be a waste of resources now that you're out here not to investigate further. You need to look inside."

Of course I'd wanted this, hadn't I? To satisfy my morbid curiosity? To address the rabid thoughts in my mind that had kept me awake, filling what little sleep I had with nightmares. Now that I was at the threshold, I found myself so afraid that even moving my hand took a kind of effort. And yet I had no choice. I had to see this through.

The bag opened with a specially designed zipper. No sound, but I could *feel* the click-click-click of the specialised teeth opening up. It's stupid, but as I unfurled the flap I could've sworn a terrible foetid stench passed over me. It lasted no more than a few seconds, but was so vivid I turned and snapped my eyes shut as they watered. Power of suggestion, I told myself as I reopened them. That was all. Nothing more. No air. No sound. No smell. I took a few deep breaths, tried not to let the incident unsettle me further, and looked inside the bag.

Multiple people watching my video feed gasped while I made a fairly unflattering noise somewhere between a moan and a cry. I'd expected something... God, at worst I'd expected something ghoulish. Blue skin. Icicles collecting around the eyelashes. Like a body found in the Arctic. But Ben... Ben had transformed. Great jagged shards of frozen blood had erupted from the eyes and ears and mouth, his jaw dislocated to an unnatural angle as an icicle the size of my forearm forced its way out. His neck was broken, his torso shredded with strips of flesh hanging off in ribbons, and his hands were clawing at his face with bizarre yellow nails. They'd even left grooves in his skin.

"What the fuck is this?" I asked no one in particular, only to realise that HQ had been talking amongst themselves the whole time.

"A malfunction in the bag..."

"Unexpected pressure..."

"Temperature changes..."

"No no, this isn't normal. Let's not pretend this is normal!"

"Guys!" I shouted, splitting the chatter and leaving silence. "Why are his arms like that?"

"Uh, muscle spasms, possibly caused by... well, whatever caused the unusual reaction in his circulatory system. Maybe that caused his arms to curl up towards his face?"

"There are scratch marks on his cheeks," I replied. "Skin under his nails. Are we sure he was dead when I brought him out here?"

A dozen urgent, alarmed voices–all desperate to avoid even the slightest hint of responsibility–told me *no*, that was not possible. But looking down at Ben's tortured face, I couldn't help but feel a bit of doubt. I was about to ask what I ought to do next when the sun rose across the station. Unlike Earth, this wasn't a gentle morning. It flipped like a light switch. Thankfully the suit reacted before it had a chance to blind me, but the temperature began to rapidly climb. I watched as something beneath Ben's skin began to writhe in the new warmth.

"That's definitely not normal."

"We can offer no further insight into the situation as of this moment. The footage you're sending us is under review by a panel of experts," HQ told me, somewhat urgently and robotically, like the person on the other end was stifling panic. "Current orders are to take samples, reseal the bag, and return to the station."

"You sure I should be taking this stuff inside?"

There was some mumbling before the same operator replied.

"Forget samples. Seal the bag. Return to the station."

"Gladly," I replied, before pulling the zipper shut.

I was keen to leave and made the journey back faster than I should have. That crawling sensation you feel when being watched, it was all over me. Made me clumsy, and I knocked myself more than once on the way back, like I was suddenly unused to the suit's controls. I just couldn't escape the notion that everywhere I looked, someone or something had darted back just out of view. Of course that was impossible, so I told myself. What could survive out in space? But it only made it that much worse to imagine something slinking into the shadows. Tapping on the hull. Stalking me every step of the way back. When I finally reached the door, the tension inside me rose. If something was going to happen, it would happen now with my back turned on infinity. I had never felt so vulnerable.

"Uh, Reynolds."

The sound made me jump. I'd been so focused on my surroundings I'd forgotten I was being supervised by a room full of people a thousand miles away.

"What is it?"

"Reynolds, we're uh… we're seeing something here we're not sure of. Being told you should hold off on returning."

Something about the voice on the other end made my stomach sink. They didn't just sound confused, and make no mistake when you're clinging to the side of a station all on your own *confused* would have been bad enough. But no, there was something else.

Fear.

"We… there's an anomaly," they added. "No one down here knows how to proceed. We're currently seeking input from higher ups. This is unprecedented."

"What's going on?"

"It began with, well… *signals* from some of the biomonitors. Specifically Ben's."

That last word hit like a truck.

"What!?"

"Yes. And the cameras are… at first, we thought they were malfunctioning. It appeared as if Ben's bag was empty. And then… Reynolds we… we noticed something. Something else."

"Guys what's going on here?"

"I'm being told I can't say more. Just… just wait."

I tightened my grip on the railing, my heart pounding. Finally, the door cycled open, and I was ready to disregard all orders when the man speaking to me from HQ practically screamed in my ear.

"Don't enter! Reynolds. Do. Not. Enter the station! What we're seeing on the cameras, you can't let that in!"

"If something's out here, I'm getting to safety before it reaches me!"

Tap tap tap.

I stopped. My brain processed.

I'd *heard* that. I'd heard something in the vacuum of space. I looked around at my hands, my feet. That couldn't be possible. Not unless...

Tap. Tap tap tap. Tap tap.

Without moving my head I turned my eyes towards the very edge of my helmet's vision and watched as a single yellow fingernail tapped gently on the glass.

The man in HQ spoke in a terrifying whisper.

"He's on your suit."

The terror that shot through me was electric. White fire coursing through my veins. Without even thinking, I reacted like I'd just found out there was a grenade strapped to my back. All instinct. No rationality. I cried out and swung around, trying to knock Ben off my back, but all I accomplished was setting off some alarms as I damaged my suit.

"Get it off!" I screamed at no one in particular. "Get it off me!"

I thrashed desperately and felt something shuffling around the exterior of the bulky suit. Finally, my eyes fell on something useful. The jet controls. I fumbled my hands into place and immediately blasted myself into the open pressure chamber, turning at the last minute so that the back of the suit smashed into the thick secondary door. I only hoped that whatever was clinging to the back of me was destroyed by the impact, but when I looked up Ben was still out there gawping at me with a mouth full of frozen blood.

Slowly, his movement packed with the eerie confidence of a predator, he prepared to enter the station.

"Reynolds, get away from the door! We're initiating an emergency shutdown."

Ben had one hand inside when the door slammed shut and cut it off. Even in space with the bulkhead between us, I could've sworn I heard him scream.

There was no ignoring Ben or the sounds he made. Not anymore. Terrible thumps that battered the station, their location changing seemingly at random. This drove the people on the ground insane. Oh I'd heard my fair share of rationalisation over the last few hours. Been sent book's worth of written material from every type of expert you could imagine. Ever since my colleague's death I'd been wrestling with all sorts of bizarre thoughts, but after the space walk it was like they'd spilled out of my head and were now terrorising other like-minded sceptics. Try as they might, no one in HQ could make sense of it.

But they didn't have the journal.

After what happened during my space walk, it became a priority for me to figure out what the fuck was going on. Those numbers Ben had recorded weren't gibberish. I'd sort of known that from the start. To read them was to feel like you were reading another language. Something secret and hidden. And while I never cracked the code, not even now after all this time, I did figure out where Ben had found it.

Light.

The trick was to dig deeper into Ben's research. Specifically, a pet project of his he'd spent nearly his entire life chasing. A little comet, a ball of ice, way out in the Kepler belt close to where the solar system abates and the great cosmic void begins. Something small and insignificant that rotated and shifted and occasionally caught the sun, bouncing photons right back at us. A glittering snowball so faint as to be invisible unless you happened to look at the right place at the right time.

Like Ben did, when he was just ten and playing with hobbyist Dad's backyard telescope.

A light in the darkness. A light that spoke to a few instruments Ben had adjusted to record each little emission. Flash on. Flash off. Flash on. Flash off. Flash on.

Tap. Tap. Tap.

Binary to hexadecimal and from there... God, something else. Something that spoke to him.

Something *out there* had spoken to him.

I don't know what scared me more. The sound of a re-animated Ben pounding away at the station, an imminent all-too-near threat. Or the thought of something in the void whispering unknown secrets to a man for the last two decades. An idea that occasionally rose over me like the tide, swallowing me whole if I dwelt on it for more than a few moments. I never did figure out what the transmission was saying, but I was transfixed nonetheless. Not just by Ben's little journal that contained hundreds, thousands, of handwritten records. But the live transmission he had set up on his computer, the one he'd converted into a sound. It was like an earworm on steroids. Like white noise made of acid, a flood of alien ideas that left me confused and drooling if I listened for too long. All told I spent no more than a few days with access to that transmission and by the end I felt like I was on the verge of melting away. But Ben... Ben had been exposed to that thing since his childhood. Spent years and years listening and recording and waiting, working towards something none of us could really hope to understand. I had to assume that transmission was responsible for his death, and even worse, what had happened to him afterwards. Had it always been the reason for his coming to space?

Had the Ben I'd known just been a sham?

The sound... the light coming from out *there*. It felt wrong. It wasn't a gentle lull or a siren's pull. It was dark and overpowering. Why had he given into it? Why had he done everything it wanted? How much of his life had been lived because of its needs and wants?

One thing I could be sure of as I spent days listening to Ben's furious rampage on the exterior of the station, whatever had spoken to him...

It was hostile, and it couldn't be allowed to come back with me.

⸻

"Reynolds, I'm being told this is going to be a bit of unconventional pickup."

I scoffed as I finished suiting up. That was an understatement.

"What did they tell you?" I asked as I pulled the helmet down and initiated the door's opening sequence.

"There are concerns about contamination," the pilot told me. "Not sure what that means. Didn't say if it was biological or chemical. All sounds a little weird if you ask me. But we're meant to pick you up mid-space walk. Is that right?"

"Yup," I replied.

"Huh. You up for that? We're told we can come about 200 metres away, but you'll have to close the rest with the suit's thrusters. Gonna be something else for you. Untethered journey from one vehicle to the next. It's never been done before"

"I'm well aware of the risks," I said. "Just keep your eyes peeled."

This time, it was his turn to scoff.

"For what?" He cried.

"You'll know it when you see it."

⸻

I made the journey with my back to the shuttle, floating in the wrong direction at a slow but consistent speed. My eyes glued to the station, looking for some signs of Ben. There was the occasional flash of something red, a slight shimmer of movement often obscured by some of the station's panels and antennae, that let me know he was still on the exterior, skulking around somewhere. So long as he stayed there, I knew I'd be okay. But the entire time I kept waiting for the other foot to drop. For the tension to finally explode into that life-threatening danger I knew was waiting for me. It came as a surprise when I finally approached the shuttle without incident. Pilot told me I was a few metres away and it was time to turn around, so I did, drifting around as gently as a diver returning to the surface.

I had my back to the station no more than a few seconds when the pilot grunted.

"Huh. That's odd."

He sounded nonchalant, but the object that hit me was anything but minor. Ben, uninterested in making the journey safely, had launched himself off the station as fast as he could. And with no way of slowing down he hit me at full speed, slamming me up against part of the door frame and sending us both tumbling out into the void before anyone had even had the time to register his attack.

This time he was not letting me get a door between us. He scrambled over my suit like a deranged insect, one that I desperately tried to swat away as the great void spun around us both. Stars turned to lines, the shuttle swooping past my helmet's field of view in almost random directions. It was sickening and terrifying, and I hoped to God I'd be able to correct the spin before it got out of control, but all of that came second to the monster who was clinging to my suit. At some point, he crawled around in such a way that I got a good look at him, the first in a few days. It was up close. Personal. Even with the helmet's glass between us, I could make out such stark and startling detail that I momentarily froze in terror, aware only vaguely of the pilot's panicked transmissions.

"Jesus Christ, what the fuck is that thing? Reynolds you need to get yourself stabilised! Much further and we won't be able to help. And whatever you do, you need to know, that fucking thing isn't coming aboard this shuttle!"

I wanted to reply, but I was busy trying to get an arm between me and Ben, who was now a profusion of jagged red crystals of varying sizes. Some as big as kitchen knives, others like sewing needles. A space suit's worst nightmare. A puncture wouldn't lead to the immediate decompression you're probably thinking of. Instead I'd have a few moments at most before the air enveloping the suit dissipated and after that my lungs would collapse, my blood would start to boil, and the water inside my eyes, nose, ears and other soft tissues would vaporise and try to escape. Like frostbite on fast-forward. But punctures weren't my sole concern. I knew I had to stop Ben's hands getting a grip on the helmet. I don't know if whatever had animated him had access to all his memories, but Ben sure-as-shit knew how to remove a helmet from the exterior, so all my focus went on keeping his nasty little fingers away from my neck. A puncture would still leave me enough time to return to the shuttle, but with no helmet, I'd be doomed to a very painful death.

So I fought the best I could, knowing everything hinged on me pushing him away. But Ben was lithe and insectile, constantly slipping out of reach whenever I got close to giving him a good shove. His fingers could easily find purchase on the suit and its many little greebles, while I was basically wielding oven gloves that offered no dexterity. I had no hope of shaking him off the usual way, but I did have something on my side. Inertia. The whole time we'd been spinning furiously, and that rotational force was just about the only thing trying to peel the two of us apart. So far I'd been fighting it, but why? I realised at the last moment I had one option left, so I jammed half thrusters on and decided to make the nearly-out-of-control spin much *much* worse.

Normally an uncontrolled spin is one of those nightmare scenarios any astronaut dreads. Humans are irregularly shaped, and once you start rotating along more than one axis, applying more force is likely just to make it worse. Correcting takes a huge amount of experience and insight, and even then, there's no guarantee you can stop it. More likely is that by the time you figure out what you need to do, the rotational forces will have you on the brink of unconsciousness. And from there, death is just a stone's throw away.

For me, it was the only chance I had.

So I accelerated the spin, and kept accelerating, holding the button down until the forces at play pulled Ben further and further towards the front of the suit. That's where inertia wanted us. Two objects in near symmetry, ready to break off in opposite directions at any moment. Ben held on for longer than I did. At some point my limbs went weak, my vision dark, and my arms fell to my side, no longer able to fight the monster off. But by then it took everything Ben had just to cling onto me and he could no longer attack or fumble at my helmet. Eventually, even he had to give in as the spin grew faster and faster and the forces trying to separate us grew too strong. It was like every rollercoaster I'd been on merged into one, and ramped up to eleven.

The last thing I remembered before I lost consciousness was the sight of Ben's monstrous face being flung off into the void.

———

I came to board the shuttle, several men and women crowded around me.

"Jesus Christ, you're a lucky sonnofabitch."

I groaned and made eyes towards the person who had spoken. It sounded like the pilot. Nice to put a face to the voice.

"I don't feel lucky," I gasped.

"You spun right towards us. We were already suited up and on our way. Timed up well. That suit was riddled with holes. Any later and we wouldn't have been around to catch you and get you into safety. As it is pal, you're going home. Medical check shows no real issues. I think you're going to be okay."

"Where's... where's Ben?"

The people around me shared a funny look before one of them realised.

"Benjamin Whateley? The other astronaut onboard. Is that what... *who* was attacking you?"

I nodded.

"Well, he's gone," they replied. "If that really was your colleague, we're... well, we're sorry. I feel like there's a story we're missing."

"I'll catch you up when I'm feeling better," I coughed.

"Well, whatever happened to him, he'll be reentering Earth's atmosphere in the next hours," the pilot replied.

"What then?" I asked.

The pilot thought for a second.

"Human body on reentry? He'll go up in flames.

"Immolation."

DRIVE THRU

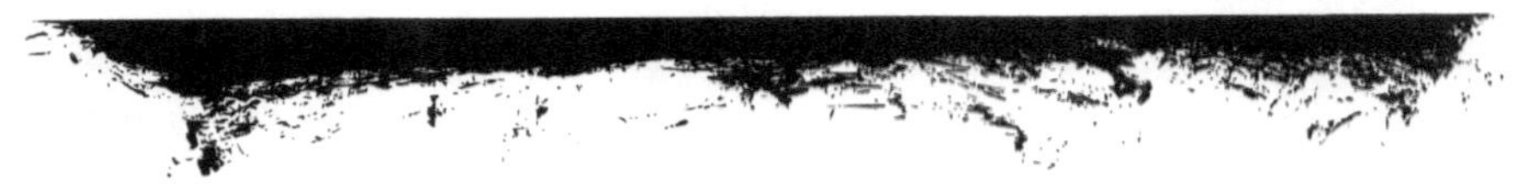

I've worked at every McDonald's in a forty-mile radius of my house. Over the years, I've gotten a reputation as a good "filler" guy. Someone you can call on to deal with sudden absences, firings, and unwanted nightshifts. I'm just about old enough that some of the managers trust me, but I've never gone far enough to get a decent promotion. I've been stuck in a kind of limbo. My Dad told me it happens. Sometimes if you agree to take the shit jobs, you become so useful to a company that they'll never fire or promote you. Up until recently that kinda suited me fine. I was on autopilot for a long time, and I enjoyed the quiet shifts and the way I was trusted by my bosses without ever being given more responsibility.

But some jobs are too much, even for me. One place, well... I don't have words. I've been there as a customer dozens of times. It's perfectly normal in the day, but sometimes I get called in to cover the night shift and it's the worst place I've ever been. For a start, they only keep one active member of staff on-site during night shifts. Apparently, it's something to do with policy to always offer 24-hour service, but the people I've spoken to have made it clear the manager doesn't want to keep the store open at night so he sticks to the bare minimum he can get away with.

One solitary person... Every time I think about covering that shift, I wonder how the hell anyone could do that job and keep a hold of their sanity. I can't even understand how anyone let it get that bad, or how anyone could ever think it's normal. I've heard of managers brushing stuff under the carpet, but...

I don't know.

Y'know night shifts are always lonely, but this place is something else. It's on a motorway junction by a small village that never recovered from the recession. Nearby there's a petrol station that isn't staffed past 11pm, a Starbucks that never even opened its doors, and a mechanic that I'm pretty doesn't do a damn thing no matter what time of the day it is. Oh, and a carwash that hasn't worked since the first Toy Story came out.

So come night time, it's just us, this little glassy McDonalds with happy mascots and bright lights standing like an island of bright fluorescent light in a sea of sepia darkness. Overhead you've got a ramp that leads to the motorway, close by are four dual carriageways that criss-cross an enormous roundabout, and between all of that there are speeding trucks, tricked-out cars zooming past blasting cheap electronic music, and... well there's nothing else. No fields, no paths, no pavements, no shops, no houses, nothing. This isn't a place made for humans, it's made for cars. And I guess that's why the McDonald's survived because the drive-thru is always busy.

But at night time it means there's this horrible atmosphere. Overhead you can hear the cars zooming by, and there are great big lampposts that bathe everything in amber, and the occasional nighttime traveller stopping for a 3am cheeseburger, but that's it. I've never worked anywhere so dead. Some nights, it's just me and I gotta be honest, it's terrifying. It's more than just loneliness, it's actually terrifying.

There's something out there.

It sounds stupid, but there is. The first time I turned up, the manager took me aside and told me I needed to fill a cup up with fat from the fryer and leave it by the open drive-thru window. I laughed, but he just groaned, grabbed a nearby cup and filled it up, anyway. He put it by the window and told me I couldn't move it. I was expecting some kind of banter, thinking it was a practical joke. But he didn't even bother. It was like he just couldn't be fucked to explain it, so he just did it himself.

That was my first night. Nothing happened, not really. Traffic died down, staff started going home, and bit-by-bit things died down until the only sound was the occasional passing engine. I started to feel severely isolated, even a little scared, which was a weird feeling to have at work. I was standing by the open window looking out on the drive-thru and the darkness on the other side started to feel like it was more than just shadow. The drive-thru was just this swervy little u-bend covered by tall hedges and at night it got no light. It was like a solid sheet of black, a total absence of light, and I was standing so close I almost touched the darkness. I wanted to reach out and shut the window or just get myself as far away as I could, but I also kept reminding myself that I was freaking out for no reason.

At least that's what I thought until I looked down and saw the cup of fat had disappeared.

I remember looking up and staring into the darkness, trying to figure out if I was tripping out over nothing or if the cup of fat really had moved. I felt my fingers start to tingle, and my mouth became dry. But there was nothing standing outside that window. Aside from the wind and sound of passing commuters, there was no one anywhere around except me. I mustered up every ounce of bravery and poked my head out the window and looked left to right, and damn near got decapitated by a car pulling up to the window way too fast, rubber tyres squealing on the road as it slammed to a stop opposite me.

I jumped a mile and suddenly the whole world returned to its boring normal self. It was just a bunch of drunk guys who wound up staying for about half an hour while they repeated their order a dozen times each. By the sixteenth time I'd been asked to remember dips, I was so angry that I'd forgotten all about the cup of fat. After that, I sort of just dismissed all my anxieties. The drunk guys were total idiots, but they did help me feel like my feet were back on the ground and the rest of my shift passed nice and quickly.

I hoped that would be the last of my creepy experiences in that place, but after that things got worse. Despite telling myself that nothing had really happened, I kept filling the cup of fat and leaving it by the drive-thru window. Each time I'd leave and come back to find it gone, I'd feel a little anxiety, and that made it hard to stay by the open window. I just felt like anything could reach out and grab me, like I could be standing there looking right at something and I wouldn't even know it.

And the sounds... Sometimes you'd catch the faintest scrape, or shuffle, or hushed breath. It's like when you know someone's looking at you, or how you're not alone in a room. I just knew on some weird instinctual level that there really was something outside in that yawning darkness. Even if it just looked like shadows moving in darkness, I could tell that I wasn't totally alone.

That's why I took to staying a little longer after the end of each shift, just to go look outside by the window. Most days I never saw something, but sometimes I'd see bits of the hedge looking broken or busted up. Nothing serious, just a few odd snapped twigs, but it definitely looked like someone or something big had scraped up against them. Of course, that could easily be a car or a van, so I was never sure. But sometimes I'd see the odd drop of fat running down the leaves, no more than a small drip. But enough to tell me something was out there.

I even managed to get a hold of the security tapes. Unfortunately, they were piss-poor quality, and all they show of the drive-thru itself (aside from me standing in a window) is total darkness. You can't make out a thing. As for the disappearing fat-shake? Well, when that happens, all the camera sees is a shadow blotting out the window. When the shadow moves, the cup of fat is gone. I've stared at that grainy footage for hours, and all I ever really saw was the faintest sense of something big moving in the darkness. But even knowing what I know now, I'm still not sure that's anything more than my imagination.

There are others, of course. I've heard a few strange stories. A while back some girl supposedly went missing from her shift, but a quick google of her name showed a news story where she'd been killed by a violent ex, although no body was found. I spoke to one guy who mentioned a kid finding a nearby drainage ditch filled with hundreds and hundreds of empty McDonald's drinks, which is supposedly where the cups of fat go. I did try looking one day but never found anything. Then again, it's a nightmare to walk around here, especially in the day. And I can't quite bring myself to abandon my shift and go looking at night.

Another story said that it's common knowledge that if a fat fryer is left for long enough, things start to live in it. One day, years back, some new manager finally went in and ordered a new fat fryer but when they emptied the old one (an ancient piece of kit that I was told had never been cleaned, ever) something black and slimy was left at the bottom. Caked in fat and looking like no animal or person anyone had ever seen, this thing slipped away when no one was looking, leaving a trail of fat between the restaurant and a nearby sewage drain. I did mention this story to one manager, and he pulled one hell of a face and told me:

"Yeah I remember that, but there wasn't anything at the bottom of the fryer. Besides, nothing could have crawled because we tipped it straight into the drain anyway, so there couldn't have been a trail."

Which I took to be a reasonable explanation, although someone else told me that particular manager hadn't even been in on that day.

But after just a few days of asking around, I had enough stories to fill a book and almost all of them conflicted in some way. None of them ever really made much sense to me. In some ways, they felt more like lazy attempts to fill in the blanks. They were just urban legends, but I wasn't happy with just tall tales. A few people even asked me: why do I care so much? And the answer was real simple:

Because I had to share my shift with something, and no one could tell me what it was. Something was out there taking that cup of fat!

I tried tying a string around the cup once but came back to it rolled up neatly by the window. Another time I left one empty cup and one full cup, only to find both cups gone when I came back. Later that night, the empty one was returned, untouched, outside the front of the restaurant doors. Writing it out now, it all seems benign, playful even. But it wasn't. I know it's hard to explain, but it didn't *feel* playful, at least not a friendly kind of playful.

For a while, I didn't have anything to back that feeling up. That is until one night I decided to do one more experiment. This time I left the cup further back from the window, by about ten feet. I don't even know what I was expecting? I just wanted to try and learn something more I guess—something about what was taking the cup. You know the weird thing is, looking back, I can tell that people were giving me pretty strong hints to leave it be. It just pissed me off. I go from place to place, never fitting in. They all have their in-jokes and their petty cliques. I just resented that I had to be so directly involved in this one. I mean, I had to be the one who actually put the cup out there, but no one was decent enough to explain why. I think some other frustrations got caught up in it all, and I couldn't quite bring myself to just leave it be.

I never saw it, at least not all of it. What I remember more than anything was the sound. It's like the image in my head changes all the time. The details move around, and the size and order of events change. But the sound was a constant nightmarish squeal. I remember that sound with perfect clarity, even as the image fades away like a nightmare on waking.

When I came back in that night, having left the cup alone for a few moments, I stopped by the doorway. Nothing had appeared, yet. But a hot gust of wind blew in from outside like an animal's breath. It tussled my hair, and I immediately knew something was wrong. I couldn't see a thing outside that window, just a veil of black. But I got the sense something was pressed up close to the other side. And then, like a dream, that something reached out, groping towards the corner of where I usually left the cup. It looked like a hand made of elephant skin? It was bony and gnarled, but the skin looked thick and crumpled like the hide of a rhino, except paler. And even though the arm was thin, like really bizarrely thin, the hand had these chubby fingers like an oversized kid's.

You know I nearly laughed? That can happen during shock. This thing was like a dream. It took a second or two before the fear caught up with me. And when it did, I couldn't even move a muscle. This hand just came out of the darkness and just started swatting around, looking for the cup. And when it couldn't find it, it didn't just stop. It kept going. I found my heart racing as it started to strain in my direction. It reached out and slowly started to stretch.

The room filled with a sound like nails on a chalkboard. And I remember thinking that none of this was possible, even as bones and skin grew and pulled themselves out of all proportion. Muscles snapped, skin turned paper-thin, revealing blue spidery veins and slick looking flesh. And eventually even the skin gave way so that tattered flesh and strips of tissue hung off... I don't even know. It wasn't bone. It was black, and pitted, like tar rolled into a long thin strip.

One foot, two foot, three, and soon much more. By the time I realised it was going to reach me, I started to scream and tried to move backwards, but I fell. My mind and body became useless to me, and I was just crying hysterically as this fat-fingered monstrosity came closer, my imagination filled with images of me being dragged into the darkness beyond even as I tried to desperately get some purchase on the slippery tile floor.

I kept screaming even after it reached the counter just above me, grabbed the fat, and slowly withdrew back into the darkness, that awful chalkboard screech fading down as the arm disappeared back into shadow.

They found me in the disabled bathroom in the morning. I didn't remember going in there, but I do remember waking up feeling as though I was still stuck in a nightmare. I opened the door and fled back home and, as if confirming my suspicions, I later found out my manager didn't say a thing about it to anyone. When I later tried getting some CCTV footage off him, he told me it wasn't available. He knew damn well what had happened. I heard one kid whining about having to clean up after me. When I asked what he meant, he talked about the "fucked up paper and rotten chicken" he found all over the floor.

The only thing I ever got out of the manager was when he got frustrated and snapped at me after I threatened to go to the police.

"No one's been hurt for years!" he cried out. And then suddenly realising what he'd said, he added, "No one's been hurt. So there's nothing to report! I've tried, plenty of times."

But I wouldn't let it go. In the end, you know what he did to get me off his back? He installed bars on the window. They had a little square where you could feed some items through, and they could even be opened from the inside to let us hand out the bigger orders. And then he acted like that was it, job done. But I remembered that hand stretching out, and those bars didn't do much to comfort me. They'd stop a random attacker, sure. But that thing that came out of the darkness?

It wasn't enough to get me back on my shift. I only had one left, but I still threatened to quit if they tried to make me do it. I only gave in when the manager himself agreed to sit in on it with me. After that, I was told I'd never have to work in that branch ever again. Reluctantly, I felt like I had to agree. I didn't exactly have other options, and my parents were pretty ruthless when it came to charging me rent. Plus... I don't know. This is stupid. But I still kinda felt like I was dreaming, y'know? I wanted to wake up. I wanted to prove that this was just a fucked up nightmare.

It was a tense shift. The manager was pissed that he had to stay up all night, and I was pissed he'd covered up what had happened, so there wasn't much conversation. The only time we interacted was when he placed the cup of fat by the window and then checked the bars. I took the time to tell him he'd have to stay by the window, because I sure as hell wouldn't. For a moment, he looked like he was going to try and have a go at me, but I think he realised it was pointless and let it go.

After all, it was just one more night, right?

Around half three, I heard a noise from the drive-thru. There was a bang and a loud cry, and I rushed to my feet, heart pounding. I burst around the corner only to find the manager stood there swearing loudly, his feet and legs covered in fat. He'd knocked the fucking cup over, hadn't he? Bang, smack, straight down his legs and all the floor. I laughed, which pissed him off, even though I was laughing from relief and not at his misfortune. I tried to explain, but he just barked at me to get another cup.

I was filling it up when this time, the screaming came back. I knew on some level this was different, so I didn't run straight around the corner. I walked, slowly, and turned to find the manager backing up towards me as that grotesque hand flailed around looking for a cup. Immediately the manager turned, saw me, and grabbed the cup I held and threw it in the direction of the window. But it just limply hit the bars and thudded to the floor where the hand, quick as a whip, followed it down. Except the cup had only ever been half-full in the first place.

I'd never had the time to fill it properly.

So those lifeless grey fingers just dabbed at a small pool of fat, somehow managing to look disappointed. And then... it snapped up, like a snake fixing its eyes on prey. The manager and I both looked down at him and saw his legs covered in fat and I immediately started to scream for him to take his trousers off. But it was too late. Before they were even around his shins, the sound started. God, it got into your head. It was like a drill piercing your deepest thoughts. It hurt just to hear. And the manager was left trying to pull his fat-soaked trousers off with one hand while he covered his bleeding ears with the other.

And that hand... it just kept coming. When it was a few feet away, I grabbed him and started to pull, but we both slipped and fell on some of the fat that had dripped off his clothes. We were both so terrified we were trying to climb over each other just get away. If we'd just taken some time, we probably could have escaped real easy. But something about that hand filled me with a hysterical need to get away.

And just like that, it grabbed him. And just as slowly as it had reached out, it started to pull him back in. It dragged him all the way, his screaming desperate and pitiful, until finally, he reached the bars.

I don't think either of us knew what to expect. But just as his knee reached the bars, he looked up at me with wide eyes.

"Open the bars!" he screamed. "Jesus Christ, open them now! Open them now!"

I ran forward and tried not to look as I fumbled with the padlock.

"Where's the keys!?" I cried, only to hear a loud cracking.

His knee had been forced through the bars. Blood was now running copiously down the metal frame and onto the counter-top, and the manager's cries were the worst sound I'd ever heard a human mouth make. His eyes were like marbles, and I realised I'd be lucky if he could manage even a simple word.

And those screams just kept getting louder.

And louder.

And louder.

It never sped up. It dragged him through, and he stayed alive for so long. Even when it pulled his thigh through, leaving long strips of gored fat and muscle dangling from the bone, even when loud thunderous cracks filled the room, even when it pulled so hard his free leg was pushed up against the side of his face, it never slowed down or sped up.

And his screams...

It pulled him through. All the way through. And what was left on the other side looked like blocks of meat and bone. The last thing I saw was his head started to crack and crumple, his face pushed together like a squashed tomato while the skull behind grew elongated and broken. He was long-dead by that point, but somehow he still looked like he was in so much pain.

Eventually, something broke, and I ran screaming into the disabled toilets. When I awoke, guess what I found?

Nothing.

No mess. No blood. No gore. Sometime ago an article was published mentioning how the manager had gone missing, but there are a few managers in this branch, and I wonder if one of the others had got here early and cleaned up? Or maybe that thing on the other side did it? I don't know. Deep down I'd be happy to call it all a dream...

Except you know what I found waiting by my car that morning when I finally left?

An empty McDonald's cup filled with bloody fat. This wasn't the kind of fat you'd find from a fryer. No. This was more like the kind you'd strip out of a cadaver, or maybe off a piece of meat. I even heard reports of a fox being found with a bloody shoe in its mouth somewhere close by. Just yesterday, someone posted to Facebook talking about an old McDonald's uniform found blocking a drainage pipe in the village.

They're still trying to get me to take over from the manager who went missing. I guess I finally found the shittiest job of all, and they think I'm ideal. Ring ring ring ring ring. The phone keeps going, but I won't answer. It's like it's just another working hazard to be swept under the rug. But I can't... I can't possibly go back to that sound. I can't keep serving that awful thing.

THE SCAR

She was charming and confident throughout the whole meal, regularly reaching across to touch my arm while making consistent, engaging, eye contact. She laughed openly and sincerely, rolled her eyes when I was self-deprecating, and spoke openly about her own vulnerabilities. Over the course of the dinner, I started to feel more comfortable and less anxious, and without fully understanding why, I noticed a strange warmth in my chest and stomach that I had never felt before. She had brown eyes and chocolate coloured hair that fell around her bare shoulders in harmonious locks. She looked like a woman straight out of a noir film, and she exuded a self-confidence that was not only attractive but, to many men, would have been downright intimidating. And yet, by the end of the date, when she held my hand, I did not find myself filled with doubts about why she wanted me, or what she saw in me. I trusted her affections in a way I never could with any other woman. Her charisma was infectious, and when we stepped out into the cold city air, I truly, genuinely, felt like I'd stepped into a fairy tale.

That was the last thing I remembered before waking up in a bathtub full of ice. The shock was so sudden there was a moment where I felt like I'd been plunged into a lucid nightmare. For the first few seconds I thought of nothing save the agony vaguely located along my left side and the stinging ice burns across my naked body. Everything hurt. It felt like I'd been in a car crash. My vision was blurry as if my eyelids were gummed together, each blink felt like rubbing sand into my eyes, and when every breath out felt like approaching suffocation.

My limbs were weak, but I pushed myself out of the ice and into a sitting position, letting out short sharp shocked exhalations as ice cubes fell down my naked stomach and shoulders. I was covered in a sickly condensation and I ran my hands over my body, shocked to find that I could barely feel anything. Desperate to escape, I started to heave myself over the edge of the bath. But without feeling in my legs, I couldn't just step out; it was like climbing a 10-foot fence.

About halfway across, gravity took over, and I slipped over the edge and fell like a piece of meat, hitting the concrete with a wet thud. My chin struck hard and drove my bottom teeth upwards into my lips with an audible clack as they cut straight through to the other side. I cried out in pain and anger and laid there, dribbling onto bloody spittle onto the dusty floor until my legs began to warm up and my eyes began to clear. I was in a warehouse, barely able to see more than a few feet in any direction, but I finally managed to collect enough thoughts to wonder where the hell I was, and what the hell had happened.

I tried to pull myself forward, although I was too numb and sore to get very far. But the mere act of movement helped gather more strength, and I found that bit by bit feeling returned to my legs, fingers, and arms. But clarity brought its downsides. There had been a constant dull pressure in my side since I'd first awoken, but as the cold receded, it felt like someone had stuffed hot coals into an open wound. In terrible pain, I sat upright and leaned back against the freezing cold porcelain of the tub. I twisted carefully until I caught a glimpse of my sides. The mere sight distressed and enraged me.

There was a fat swollen scar cut across the soft fat of my flank, the ridges as thick as a finger, the skin molten and jagged, the tear pink and bloody. Stitches as wide as shoelaces pierced the skin and bound the walls of the scar tightly together. I got the sense that if I put any real pressure against the fissure, my finger would push right through and I would feel my innards swishing around inside.

"What the fuck!?" I cried, my words slurred and pathetic. "What the fuck!? What the fuck!? *What the fuck!?*"

—————

"What happened?"

"I don't know. I just need you to come get me."

"James I don't get it. I haven't heard from you in over a—"

"Annie please just come fucking get me please. Something happened. I don't know what but please just come fucking get me I sent you the pin on google maps just come get me."

"I've never heard you sound so—"

"*Just come fucking get me!*" I screamed and then hung up. I was shaking, standing in the rain as my stomach churned and my head throbbed. I had limped a mile and a half along a desolate road until I came across a small spot where I got reception. I had been crying on and off for hours, and I genuinely wondered if it would have hurt less to die.

The warehouse I had woken up in was abandoned. There were no signs of life except for gory surgical instruments and a terrifying dentist's chair modified with restraints and straps. Fresh spatters of blood coated the floor, newer stains layered over older burgundy coloured ones, and a quick look at my wrists confirmed they were bruised and marked from being tied down. On a nearby table were the clothes I'd been wearing from the date, and while my wallet and keys were missing, my phone was neatly placed on top of the folded jeans and jacket.

They had even been laundered, along with my socks and underwear. There were even a pair of walking shoes in my size (but which were not mine) placed carefully beside the clothes. I took them, having little choice, and quickly escaped, only to find myself abandoned in the middle of a huge forest with nothing but a dirt road to follow.

It took hours to get decent phone reception, and then another six before my sister finally found me. She was winding the window down to ask an endless series of questions when something caught her eye.

"What?" she stammered, and a quick look at my side revealed that my jacket was coated in pinkish pus that leaked from my side.

I went to explain but found my strength suddenly leeched from me. I collapsed on the spot.

"How does no one know this woman, Gary!?" Annie was pacing in the background of my vision. I watched her as if she was a TV show where the volume was being slowly turned up. "She *assaulted* my brother. I need to know who the *fuck* she is! *How could you not know who this woman is!?*"

She was growing angrier by the minute. It had been like this for days, maybe longer. She'd been the one to set me up on the blind date, and it was clear that she felt guilty. She had knelt beside me often as I lay on her sofa and promised me all kinds of things. If she knew she would never have arranged the date, this woman wasn't a total stranger, people vouched for her, they worked at the same company for years, she'd seen her dozens of times taking the lift, they'd even all gone out for Caz's hen party!

It had transpired early on that the woman who appeared was not the woman my sister worked with, but I was still confused and struggled to care. Days had come and gone. I knew I was pumped full of drugs, and they were messing with my head. I had only fleeting memories of a hospital stay, but Annie later told me I was in there for two weeks before being discharged. As time went on all I wanted was for a sense of normality to return. I wanted to see the world with lucid eyes, clean from the fog and confusion caused by illness and drugs. But when it finally happened, it felt like being hit by a truck.

"Fuck you Gary, *you're* being unprofessional!"

Something about her voice woke me up in the moment. It wasn't just a fluttering of my eyes; I surfaced from the confused shadows of semi-consciousness and emerged into my own mind with a thousand questions. I was already pulling myself upright before my sister had time to hang up the phone. My hands roamed freely, touching and groping the couch, then the blankets, my chest, and finally head and face. I couldn't balance the myriad of voices and thoughts that popped into my head, and it took a few seconds before I finally groaned the words,

"My cactus," I croaked. "Water."

My sister had been momentarily frozen from shock, but something about the absurdity of it all caused her to laugh, then cry, then run over and hug me. I blinked my ears clear and tried to speak again.

"I'm sorry about your sofa," I groaned, picking my hand up from where it had been propping me up. Something had soaked through the fabric and stank of sickly-sweet infection, and I realised with disgust that it was coming from me.

"Don't be silly," she sobbed. "I'll get a new one."

Gingerly, I sniffed my palm.

"Can we burn this one?"

An hour later and I was wrapped head to toe in a blanket, shivering from fever, but lucid for the first time in weeks. My sister had made me a cup of tea and as I sipped it, I savoured the feeling of warmth in my belly.

"Do you remember anything else about her?" she asked.

"No," I said.

"The police told me they're trying to find her but... I don't know, what with your history, I wonder if they'll even look that hard."

"She didn't even take anything," I said.

"She cut you open, and we still don't know why!" Annie cried with great incredulity. "We don't know if there were a gang of them or if she's just some lunatic or what? James, this... what happened to you is serious. This all of *this,*" she waved her hands in my direction, "is very serious."

"I just want to go back to normal," I said, pulling the blanket closer around me.

She reached out and gave my hand a squeeze. For a moment I thought she was going to tell me it'd all go back to normal any day now, but she closed her mouth without saying another word and I realised it was a promise she couldn't keep.

The scar was huge. It was easily eight inches end to end and crossed my left side at a diagonal turn. It was just below my ribs where it bellowed aching agony into my abdomen. It was a throbbing, pulsing mess of sharp and blunt pains that hurt no matter what I did, pinging away at the edges of my awareness like a discordant rhythm. Over time, the broken skin had swollen so much that the thick stitches strained against their respective holes, warping them into distended oval shapes that looked close to tearing. The stitches, for some reason, were unspeakably sensitive. Not only did it hurt to pull at or pluck them (as you might expect), but even brushing them sent lancing waves up through my ribs and into my jaw where the pain settled like a toothache. The gentlest prod was felt by them, and it made little sense to me as to how I could so clearly feel something that was not part of my body.

Poking the wound hurt like hell, but I found myself able to give it a more thorough examination that I had in the previous weeks and, most unusually, I found the surrounding flesh to be hard and ungiving. It felt to me as if something were buried in the wound, almost as if I was feeling a piece of wood beneath some fabric, and desperate to know more I pushed harder and harder until my finger slid between the folds of skin and sank a quarter-inch into the cut. It hurt less than I imagined it would, and I could feel something strange embedded in the flesh.

It had an irregular surface like a stick, but was hard like rock. It was jagged, starting wide at the base and tapering to a serrated edge buried in the other side of flesh. Carefully I ran my finger sideways along the cut and found similar pieces of hardened material lined up in rows. Tracing their outline made a zig-zag shape that followed the cut like a zipper on a jacket, and when I finally managed to get a small glimpse at what it was beneath the skin, I saw something the colour of nicotine-stained fingers.

My skin crawled with disgust. The violation was rank. I couldn't contain myself and I became overcome with a kind of panic, a strong repulsion towards my own skin. *Something's in there*, I thought, *and I have to get it out.*

I became desperate and tried to leverage it open with both hands, pushing fingers from both hands in deeper and deeper, even as the pain overcame me. Overeager, my hand slipped and my finger caught a sharp edge along the way.

"Fuck!" I cried and snatched my hand away, it barely hurt, but something in my stomach began to ache. It hurt like I hadn't eaten for days, lurching as if I was in a roller coaster going over an enormous drop. It grew from a mild sensation to an overwhelming nausea in less than a second, and the pain became a kind of dynamic sensation I couldn't possibly hope to describe. Stumbling over, I had to prop myself against the mirror where I managed get one last look at my side. What I saw struck me as some kind of mad hallucination.

The scar was moving, the flesh of either side undulating as a small drop of blood rolled along the edges. Not only did the skin start to curl back, revealing a long row of jagged teeth an inch or two in length, but the stitches plucked themselves from their nested pockets and writhed in the empty air like the cilia of a jellyfish. Even without my intervention, the wound continued to open, slowly spreading apart to a few inches wide. By the time I registered the gullet leading sideways into my body, I passed out.

———

"Got your appetite back!?" Annie proclaimed happily as she stepped through the door. I looked guiltily at the six or seven plates piled up on the kitchen table, filled with bones and scraps of inedible waste. "When you called me up asking for food, I didn't realise you were going to clear out the whole damn fridge."

"Sorry," I mewed.

"Don't be," she smiled. "You lost so much weight I didn't even recognise you. It's good you're eating again."

Without thinking one of my hands strayed down to my left my side. I ran my hand over my t-shirt and felt something unusual beneath the fabric, something that was neither part of my body nor the wound. When my sister turned away, I pulled the t-shirt up and saw a half-eaten fry stuck between the teeth. Almost as if in reaction to the light and sound, the scar's lips started to churn away, trying to dislodge the piece of potato. Gingerly I snatched the chip away from between the jaws and went to throw it away but was stopped without realising why.

My sister turned, and I dropped my shirt as quickly as I could. She looked at me for a moment, puzzled over my sitting there with half a fry in one hand and a look of unrelenting terror on the other.

"You don't have to be ashamed if you've been lying there and eating like a pig," she laughed.

I tried to ask her to take the piece of food away from me, but I couldn't make the words leave my mouth. I stared at it and felt a growing pang of hunger ringing outward from my chest, as if my belly was an enormous empty brass bell being struck from within. My mouth was filling with saliva so quickly it was like a continuous flow of milkshake, and in the end, I gave in and threw the chip in my mouth and swallowed it whole like a dry pill.

My sister burst out into laughter.

"Just like when we were kids fighting over food, eh?" she chuckled. "Like that time we found a snickers under the sofa?"

"Mm-mmm," I agreed, my lips pressed tightly shut.

She turned and began packing away the shopping. Subconsciously my hands returned to my side, and I felt something unusual once more. Pulling the shirt up I stared down at the same half-a-fry sticking out of the side, and like the first peel of thunder before a terrible storm, my stomach let out a nauseating growl of hunger.

"Can you pick up some more meat?" I said.

"Yeah sure," she chirped over the phone. "The doctor said you might have an iron deficiency. God knows how much blood you lost when those wackos... well... look anything you need, I'll get okay."

"Thank you," I said. "I'm going to go lie down now."

"Okay, see you when I get back tonight!"

I hung up the phone and opened the door of the fridge. All around me lay open packets of steak I'd stuffed hungrily into my face all throughout the morning. Without thinking I itched my nose and my fingertips came away bloody. When I checked a mirror, I looked like a Halloween decoration, my mouth and nose covered in fresh blood. I peeled my lips back and stared at my teeth, repulsed by the brown clotted plaque that stained my gums.

With the regularity of clockwork, my side began to ache, and I pulled my t-shirt up in time to see the wound's lips writhing and moving like the mouth of a toothless old man sucking on hard-candy. A second later and it spat out the first bone, and then another, and then another. Over the course of fifteen minutes, it carefully spat out hundreds of bones, most from a whole uncooked chicken I'd eaten just before calling my sister. By the time the wound was done expelling bones, I felt close to collapsing, but I pulled myself back to the kitchen, where I grabbed my phone and called Annie once more.

"Hey," I said breathlessly. "Can you only get boneless stuff?"

"Of course," she said. "What about chips or anything like that? Bit of bread? I could cook up burgers real easy using the grill."

The thought of bread nearly made me pass out on the spot.

"No," I replied. "Maybe it's the gluten or something. I don't know. But please, no bread. No fruit. No veg."

"Okay," she said, and for the first time, I detected a curious tone in her voice, something approaching concern. "Only meat... again."

I was awoken to a sound a bit like a violin. I was lying down when it came from a nearby window, and I looked up to see a silver cat staring at me with indignity. My sister had told me about the neighbour's cat. She'd warmly suggested that if it visited I let it in and feed it, much like she does when she's feeling down. With bigger problems on my mind, I first tried to ignore it, but it was patient and wouldn't let up. Perhaps it was the sight of all the meat and bones that lay half-eaten across the kitchen island, but the cat was determined to get in.

"Alright," I grumbled, standing up just as the cat began to loudly paw at the glass. "Alright alright alright I'm coming—"

As soon as the window was raised, the cat burst into the room like lightning before quickly settling down on one of the countertops where it purred and started chewing on some bones. I shuffled back to the sofa and sat down, then lay down, and then, without quite remembering when, I fell asleep. It felt like barely a few minutes had passed when I later awoke, finding the cat nearby, purring and mewing at my face.

Confused, I sat up and it jumped gracefully between the coffee table and the sofa landing silently to my left. For a brief moment I scratched its head and enjoyed its company, right up until it nuzzled against my side.

I'm still not sure what happened in what order. Everything came so quickly, and those first few seconds blinded me with pain. I could barely think or see; it felt like my entire nervous system was being pumped full of electricity. I briefly registered a tearing wet sound and when I looked I saw my t-shirt was sopping wet with blood. The cat was wailing and everything was a confused spatter of blood, fur, and the mustard yellow cotton of my t-shirt.

Quickly, the initial burst of energy died down. The cat's cries became less manic and more pathetic, turning into the long-drawn out cries of the slowly-dying. I soon realised that something had torn a hole in my clothes and the cat was half-buried within it, its front paws still feebly scratching at my soft skin. Meanwhile, the back legs twitched and jerked, and I became uncomfortably aware of a crunching sound.

Somehow, I could feel the mouth and its movements. The spasms along the scar's opening felt very much like a part of me, but distant, like when you get an injection at the dentist and you spend hours afterwards running your tongue along your cheek. Quietly trying to hold back tears, I got up and walked to the bathroom where I could use the full-length mirror. I had to thread the remainder of the cat's body through the gaping hole in my shirt before I could pull it up, but when I did, I saw that strange mouth had grown more pronounced, jutting out of my side like a rising hill.

Caught between the powerful lips and bony teeth was half a cat, and slowly the mouth wormed and chewed away at the now-dead animal. It reminded me of someone slurping up spaghetti and stopping to chew on a mouthful.

I could feel it. I could feel its death throes inside me. The urge to vomit rose up quickly at the realisation, and I ran over to the toilet and began to wretch. However, something was wrong. I wasn't being sick out of disgust, something else was happening. I started to gag, and my heaving was painfully violent. As I crouched, hanging over the toilet with heavy rivulets of spit dripping into the bowl, I started to feel something hard and strange rising up out of my throat. It took nearly an hour of near-suffocation—eyes screwed shut as I tried hard to "be" somewhere else to endure the pain—before something plopped out of my mouth and clinked against the porcelain.

I wiped away the tears in my eyes and fished it out.

It was the cat's collar.

———

"You haven't seen her at all?"

"No," I said as she forced a bag of chicken nuggets into an overstuffed freezer drawer.

"Now are you sure you don't want me to cook any of these up?" she asked, turning to look over her shoulder at me.

"I'm not hungry," I answered and for once, I genuinely wasn't.

"It's just apparently Elle said she let her out last night and she almost always comes straight down here. She's a little silver thing? With a small red tag on her collar that's shaped like a wax seal. Are you sure you haven't seen her?"

I guiltily thumbed that exact same name tag in my pocket.

"Nope," I said. "Why would I lie?"

Annie didn't respond, she just kept packing away food.

"Have you been cleaning in here?" she asked suddenly. "It smells of bleach."

"No," I shook my head. "Haven't done anything of the sort."

I laid down and pretended to sleep, desperately hoping she wouldn't ask any more questions.

It was the small black eye of a mollusc; a pearly obsidian orb embedded just above my lowest rib. Around the edges was a line of faint hairs that left me breathless when I touched them. There were no lids to blink, but the hairs moved eerily in the air, almost as if floating in the slow current of a river. When I tapped it with a pen, the eye sank back down into my skin and disappeared, only to return like a soap bubble several seconds later. Below it the mouth continued to writhe and grunt away, the bone protrusions of its jaws having since grown jut out of my profile by a good four or five inches.

Gently I prodded the mouth, but it did nothing. I could feel the pen. I could feel the hard plastic against skin that I swore wasn't mine anymore. It felt like a part of me, so I put the pen down and poked it with my hand, snatching my finger away in anticipation of a lethal snap. But nothing happened. It continued chewing the air absent-mindedly. To get a better look at the discolouration I turned back to the mirror and lifted my arm above my head, noting how the pink and yellow skin of the mouth strained against a bony underlying carapace. As I watched, another small black orb floated to the surface of my skin, then another.

I raised my arm higher and several more popped up audibly amongst the soft nook of my armpit. They bubbled out so quickly I wasn't even sure if it would stop, but once the growth the subsided I was left with a fist-sized lump of black featureless orbs buried in my armpit like a blackberry. Around the central mass, new hairs grew, as did a bony crater with similar ridges to the mouth below. Gently I tried to lower my arm, but past a certain point the orbs became too sensitive. I tried a few times, going as far as to try and force my arm down but before my elbow was in line with my jaw, the pain became unbearable, shooting across my collarbone and straight down into my stomach where it settled like a punch to the gut.

Behind the locked bathroom door, I could hear my sister enter the apartment. I had no idea how this was going to work, but thinking quickly I grabbed a large towel and stuffed it under my arm. When I entered the living room I looked like I was trying to haul a log and my sister wordlessly turned her head in confusion.

"Are you okay?"

"Yeah," I answered a bit too quickly.

"How's...?" She gestured to her side.

"Fine," I replied, breaking eye contact to walk over to the sofa. "I'm just not feeling well."

"You don't look like you have much of a fever. Is it healing okay? It's not infected again is it?"

She stepped forward and for some reason I found the sight of her coming towards me utterly terrifying. I was filled with a peculiar, almost primal, desire to flee somewhere dark. For some bizarre reason, I saw the sun being eclipsed by a large object swimming towards me. In a split second the image flashed in and out of my mind and left me dazed leaving plenty of time for Annie to reach out and lift my shirt up. Before she got any further, I lashed out and slapped her arm away.

"Jesus Christ Jacob, what's the fucking matter with you?" she cried, more upset than angry. The tone in her voice caught me off guard and when she reached out once more, even faster this time, I was too slow.

Before I could react, the wound did. My body lunged out to meet her, pulled as if by invisible strings.

Bone cracked.

She gave a short sharp cry of pain, followed by another longer scream that rose in pitch like a violin concerto. It never stopped; she just kept screaming at the sight of what remained of her hand. I looked down at my side and saw the t-shirt torn apart and the fat bony mouth chewing clumsily at three fingers and a chunk of palm. Someone was saying *no* over and over, and it realised it was the sound of my own voice filled with regret and horror.

I reached out and grabbed her hand. I don't even know what I was going to do—stem the blood maybe?—but her screaming intensified and she fell over, trying to get away. I was crying now, salty tears streaming down my cheeks, and stepped forward in another vain attempt to help. She cried out and savagely batted away my hand, scrambling backwards in a desperate crab walk until her back thudded against the wall.

"Get away," she sobbed. "Get away get away *get away.*"

The words broke my heart, and I felt a knot in my throat. I tried to take a step backwards, to walk away and go God knows where, but something stopped me. The pain in my side flared up. It felt like something was wrenching sideways against my rib cage.

"No," I mewed and felt it lunge once more. This time it pulled me a few feet towards Annie, who was screaming at a feverous non-stop pitch. "No no no please no!" I cried, and this time it pulled me so hard it didn't stop. I flailed across the room, trying desperately to gain purchase on anything around me, dragging plastic bags full of food to the floor as I was yanked closer and closer to my sister. That thing was grumbling so loudly it filled the room, growling with an inane, stupid hunger.

I couldn't look, not even as it latched onto her head with a soft crunch. She kept screaming, kept crying into the darkness that ate her face, stripping away the soft skin, the muscle, the cartilage, and then finally the bone. Something hideous had punched out of the things mouth. I couldn't see it but I could feel it and knew instinctively it was a proboscises. It writhed through her skull, grinding and boring through anything in its way, popping eyes and draining the fluid before gouging deeper and deeper towards her brain.

It drained it in minutes, and when her screaming finally died down, the only sound in the apartment was the breathy gurgle of her spinal fluid being slurped up by the tuberous growth. Satisfied, the mouth let go and belched, then nestled back into my side with the affectionate wiggle of a sleeping cat. I knew what I was going to see when I faced my sister, and my fear was soon confirmed. There was nothing but a skull surrounded by a ragged hood of skin and hair.

Even in the silence, I could still hear her scream.

THE SHIMMERING TREE

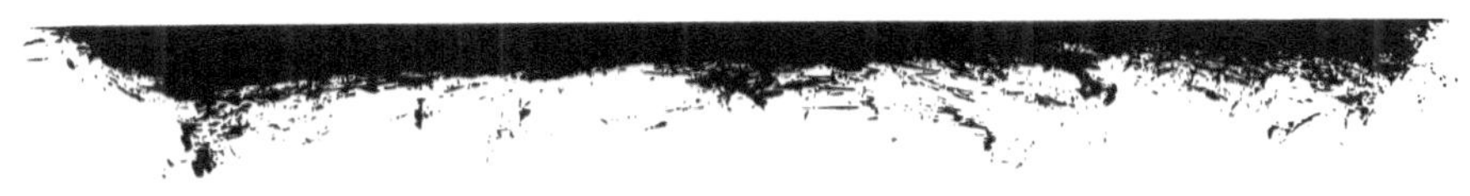

1 *9th February 2009*

Michael,

I thought I would let you know that I've been at Mum's the past few weeks sorting through everything. I want to apologize for not saying anything at the funeral. David shouldn't have said what he did, but you've got to understand that he's the youngest and it's been very hard on him. You always were their precious favourite, and the rest of us couldn't help but be a bit jealous.

But it still wasn't fair for me to just stand back and let him speak to you like that. And I want you to know that I'd like to try and fix things between us. So I thought I'd pass this onto you, as just a little peace offering. It's your birth certificate. You'll have to forgive that it's come in an envelope with some other stuff, but I just didn't have time to go through it all. I'm sure if Mum kept anything, she did so for a reason. At the very least, I hope you can appreciate the gesture.

Let me know how things are going out there in Asia, and if there's anything else you'd like me to send over to you, okay?

With love from your sister,
Sarah Nettleworth

———————

16th November 1959

Dear Angela and Liam Nettleworth,

I would like to thank you for your gratuitous donation to the institution. However, I must emphasise that the service I, and the other Archivers, have offered to you is unrelated to my 'day job' as the museum's curator. I trust that you realize the *actual* payment owed to me and my associates at the Archives is still due, and that you have not mistakenly made a donation to the wrong institute.

Nonetheless, as a sign of good faith, I would like to direct you to a safe at the bottom of the Crossroads Manor found in the Hebrides of Scotland. The Manor has long since burned to the ground, but if you are persistent, you will find that a basement still stands, and that somewhere within that basement is a safe. Once the Archives have written to me to confirm receipt of your true payment, I will deliver to you the key to the safe. Within that safe are the full three volumes detailing the true name of The Shimmering Tree. Vocalization of this name will summon the tree. Exact pronunciation is not important, but it is not recommended that you test the limits of common sense. A simple phonetic oration will be satisfactory.

I cannot stress to you enough that you will need a third person, one whose absence from society will not be noticed, otherwise one of you will act as the initial host for the tree. You need only look at the desired host during the final page or two of the readings to designate them as the desired vessel, but nonetheless you should be careful not to accidentally designate somebody else. Below, you will find a detailed description of the tree compiled from notes found in the Archive, although some details have been drawn from my own experiences as an Archival observer.

The tree is made of bone, muscle and nervous tissue, and will spring up out of the flesh out of whoever has been marked as a host. Its incubation is barely a second in length. The designated individual will stop what they are doing, and occasionally emit a small sigh, or groan, suggesting confusion or even just indifference. To the observer, it will then feel like an explosion when the tree emerges from the body, as it is almost always noisy, and violently fast. Although it is important to note that what this observer witnessed was not necessarily destructive or staggered but was instead the smooth and fluid transformation of flesh compressed into a remarkably short period of time. It is not uncommon to vomit during this initial stage of growth. Where, anatomically, the tree will emerge from, and the exact nature of its composition, will vary significantly from person to person. The archives note a preference for the torso, but this observer has seen it spring up from an array of other locations.

The tree will then take several minutes to grow to full size after the initial growth, and often resembles a fleshy coral. The colours observed can change, but they typically feature metallic purples, blood reds, and putrid greens. This slowed period of growth is the second stage. During this phase, the tree will also assimilate the flesh and tissues of any nearby mammalian species, and if in desperate need, it will also consider the assimilation of lower order animals such as flies and spiders. During this second phase of rapid growth, it will typically expand to around sixteen feet in height, although its exact size can vary considerably. Importantly, the tree has been known to exhibit restraint in certain situations where the necessary construction materials are limited, as it will avoid the complete annihilation of the host if possible. In one case where an infant was used, the tree grew to only three feet in height.

The host, meanwhile, will undergo distinct and separate transformations. They will typically fall to the floor, given the force of what is occurring, and lay flat while their nervous material is ejected from their skin as an outward growth. In particular, tendrils will extend farthest from areas of greater sensitivity with the greatest lengths emerging from the fingers, toes, facial features, and genitals. This nervous material will branch out in a fractal pattern, much like the roots of a tree, and make contact with as much of the external environment as possible. During this period, the host will usually vocalize tremendous distress for as long as it is physically possible. The archives note that it is typical for the tongue to swell up and become part of the extending nervous tissue, which will block the passageways and prevent further vocalizations. Interestingly the tree will manipulate the host's structural composition, creating new airways, in order to avoid asphyxiation.

It cannot be stressed strongly enough that one should not come into contact with these nervous tendrils as they are responsible for the tree's assimilation of extraneous matter and are surprisingly agile and aggressive. It will usually be necessary to vacate the area and return later once the second stage of growth has stopped. After this, between the second and third stages of growth, is a period of inactivity during which the tree will be amenable to conversation.

The tree utilizes a series of pipes and organs appropriated from the host to pass air over its frills, and tendril covered branches. These small cilia like projections are able to vibrate at a range of frequencies and will produce a remarkable visual and aural effect of sound and light which corresponds to the tree's speech. It is wise to ensure that the tree has emerged from a host who speaks a common language with yourself. If you do not do this, then the tree will essentially be unable to converse in your own tongue, and there will be a language barrier. It is not wise to waste the tree's time. You should submit a request quickly, but if you cannot—due to the aforementioned linguistic problems—you should leave and return quickly with another host who can speak the same language as yourself. It will not take long for the tree to appropriate the correct linguistic skills from your second offering. You can then initiate your request.

Regarding requests: The tree is able to grant limited requests regarding reincarnation, recollection from past lives, precognition, and the location of lost objects. The location of such objects can be presented in any format, including annotations on a map (bring a pen if this is your intention). The tree also possesses other skills, but a request must specify exactly what it requires. It is not possible to 'browse' the tree like a catalogue, and so without a comprehensive list of what else the tree can achieve, which, sadly, the archive does not possess, it is suggested that one should adhere to those I have suggested here. Otherwise you might risk becoming another offering.

Once the request has been satisfied, the third stage of growth will initiate. The tree will proceed to manipulate the host further and prompt the growth of several large veiny, membranous sacks proportionate to its size (typically eight feet across once inflated). These sacks will inflate with a gaseous matter distinct from normal air, which when heated by the tree, using means unknown, will provide it with a means of escape via flight. The tree will usually demonstrate a terrifying capacity to reorganize inorganic matter during this stage, as it will quickly and fluently dismantle any and all obstructions using its branches and roots during the ascent.

Exactly where the Shimmering Tree comes from, and where it goes, remains a complete and utter mystery. It does not require a physical precursor, and as far as this observer can tell, it seems to occur as a result of spontaneous matter reorganization. How it achieves this is beyond comprehension, but it has been suggested by older members of the Archives that the tree is the result of an unknown entity's will being imposed upon reality; twisting biological material into a desirable form, from unknown and unseen dimensions.

This is important to consider as the tree does not actually require summoning to enter our existence and has been known to emerge spontaneously from those who have upset it after the arrangements seemed long finished. As part of our earlier correspondence, I have made it clear to you that you might wish to gather large quantities of ammonia and copper for use as a deterrent should the tree seek to use you as a construction material during the initial summoning. But if you happen to draw the tree's ire at some point after this, you may wish to consider self-termination or euthanasia. As mentioned above, the tree doesn't need an invitation nor a host to manifest, and without unlimited repellents, one can only delay the inevitable. The Shimmering Tree is not deterred by distance, or time, and if you abuse its goodwill, your options will be limited.

Exactly what qualifies as an abuse varies. Historical examples of unsolicited growths found in the archives list a Scottish Presbyterian preacher from 1639 who used his gifts to oppose King James VI's reformation of the Bible, a traveller from the 1940s who tried to convince a child that Santa Clause was real, and a stockbroker in 1949 who wrote a book about economic theory that heaped endless praise upon unregulated markets and capitalism. The current theory is that one should avoid attributing the nature of your successes and gifts to any single specific thing, whether it is a fictional person or an ideology. It is well known amongst those who have performed a successful summoning of the tree that one should instead attribute any new-found success, or talents, to "hard work, perseverance, and faith in a higher spiritual power". The ambiguity of this phrase has, so far, never been known to invoke the tree's ire.

Finally, I would like to highlight to you that the tree itself, despite the myriad of rules that surround it, is surprisingly amiable and quite conversational. It seems to enjoy the acquisition of knowledge, although it most certainly possesses eclectic, and unpredictable, tastes. Archives indicate that the tree once engaged in a several hours-long conversation with a young man regarding the taxonomical classification of sea cucumbers. Do be careful, and don't allow yourself to become enamoured as the tree will not hesitate to assimilate individuals who stray too close, or who have appeared to let their guard down.

Ultimately, I wish you luck in your quest. I simply cannot say whether what you have asked is within the tree's powers to grant but considering its capacity to manipulate flesh, I suspect that it is. However, the risk of such a request is positively enormous. There is not only the obvious dangerous possibility that The Shimmering Tree will take offence and try to assimilate you, but I am personally distressed at the possibility it might actually acquiesce. I really do suggest you stick to the usual wish of wealth and power. Most of our clients find this quite fulfilling all on its own. I am aware of the pain and tragedy you have experienced as a couple, and I must send you my condolences. But I would be derelict in my duties to you if I did not highlight the potential for disaster in asking The Shimmering Tree to reverse your recent miscarriage.

I beg you to reconsider.

CLICK CLACK

"**W**hat is it?" Andrew asked. He had noticed me stopping by a small pipe. I reached out and plucked a small piece of red and silver metal that had been perched on a steaming pipe, close to chest height. It was folded into the shape of a deer.

"My father makes these out of coke cans," I said, holding it in front of my torch. "He gives them to us at Christmas and on birthdays. They're little things but... they build up over time. I have dozens all lined up. He must have left this for us."

"So we're on the right track," Caz said. "His directions are actually right?"

It had been six days since my father had gone into hiding in the London underground, but this was the first time I thought I might actually find him. Quietly, I pocketed the little figurine and tried to kindle the feeling of hope it gave me.

"He must mean a lot to you," Caz whispered.

"He's kind," I replied. "Everyone hears 'schizophrenia' and they think 'psychopath' but that's not true at all. He lives in a scary world filled with voices and strange patterns. He's vulnerable, not dangerous. He must be having a bad episode to come down here."

"You said he's done this before though," Andrew said. "At least that means he knows what he's doing."

"Yeah," I replied. "It's just he was 43 when he last spent some time down here. He's 65 now and struggles with stairs." I held up the bizarre list of directions he'd left me, some of which included ten-foot drops onto hard concrete. "How's he going to manage this?"

"I've never heard of a telecoms bunker anywhere in this part of the underground," William said.

"If he's where his letter says he is," Andrew interrupted, flashing his brother a dirty look. "We'll find him. We know everything down here."

"Yeah," William stammered, quickly adapting. "No one knows this city like we do."

"How deep are we now?" Caz asked after a few minutes of silence had passed.

"Honestly I don't know, but I'm gonna guess about 60m," William answered.

"There's a kind of quality to the air past a certain depth," Andrew added. "You learn to recognise it."

"I never even knew this was all down here," she replied.

"My dad was obsessed," I said. "He used to research all the stuff hidden down here, but this bunker was his favourite of them all. When I found his directions, I knew what it was going to say before I even opened it. He's the smartest man I've ever met, funny, passionate, and he's... he's just got this *spark,* you know? But he overestimates himself. He thinks he's invulnerable, and I know he's going to get himself hurt down here."

"You're a good son," Caz said.

"You came to the right guys," William added, turning over his shoulder to smile at me.

Silence returned, and I kept my eyes down, trying to ignore the harsh monochrome concrete tunnel and the way it made me feel. Eventually, the two brothers led us to a creaking bulkhead that hung open on rusted hinges. Carefully William squeezed past the stiff door before crying out for us to follow. I soon found myself standing in an enormous reservoir, easily the size of ten football pitches. One of the nearby walls was inscribed with the letters: *ACWW Ansley Wells Reservoir 1867-1869* and I excitedly told the others:

"This must be the reservoir he mentions in the letter."

All around us dozens of red-brick pillars reached out of the water and into the vaulted roof, all perfectly aligned in diminishing rows. Andrew pushed ahead with a map held open in his arms, muttering quietly to himself.

"It shouldn't be here," William said after glancing at his brother. "I thought it would be a small side-tunnel, something unmarked, but there's nothing, *nothing* in any documents about this. I figured he was just a craz—"

"Ahem!" Andrew coughed loudly, and William immediately shut up.

"Could you have just not heard about it?" Caz asked.

"No," Andrew answered. "We'd know about something like this. If there was even a whisper about this, the urban exploring community would be all over it. This is... it's incredible. If we knew about this section of tunnels, we'd be running tours down here every other day of the week. So would everyone else."

"But is there a route through?" I asked. "I mean if the instructions he left me are accurate then... I mean, doesn't that mean we have a good chance of finding him?"

"Yes," he replied. "So long as we find the manhole and ladder your father described."

"Come on," William said, and one by one we all began to march through the ankle-deep water. Only we didn't get very far before something caught my eye.

"There's something under the water," I said.

"What?" Andrew asked.

I walked over, knowing it'd be quicker to show them than explain. The water wasn't very deep, and I gingerly reached out to pick the object up.

"It's an axe," William said, not very far behind me. "Weird."

He left and I could hear him telling Caz not to worry. Andrew, however, who had also spotted the unusual mark along the handle, stayed right next to me. He gave me a knowing look, and I nodded before dropping the axe back in the water.

It was blood, soaked into the very grain of the wood.

———

Click clack

    He'll break your back

    Follow his laws and stay on track

The words were spray painted in stark white lettering across the pitted interior of a drainage pipe.

"Creepy," Caz whispered before nervously chuckling. We all tried to laugh it off as well, as if we could somehow send the fear packing by bad acting.

It broke the spell enough for us to carry on. The pipe was wide enough for all four of us to walk abreast, and so far my father's instructions had not failed us. As we expected, we soon came across a rickety ladder rising up from the centre of the pipe to an already opened hatch. It was about a thirty-foot climb to the top and the two brothers wasted no time in setting out the order of ascent. It was to be one at a time, just in case the ladder could not hold much weight.

I was to be last as I weighed the most, and I patiently waited as one by one the others climbed the ladder and disappeared. Just before Andrew left, he stopped and saw me flick the torch nervously towards the darkness. He and I both knew there'd be a few nervous moments where I would be all alone.

"Are you okay?" he asked.

"Yeah sure," I answered. "Let's just be quick about it."

He nodded and began to climb, his footfalls appallingly loud. I waited patiently for him to climb, only when he was about half-way up we both heard a distinct sound from up ahead.

Click clack.

It was a single short exclamation amidst the silence.

Click clack.

There it was again, louder this time. I couldn't see further than a few metres in any direction and my chest was tight with panic.

Click clack.

The water at my feet surged. I watched, confused, as it started rising above my ankles. I couldn't be sure, but it appeared to be running uphill, although I hoped I'd just gotten turned around and couldn't tell up from down. That made sense, I figured. More sense than the idea that the water was somehow fleeing something in the dark, something out there that had a presence I could feel crackle with an invisible charge. A presence that lingered directly on the mind as if it bypassed the senses and spoke to some primeval need to hide…

As soon as Andrew gave the all-clear, I grabbed the first rung and started climbing.

Click clack

I stopped without meaning to. I was half-way up, but the sound was so close I had to look down and check. I could see nothing except churning water.

Click clack

It was so loud this time it didn't even echo, like something spoken just over my shoulder. I decided not to wait and see and scrambled up the last few rungs, my grip shaky and clumsy. I kept worrying I was going to fall, but some primal need to flee had seized me and was urging me on.

Click clack
Thump
Click clack
Thump

Something was climbing up behind me. I felt my whole body tense up with terror and I practically leapt clear of the last few rungs. As soon as I was clear of the hatch, I grabbed the cover and slammed it shut as hard as I could.

"Who was down there?" Andrew asked.

"Nothing," I said, not sure I wanted to even trust what my eyes had glimpsed as I'd panicked in the dark.

My torch filled the room with a chalky light. Behind me a pipe dripped while Andrew swung the door shut with a keening rusted howl. We had finally found the bunker, or at least the door my father described, and found ourselves in a small room. Moving our lights, we saw three cots, the mattresses half-covered with bunched up khaki sleeping bags that cast lumpen drifting shadows. In the centre of the room was a table with a frayed pack of cards and a 10,000 piece jigsaw placed face down.

"I thought it was a World War 2 bunker?" Caz asked as she lifted an old Walkman CD player from beneath a pillow. "Unless someone has been here since?"

"The last time my father would have come down here was around 1996," I said. "The letter makes no mention of seeing any-one living here. He said it was filled with gas masks and uniforms and paperwork from the 50s."

We carried on into the next room, where we found a small canteen. From there, the bunker opened up into a labyrinth of industrial tunnels, their walls covered with lifeless dials and steel lockers. Choosing at random, we followed one of the tunnels to a small dormitory with just four bunk beds, all unmade and empty. At the foot of one of the beds was an unlatched and open trunk filled with women's clothes. Buried beneath the underwear and overalls was a small book titled *Millennial Apocalypse: The Y2k Bug and The Modern Mayan Prophecy.*

"Y2K preppers," I said.

"Clearly it wasn't just your father who knew about this place," Andrew replied. "Someone else must have thought it was a great place to hide out."

"The Y2K bug was the only apocalypse he didn't believe in," I chuckled.

"How long do you think they were down here?" Caz asked.

I walked up to a nearby corkboard where a calendar was pinned and fanned through the pages. The last date marked was October 24th, 2001; the small square crossed off with a purple felt-tip pen. All the dates before that were marked off, going all the way back to January with mentions of birthdays, anniversaries, and even Easter.

"Did they seriously spend all that time down here?" Caz asled.

"At least one of them was," I replied, gesturing to the calendar.

"Let's keep going," William said. "I want to get a sense of how big this place is."

We carried on exploring for at least another two hours. We found another dozen beds, although not all looked used. One of the larger rooms had been turned into a kind of communal living space complete with tables and benches, and another was a small gym filled with fold-up exercise equipment. Surprisingly, very little of the bunker was dedicated to living space. The vast majority of the rooms were used for storage, and we found whole walk-in freezers filled with desiccated and rancid meat that swung gently in the dark. Beneath them, people-sized sacks of grain and oats were stacked like firewood, their contents mushy and rotten.

There were generators, water filters, distillation units, lathes, presses, six kinds of fuel, books, and enough medical supplies to shame a hospital – there was even a room with half-a-dozen UV lights wired up over some long-dead plants. This wasn't a half-arsed effort at surviving the end of the world. They'd been tremendously well-prepared.

But now they were gone.

Despite searching for hours, we kept finding new doors, new rooms, even whole new floors. The bunker seemed endless. Eventually William and Andrew decided we needed a break. I was standing at the threshold of the fourth sub-level, desperate to continue looking for my father, when they convinced me to step away and return to the entrance so we could regroup and discuss what we'd found. Begrudgingly I agreed, and we began to retrace our steps only for something strange to catch our attention from up ahead. It was a sound coming from the entrance up ahead. I turned the corner with my breath held, waiting to hear that dreadful sound I'd heard in the tunnel.

Only what I found was somehow even more surprising.

"Dad!" I cried out, rushing ahead to greet my father. He looked startled for just a moment, but he didn't turn to greet me. He never took his attention from the door that he was so desperately trying to pull shut. His face looked stretched out of shape, and it took me a few seconds to realise it was because he was scared in a way I'd never seen before.

"Dad it's okay, it's me," I said, taking a step forward. "These are my friends. We've come to get you out."

"No!" he cried. "We have to close it! We have to stay!"

I was about to ask why, but then I heard it.

Click clack.

Without realising I became a man possessed and rushed forward to help my father, spurred on by the memory of that *presence* in the tunnel. From where I stood on the other side of the door, I could see nothing, but I knew everyone was confused and crying out their questions. I ignored them, pushing as hard as I could on that rusted bulkhead.

Click clack.

I heard Caz scream, and I was suddenly thankful I was behind the door. Suddenly William and Andrew were beside me, white with terror and pushing with all their might. Caz joined in too, and with all of us at it, the door finally swung shut and my father twisted the lock, sliding thick metal bars into place.

"I thought you said there was nothing down here!" Caz cried, turning to face our guides. "What the *fuck* was on the other side of that door?"

I decided to let William answer that and instead turned my attention to my father, who was on his knees, gasping for breath.

"What's going on?" I asked.

"I'm so sorry," he said, tears in his eyes.

And with that, he shoved me aside and ran sobbing back into the shadows.

———

"Is it... is it a person?" she asked, staring through the tiny portcullis embedded in the door.

"Does it look like a person?" William said, his tone close to exasperation.

"Well it has two arms and two legs," she answered. "There's a head... I think. It's just waiting."

"Well it must be a person then," he said with a facetious shrug. "Why don't you go out and ask them about the weather?"

"We don't have the answers," Andrew said, stopping the argument before it began. "We don't know anything, but I think if we all took a vote, no one here would want to try and get past it."

"I certainly don't," I said, aiming my response at Andrew. "Maybe we'll just get to laugh about this when we're back up on the surface, but for now I can't think of anything worse than going back the way we came. At the very least, I'd like to try and exhaust all other options because whatever is out there, it's scaring the ever-loving shit out of me."

"Do you think there could be another way out?" Caz asked.

"It's worth checking," I replied. "And I still need to find my dad."

"This place is one of the largest underground facilities I've ever seen," Andrew said. "It makes sense it'd have more than just the one entrance."

———

"Is this what I think it is?" Andrew asked.

We huddled around him and stared at the haphazard sketch on one of the walls. At a glance it looked like a squarish mushroom or a top-heavy wine cork, but the more I stared the more details resolved themselves.

"Dorms, cooking, food, grain..." Caz muttered as she squinted to read the faded writing beside it. "First level."

"It's a map," I muttered. "The preppers must have been exploring this place just like us."

"That's what I thought," Andrew replied. "But... look, floor two they've got storage, fuel, cleaning supplies, electronics. On floor three they have filtration, water, distillery, UV lamps. On floor four there's just sewage."

"But it keeps going," William said. He pointed towards the lower levels on the map. The lines were rough and covered with question marks. The map was clearly unfinished.

"There's more here," I said, showing everyone a notepad I'd been flicking through.

Floor 5: Some metal caskets, vases, nice paintings. Duplicates of ones I've seen in the London Museum. Museum ones fake, these ones real? Vault to protect valuable culture, perhaps?

Floor 6: Funny looking computers. Don't need to worry about 2k bug at least. They run on vacuum tubes. All busted up.

Floor 7: Loud machines down here make my teeth itch. Purpose???

Floor 8: Filing cabinets everywhere, mostly empty. Some government documents remain, all redacted, logo and department thor-

oughly scrubbed. British and American flag on wall, both look weird. Wrong colours, wrong number of stars, wrong stripes. Illuminati?

Floor 9: Too dark to see, torch low on battery. Will return later. Could at least see stairs to another floor. How deep is this place?

"They don't make a single mention of a way out," Caz said.

"But they didn't explore it all," I replied.

"Is that even possible?" she asked. "How could they live here all this time and not explore it all? How big is this fucking place? If I didn't know any better, I'd say it was built from the bottom-up"

"We'll just have to go see for ourselves," I said.

During our descent, we each made our own worrying observations. Caz, for example, observed that many of the paintings on floor 5 were not duplicates but rather slight variations of famous paintings. When asked if they were fakes, her response was a little strange.

"No, I don't think so," she said. "This, this is a near perfect carbon copy of one of the early sketches of a Monet, except it's a full canvas painting instead of just a preliminary outline."

"Well maybe the fraud used the wrong version?" William asked.

"I doubt it," she replied. "The sketch was unearthed just a year or two ago."

We carried on, stepping over obsidian caskets, redwood trunks, human-sized urns, and mouldy sagging cavasses until we reached floor 6 where we found ourselves surrounded by an unusual army of upright machines with glass faces. They looked faintly like computers, but lacked any kind of interface that I could recognise. As described in the journal, a few of them had dusty and cracked vacuum tubes but others lacked them. I might have thought them little more than novel antiques were it not for one of the machines that bore a tiny inscription reading *Magnetic Resonance Safe Display*.

I didn't tell the others; the anachronism confused me, but I didn't know what it meant. As it was we were forced to hurry through floor 7 to avoid the wretched smell of o-zone emanating from an army of humming machines, their glass portcullises glowing a peculiar blue that pricked the skin if you strayed too close. William even burned himself wiping some dust from one of them, and in doing so revealed that a strange four-fingered streak along the glass had somehow been made on the inside.

It was almost a relief when we found floor 8 filled with nothing but endless filing cabinets. Unlike the journal description, we found them to be empty and were left to silently make our way through their disorderly arrangement, zigzagging through them until, finally, William cried out,

"Where's this stairway the journal mentioned?"

"God knows," I replied. "This place is a maze."

"I'm not sure I even want to find it," Caz said, her voice carrying strangely in the dark.

"Why's that?" I asked.

"If there's another way out, there's another way in."

I can't say why it hadn't occurred to me before, but the thought hit me like a breeze block. I stopped dead in my tracks, as did William and Andrew, and only Caz was left pottering around, oblivious to the effect her sentence had had on us.

"You don't think...?" Andrew muttered.

"Guys," Caz said. "I think I found something."

She was stood by a wall of lockers that had been pushed over and dragged to fill a small stairwell. It had all the makings of a hasty and desperate barricade.

"Should we...?" I asked.

Click

What immediately followed that sound couldn't have taken longer than a few seconds, but there were a million thoughts running through my head and the events played out like in some kind of slow-mo.

In the harsh silvery light of my torch—the air thick with raining motes of dust—one of the cabinets was thrown and sent tumbling down the pile. I became paralysed by an electric terror that seized me, my eyes wide and my mouth open in a silent cry.

Clack.

Another locker was lifted up and thrown aside, falling end over end like a domino.

Click clack.

A hand emerged from beneath the pile of twisted metal, its palm pale and strangely large. It pushed more and more of the lockers away until, at last, a head appeared. It was dangling lopsidedly from a broken neck with a slack pair of milky eyes and a drooling mouth. That sagging wretched head was adorned with a policeman's helmet, and from the neck down he wore a buttoned-down constable's uniform like something straight of the Victorian era. Bound to his hip was a strange-looking baton connected to a rusted power-pack by dozens of coiled copper wires.

He was huge, not muscular, just... large, like he came straight out of a different world. His enormous groping hands looked big enough to crush my skull and, as if ready to signal his intent, the monster's head snapped from right to left—*CLICK CLACK—*and he took a step forward.

William acted first, leaping forward into a running jump to kick the strange figure back into the stairwell, but it was like moving a tree. He struck the giant with a quiet thump and fell backwards onto the floor. He was scrambling to get up when the constable's giant hand wrapped around his head and lifted him from the floor. Wasting no time, Andrew ran forward, pulled free a knife, and began trying to frantically free his brother. But the blade did nothing—no blood, no pain, no change in grip. It was like he stabbing at straw.

I felt a gentle tug on my sleeve and nearly screamed, but the hand that reached up and gripped my own felt warm and somehow familiar. A glance down showed my father staring up at me, finger pressed to his mouth. He was crouched in darkness. He pulled me away just as Caz started screaming and a loud crack reverberated through the dark. My father grabbed me and stared into my eyes. Silently he mouthed for me to follow. Hesitating, I turned back, but all I saw was a confused display of criss-crossing lights, and the desperate sounds of a struggle.

"It's the only way," my father whispered and, much to my shame, I followed. I wasn't sure what to expect, but it was my deepest hope he'd take me somewhere safe. In reality, he dragged me into a small nook made by the endless rows of cabinets, and he made us both crouch down in the darkness. There wasn't really anywhere to hide properly, and all we could do was hide and wait and hope that whatever was looking for us wouldn't look very hard.

It felt like a long time, waiting there. There was a terrible tearing sound, like paper being ripped from end-to-end. Screaming turned to painful wails, then grief-wracked sobs, and at last a quiet, despondent, silence. Whether the others had hidden, ran, or died one-by-one, I couldn't say. A broken headlight lay somewhere on the floor where it cast dismal shadows, and I nearly gasped when I saw the wretched silhouette of the helmeted-giant taking another step.

Click Clack

Each footfall was punctuated by the stomach-churning sight of the monster's snapping from side to side... I swear I could *feel* that thing looking for us in the darkness, the same way you can feel someone looming over your shoulder. It was like a person magnified, not just in size but in spirit and intent.

With each step it took, my father tightened his grip around my wrist until, at last, the terrifying crescendo came and passed, and I watched the faint blue shadowy outline of the ghostly constable pass by our hiding spot without turning to look our way.

"It's not stupid," my father whispered, so quiet there was barely any breath to his hushed plea, only the wet sounds of him mouthing the words. "It knows we're still here. Be *quiet*."

He moved ahead of me on all fours, and I followed. He turned left at the end of the lockers, towards the stairwell, and I nearly panicked at the thought of turning my back on the monster that still *click-clacked* somewhere in that very room. I couldn't say if I was particularly stealthy; my breath was held most of the time and my heart felt like it was battering against my ribcage. But we reached the stairwell in safety, and I blanched at the feeling of something wet and warm along my hands and knees.

But my father didn't stop, and in fact he made sure to turn and beckon for me to follow even as we passed the pulped remains of one of my former party members. The tussled blond hair made me think of William, but the bubbling mess of broken bones and pulped flesh meant it could easily have been Andrew, or even both of them crunched together like two corpses fed through a trash compactor.

Feet first, and on our stomachs, we backed down through the hole in the barricaded stairwell. The last thing I saw before my head ducked beneath the portal was a light glowing in the distance. With horror, I realised that the monster had lifted up some kind of lantern to bathe us in light.

Click clack

"Please do not be alarmed!" it cried. Its voice a robotic transmission that sounded deeply warped. Even from afar, I was certain it came from no human mouth, certainly not the slack drooling orifice I had glimpsed on its face. It was the kind of voice you'd use to force civilians into a bomb shelter, or even out onto a firing line. I inherently distrusted the speaker and whoever had authored it into this world. "Travellers! Do not panic! Risk of contamination is minimal. Entropic parasites are not present in this location. Goosehead infestation is under control. Please present yourself for examination by an officer.

"Vigilance is the price of safety.

"This is our last resort.

"There is no other refuge."

"Does he eat them?" I asked, staring at the rows and rows of cages filled with desiccated remains. Some had been split open at the legs like wishbones, one had been forced through the unyielding metal bars and gored brutally in the process, but most looked like they'd starved to death. Approaching one, my father bent over and picked up a piece of paper and held it up to me. It was an unremarkable form with dozens of boxes, only they'd been filled in with a desperate scrawl and the fingers that gripped it had clearly been wet and greasy.

Arrest report 203887

Infraction: failure to present Prosiah ID to arresting officer. Non-compliance with police is grievous offence.

Initial scans show lack of vaccination nanites. Translocation without prior vaccination is grievous offence.

Personal possessions suggest culprit has stolen from locals. Breaching integration protocols is grievous offence.

Suspect details are transcribed below.

Name: FUCK YOU!

Citizen ID No.: What the fuck are you on about!?

Initial statement: What the fuck is wrong with you? Let me go!

Notes from arresting officer: I'm very cold.

In the corner of the room there was a bizarre copper coffin that stank of decay and mould, wired up to a strange machine that hummed like those we'd found in the glowing blue-room. From the size of it I guessed it belonged to the policeman chasing us, although I could scarcely imagine why the floor was riddled with rusted and bent nails that would pierce the flesh of anyone who lay within. Then again, I remembered Andrew stabbing at the forearm and producing only a vague cloud of dust, and I realised that whatever was hunting us clearly had a high pain threshold.

We carried on downwards, passing through what I considered to be the policeman's "workshop" and into a larger laboratory-like structure and a meeting hall plastered with faded propaganda posters. One showed a smiling policeman much like the one who chased us, looming over a menacing figure who was too faded to see. Behind the policeman was a red-headed cartoon of a woman, clutching his coat tails for safety.

"Seen a goosehead? Find your nearest ReConned Officer!"

And in smaller print beneath:

"Reconstituted officers are immune to the entropic blight! Seek one immediately if you believe a goosehead is in the vicinity. DO NOT TOUCH THE INFECTED."

The policeman in the poster was enormous, and clearly alike to the one who haunted us, but his head was set normally, and he looked quite cheery. His face was alert, intelligent even. Close by, another poster showed a similar looking policeman looming over a London skyline, a stern paternal expression worn on his face. The poster read:

"Even the meekest man may have the heart of a lion! Stand up against the plague. Resist the entropic parasites. Science can elevate the flesh, but this nation needs YOUR spirit! Something worse than death stalks London, do YOU have what it takes to stem the tide of parasitic assault?

"Keep your country safe. Keep your family safe. Inquire about reconstitution at your local constabulary."

I turned my light to the final poster. It depicted a rowdy looking soldier winking at a woman who walked past with a smile. Just below was another panel showing him at a clinic, the doctor vomiting while the soldier's skin slowly started to drip from his bones.

"The locals may look like us! They may talk like us! But they are NOT from our world.

"FOLLOW TRANSLOCATION PROTOCOLS! Keep your family safe. Keep your country safe. Do NOT fraternise with the natives!"

I jumped when a few seconds later my dad spoke aloud. I turned to see him holding a piece of paper in his hands. He read from it aloud.

"Word came down from HQ on what to do with Officer 217. Support told me that ReConned officers without executive function are a nightmare to contain, so I guess we're not the first to deal with this. They say if we ship him back, they'll be able to kill him. It may seem small with everything going on, but with the future so uncertain we can't have a ReCon walking around in eternal pain. It's dangerous to everyone and, not to mention, very cruel.

"As soon as the next safe opening comes along, we'll send him back. If there's still a HQ, they can sort it out. If not, then at least we don't have to worry about him giving us away. By the way, I saw you practicing in the mirror. Your accent is getting better. Any day now and I'll arrange a visit to the surface."

"What the hell does that mean?" I asked.

"God knows," he answered, before taking my arm and leading me to a stairwell in the corner of the lab. When we descended, we found ourselves at another floor that strongly resembled a metro station. It bore the sign:

"Outpost 18997." But graffitied underneath were the words: "The Last Stop! Nowhere else to go!"

Gas masks littered the floor, and the railway was clogged with a thousand bleached bones whose screaming skulls looked out from behind cracked and broken visors. They were all reaching for the platform. Turning my light on, I could just about glimpse a broken-down carriage some distance away. Like the other machines in this place, it bore strange tesla coils and copper orbs that I imagine once crackled with electricity and power, but which were now either thick with rust or covered in sickly Verdigris.

I nearly gasped when a breeze flowed through the tunnel and tousled my hair. For a fleeting moment, I thought about abandoning all sense and running into it with open arms and joyful cries, but we were nowhere near the surface. And why were all the skeletons fleeing towards us?

"Dad," I asked, finding myself able to give voice to the thought for the first time since we'd been reunited. "What the *fuck* is this place?"

"Just a bunker," he sighed. "I thought... I don't know what I thought. Just about anything except *this*. I'm starting to think," he gestured towards the tunnel, "that tunnel doesn't lead home at all."

"At least not our home?"

"Right."

Click.

"Fuck," I hissed.

Clack.

"I thought there'd be a way out," my dad said, his face bunching up, close to tears. "Oh God, I'm such an idiot. I thought I'd be safe. I thought..."

"Come on," I said. "We simply have no other choice."

The tunnel ended in a wall, only the breeze kept on coming. It smelled odd, a little like the dust filled air of a construction site. Dad reached out and touched it and we saw the whole wall ripple like water. If we hadn't been running for our lives, we might have even felt awe and wonder.

Click clack

"Here we go," I said, taking a deep breath. Dad turned to look over his shoulder at the source of the noise, only to pull his pull his hand back from the illusory wall.

It didn't come back alone.

Something was on the end of his finger. Something that looked a little like the spots you see in your eye on a sunny day, or like the little worms that haunt the corner of your vision. Only it wasn't flat like those visual flare-ups. It was thick, three-dimensional, and about the size of a leech. It looked a little like something alive and made out of a mixture of KY Jelly and the rainbows you see on oil. Before either of us had a chance to ask about it, it began to engulf his hand.

"Shit shit shit," he hissed. "Get it off! Get it off!"

Dad tried to flick the thing off like a bit of snot, but it didn't react to inertia or even gravity. The way it bubbled and moved around his skin, it didn't even look like it could interact with his hand, like it wasn't made out of the same matter as the rest of us. It got about half-way up his arm before he started screaming.

Click clack

The constable was visible now, working hard to keep its feet steady on the mountain of bones. It was taking its time. But then again, we didn't have anywhere to go, so what was the rush?

"Get it off!" Dad screamed, collapsing to his knees. He held his arm up, and I saw that there were holes punched clean through his flesh like he was a piece of swiss cheese. By now the worm-thing had swallowed his whole arm up to the shoulder, its quivering translucent flesh expanding by the second. Every second or two it would seize up and appear to strain with effort, and another geometrically perfect hole would be punched into my father's flesh, bisecting bone and muscle like it was nothing more than paper.

"Infestation detected!" the constable cried, and I turned to see him closer than ever before. "Biological vessel has breached translocation. Containment protocols have failed."

He reached down and grabbed my father's skull like it was an orange, and he lifted him off the ground effortlessly.

"ReConn Officer 217 preparing for unscheduled emergency translocation."

Click!

The monster's head lurched towards me on its broken neck.

"Do not attempt to flee before the arrival of further police presence. Doing so will only increase the severity of your sentencing. Remain where you are."

Clack!

The neck snapped back, and without further delay, the monster stepped forward into the rippling wall, taking my screaming father with it.

It is not, it turns out, all that uncommon for people to go missing in the underground. Andrew, William, and Caz were not asked after, at least not by the government. Their families have tried to hire private investigators, I understand, but for the most part nothing looks odd from the outside. They held tours underground in dangerous places. They'd had one or two close-calls before (which I'd never heard of when first hiring them), and the police weren't at all surprised it had ended badly for them. I never even had to come up with much of an excuse. I told them about the drainpipe, the one with the ladder, and said it had flooded while we were part-way through it.

After that, nobody asked any questions. Well... except for one. He was a policeman, a normal looking one. And he turned up at my door three weeks after it had all died down while wearing a smile that made my stomach churn. He looked decent enough, I guess. I hadn't wanted to think too much about anything down there and after telling so many lies, a part of me started to believe them. Maybe we had nearly drowned? Maybe I had spent two delirious days stumbling around while half-dying of pneumonia? It made a lot more sense.

But this guy, he didn't look right. Not so much in the face, but in the way he looked at me, the way he smiled. He said he had a few more check ups to do and entered my home with a polite manner, but one which didn't really let me protest. He just entered, nodding and speaking the whole time about the weather and the upcoming easing of lockdown and the smell of good food cooking in my neighbour's kitchen.

Nothing about it was right. Nothing at all. Least of all the suitcase in his right hand that looked *nothing* like the kind of thing a cop should carry. It was old, battered leather with a funny little lock made of oily brass. When it clicked open, he kept its inside facing away from me, but I caught a glimpse of some wires, maybe even a glass tube.

"What are you doing?" I asked.

"Just a test," he said with a smile and an hard-to-place accent. "All sorts of things down there, I reckon. All sorts of funny bugs... *parasites*. Just want to make sure you didn't bring any of them back with you. One day, I hope someone will go down and block all that nonsense off. That way we never have to worry about people getting hurt again. But uh... well, some people can be sentimental about history."

His eyes, turned down towards the mysterious case, were filled with tension. At one point, I shifted uncomfortably in my chair, and he flinched. He tried to hide it, but I got the sense if I reached out and touched him, he would've screamed the house down. Only all of that changed when a little ding rang out from the whirring machine that he wouldn't let me see. Suddenly the case snapped shut, and he was reaching out to shake my hand.

"Oh so good!" he cried, and I could see the relief in his face was coming from somewhere deep inside his soul. "No infection," he said. "Clean bill of health!"

"No parasites," I replied, "entropic or otherwise." And he stopped dead like I'd slapped him hard. That creepy forced cheeriness disappeared, and he looked at me with so much sadness in his eyes.

"Was anybody down there?" he asked.

"Nobody alive," I answered.

"We thought as much," he replied. "Nothing down there worth saving, I suppose?"

"No." I shook my head.

"Well," he said, trying but failing to look unphased, "I suppose we're here for good."

And with that, he left, his strange little suitcase tucked under one arm.

THE MURAL

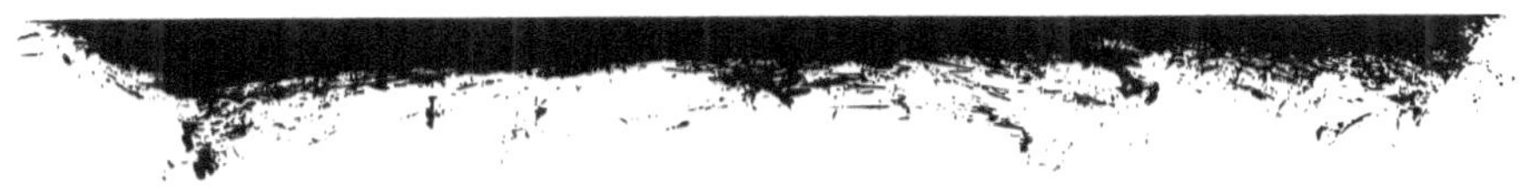

“Are they going to pump this out?” Alec asked as he stepped awkwardly into the flooded basement, the water rising to just a little below his knees.

“I don’t know,” I said.

“Aren’t they renovating the place?”

“I don’t think so,” I said. “It’s just this mural they’re after.”

“Well we’re gonna need it dry,” Alec grumbled. “Can’t run electricity down here like this. Gonna need it for the imaging equipment, too.”

“Yeah,” I agreed. “Plus, God knows what’s in this water. Some of these tunnels must lead off to the catacombs.”

“You can’t be serious!” he cried, his flashlight suddenly snapping from one bare stone wall to another. “Are there actually bodies down here?”

“It’s a church,” I said. “They buried people here. Not recently but, yeah, it has catacombs. Don’t worry, they’re not just stacked up like firewood in some room. There’s gates and stuff to stop people desecrating them.”

Alec shone his light at the water lapping around his feet and curled his lip. It was the colour of old coffee.

“I don’t know how anyone can expect us to work in these conditions.”

"For the money they're paying, I'd work waist-deep in the Thames," I told him. "The guy's last painting sold for seven million. You know how excited the church was when they found out he'd been down here in the seventies? Whatever he put on the walls, they charged him with vandalism then. But now there's money on the line, they want whatever he did restored, packed up, and sold."

Alec huffed. "Where is the damn thing anyway?"

I stopped momentarily to get my bearings.

"Down here."

I waved him on, and we delved deeper into the basement as I led us through a strange mix of large rooms and awkward tunnels carved directly into the rock, some of which you had to stoop just to fit in. Many of the rooms we passed had old boxes in them. One had furniture draped with once-white sheets that were now mouldy and stained. Another had an old piano, the lid still up. Thankfully, it wasn't far. A few minutes at most. Once we found the door, we both put our shoulders to it and forced it open. Water must have built up because it came pouring out at waist-height and nearly took us both of our feet.

"Fucking stinks!" Alec cried over the roar of water, but I ignored him. Once it was safe, we stepped inside, and it was as if our lights grew dimmer and the air colder. A distinct sense that we'd crossed a threshold. A long and empty room where the only sound was water dripping somewhere in the distance. I was about to suggest we'd taken a wrong turn, but then I saw one of the walls had been painted black. And there was something strange about it.

It was only when you let your eye linger that you saw the brush strokes, each no thicker than my thumb. They covered every inch of it and caught the dim light of our torches, shimmering with brief flashes of iridescent colour that were impossible to focus on. The longer I looked, the more I saw great depths in that work. The texture alone was remarkable, like you were up high and looking down on a vast stretch of unbroken ocean. Roiling waves made of slick black water. And the colour... The closest comparison is what you see when you close your eyes. The whole thing made my stomach churn, but there was no denying its artistic merit. The kind of thing I could imagine hanging on a wall in the Tate modern. No wonder the church wanted it restored and transferred out of the basement. But it would be no easy feat. It was huge.

"I don't... I don't feel too good."

Alec wobbled momentarily before collapsing. I had to rush, but I managed to catch him before his head went beneath the water.

"Shit!" I hissed as I struggled to hold his weight with my arms beneath his shoulders. Panicking, I looked around for somewhere to put him, but the room was empty. If I let him go, he'd flop down and inevitably drown, but he was a big guy, and my arms were already getting tired. I had no hope of making it all the way back to the stairs, but I remembered that room was nearby. The one with the furniture. It'd have to do in a pinch. Struggling to keep him upright, I dragged him slowly through the murky waters.

It wasn't easy. While the ground was firm, it was still irregular, and I was walking backwards through knee high water. My mind fluttered through all the possible outcomes of this situation and inevitably focused on the worst. He could drown. Get an infection. We could get lost. Those tunnels were tight and confusing. I could imagine it so very easily, the fear and panic of going around in circles. Rough hewn stone wrapping in on itself so that every turn takes me back to that place as my arms grow ever more tired. What would I do in that situation? I wondered. Would I let him drown? Or would I keep going until I collapsed from exhaustion? And how long would I last? A few hours? A day? Maybe more?

It was a silly idea, but it got my heart racing. Tried telling myself I had it under control. I had a plan. A good one. *Get him upright in one of those old chairs.* He'd probably just fainted because of the air down there. Maybe he was more sensitive to it than most. But while I tried to keep my eyes on him, watching for any signs of consciousness, I kept looking up at the tunnel ahead. With each step, the darkness felt heavier, and the lapping of the water grew so loud it seemed to almost hurt my ears. And yet at the same time I could hear my every breath as clear as if I was standing in total silence. Without any real reason for it, a cold dread crept over me. I didn't feel alone down there. No matter how hard I tried to dismiss it as a childish feeling, it just kept getting stronger. Each time I looked up, I expected to see something. God only knows what I thought would be waiting for me. But it didn't matter. The mere thought there was something in the dark or lurking beneath the water was enough to make me hurry, even as I kept reminding myself that was a great way to make a mistake.

Thank God it wasn't far to the room with the furniture. There was no door, so I simply turned and plodded backwards until I saw a chair that looked good enough. Sure, it was disgusting and green with mould and mildew, but all it had to do was hold his weight. Alec is a good six inches taller than me and built heavier too, so by the time I lugged him onto the chair I was exhausted and had to stop and catch my breath. Hands on my knees. Entire body trembling. I took a few seconds to comfort myself before leaning over him and calling his name.

"Alec," I cried. "Alec!" I gave him a few gentle pats on the face. He seemed to stir, but I couldn't say for sure. "For fuck's sake," I hissed, hearing just the slightest hint of alarm in my voice and trying to suppress it. "Alec, wake up and let's get the hell out of–"

Someone pressed a key on the piano and everything inside me came to a screeching halt. It was dull and off-key, but there was no mistaking the sound that had come from the nearby room. The thought of there actually being someone else down there made my skin tight and my head ice cold. Took every ounce of willpower I had to stand upright and look towards the doorway.

"Mike!" Alec groaned and I damn near jumped out my skin. I don't feel well." he muttered while rubbing his face. "It's so dark in here. I think I might be dreaming."

As the initial shock left me, I was flooded with relief at no longer being alone in that horrible place.

"You fainted," I said with as friendly a laugh as I could manage. "Must be the air down here. We'll need respirators from here on in."

"I'm cold," he moaned while pushing himself upright. "I want to go home. Can I go home, please?"

"Damn right!" I said, while taking his elbow and leading him to the exit. I felt a lot safer knowing it wasn't just me facing the darkness, but I still found myself hesitating as we passed the next room along.

"What is it?" Alec asked as I paused to look at the old piano.

"Nothing," I muttered before hurrying us both along.

Someone had closed the lid.

———

"It's like a different painting when photographed." Marie pursed her lips as she looked at the camera display. "Something to do with how it catches the light?" She picked the tripod up and moved it several feet to her right. She pressed a button, and the flash went off in the dark room like a bolt of lightning. For an instant, the whole place was laid bare. Roughly hewn stone and stagnant water. "Look." She called me over. "It happened again."

I stopped my work setting up the fourth pump at the far end of the room and wandered over. So far I'd managed to pump out most of the water, but it still lay an inch thick along the ground. Of course, the rest of the tunnels were still flooded. No hope there. So the room itself was sealed off. Sandbags at the only doorway with further waterproofing from rubber tarps. I'd since spent days trying to figure out where the last of the water in that one room was coming from, and had been so busy chasing leaks that I'd had to hire Marie to help with imaging.

"Looks funny." I said as I leaned over her shoulder and looked at the latest picture. The wall appeared as an explosion of psyche-delic colours. Closer to a tie-dye t-shirt than the black obelisk it was in-person. "But it's a weird piece. Very textured, and the paint itself is quite unique. I'm not surprised it behaves strangely under a camera's flash."

"But look at it," she said.

"I did," I replied while wandering off, unwilling to stare too long. "It's weird."

"I don't like it," she said before quietly moving the tripod another few feet along.

"Me neither!" I snapped as I knelt down next to the broken pump. "So let's get on with it. I need all the help I can get."

"Alright." She tutted. "Where's your partner in crime then?"

"Alec's not been feeling well," I said.

"Ah that's a shame. Always liked Al." Another flash. For a brief moment my silhouette was painted on the wall opposite the mural. I could have sworn it was a different kind of black, as if my shadow had texture. Brush strokes, even. Before I had time to think about what I'd seen, Marie was suddenly standing by me. "Still no luck with that pump?"

"Driving me nuts," I said.

"Well I want to set the x-ray up now. Won't take long. But we'll need to leave the room each time. Or at least I will, since this is something I do daily."

I thought about staying in that place alone.

"Fuck it I'll join you," I said.

"Well before we get going, I'm gonna need help getting it into position."

"Sure thing," I said as I took her hand to get up.

It was a big unit, designed to capture high-resolution images of what lay beneath paint and canvas. Essential for seeing the early work of a painter. In the few years I'd spent in the archives of the National Gallery, I'd always enjoyed documenting the strange artefacts found beneath famous paintings. Sometimes you could even see a timeline of the artist's process. Preliminary sketches. Features removed. Background details added late into the process.

Most people don't realise there's more than one Mona Lisa lurking under all that paint.

"Okay," Marie said as we manhandled the machine onto the first little yellow marker she'd put on the ground. "First of four. I'll hit the timer, then we make our way to the corridor. It'll beep when it's done. Good to go?"

I nodded, and she hit the button. We walked briskly to the exit and climbed over the barricade, pulling aside the plastic sheeting I'd draped over the doorway. Just as Marie was on the other side, we heard the beep telling us it was done. Then we were back inside, where she removed the plate, put it into a waterproof duffel bag, and the process began again. Each time we moved it further down into the long room. Each time it took a little longer to get back to the exit. It was a pain-in-the-ass, but necessary.

"Last one!" Marie exclaimed when we finally hauled onto the fourth yellow marker. "I'm actually curious to take a closer look at these pictures, you know?" she added before pausing to look at the mural. "It's horrible to look at, but you have to admire the skill that went into it. It's almost, well... *familiar*..." her words trailed off, and she slowly tilted her head. I had to give her a nudge to remind her to press the button. She laughed, pressed it, and with that we were both marching back towards the exit. I quickly climbed over the barricade once more, turned to help Marie, but found myself staring at an empty doorway.

The machine beeped to say it was done, and I poked my head through the tarp and looked around but couldn't see her. Confused, I climbed back in and scanned the room. Nothing. The machine was still there, humming away. But no sign of the woman who, until just a few seconds ago, was right behind me.

"Marie?" I called out, but there was only the sound of dripping water. I was baffled. I couldn't understand where she had gone. She couldn't have gotten past me into the hallway. It just didn't make sense, but as the seconds turned to minutes, confusion was replaced with a chilling panic. "Marie!?" I shouted again. And then again. And again. Each time, my voice got a little louder, and the repetitions grew closer together until I was pacing furiously just screaming her name over and over again. My voice grew hoarse. I even stuck my head out into the corridor and cried out, but there was never any response. I checked every inch of that place and when I didn't find her, I checked every inch again.

Part of me started to visualise her eventual return, to hope for it. Started to imagine that moment of relief. The sight of her appearing at a doorway before explaining where she'd gone. I held onto that fantasy so hard that at times it felt as if I was alive in two worlds at once. One where Marie and I were laughing about a slight misunderstanding, and another where a woman could disappear into thin air. *Surely the latter isn't reality*, I thought to myself as I shouted over and over.

This one has to be the dream.

But if it was a dream, I wasn't waking up. And eventually I accepted that I had to go get help. I didn't even grab my things before stepping out into the corridor. I was in a rush, desperate to get this nightmare over with. To get help and to find Marie somewhere safe and sound, but I only made it a few feet when I heard her voice call out to me from behind.

"Mike. I don't feel so good. Am I dreaming?"

She was leaning on the doorway I'd just left, eyes sunken and cheeks sallow. Even her hair looked thinner. She looked like a woman who'd just spent a week on a desert island.

"Jesus Christ!" I cried before running over and grabbing her. She was close to collapse, wobbling back and forth and clutching the door just to stay standing. "Where the fuck did you go?"

"It's so dark in here. I want to go home," she said in a quiet drone, like a child that'd just been pulled out of a car crash.

"Alright, alright," I said. "Let me... what is that?"

She was holding something in her hands. It was one of the plates from the x-ray machine. She didn't even register me taking it from her. Down in the dark it didn't look like much, and being in a hurry, I simply tucked it under one arm and helped her over the barricade and into the water.

Everything that followed was a rushed blur. I took her into the church, sat her on a pew, and called for an ambulance. Paramedics quickly arrived and rushed her off, asking a few questions here and there about what I think might have happened. I had no real answers to speak of, but when I mentioned that she didn't have her respirator on her, they all seemed to take it as a given that she had carbon monoxide poisoning. That was the official diagnosis for Alec, and I recognised a few of the paramedics from when I'd called them out for him, so they must have connected the dots. But CO poisoning didn't explain why she looked so thin and... I don't know. Broken? She looked worse than awful. Seeing in her that state had terrified me.

At least she's in safe hands, I told myself as I watched the ambulance doors close. I decided it was time to call it a day and went to grab some of the things I'd left on a nearby bench when I saw the slide Marie had been holding. The light was a little better in the church, especially since it was midday, and that broken roof filled the place with rays of amber light. I took the x-ray and held the black plate up, squinting to see what it showed.

It looked like a hurricane of swirls and spiralling bone-white shapes. A confusing mess of strange distortions that reminded me distantly of the background of Van Gogh's starry night. Only there in the middle of all those swirling roiling lines and growths was a woman. Marie, in fact. I was sure of it. And she had both hands clutched to the side of her head like she was screaming for her life.

"You saw it?" The old man who'd answered the door was practically skeletal, but he wasn't infirm. He glared at me with twitchy anticipation of my answer. He seemed ready to explode. "You saw the mural?"

"Yes."

"When my secretary got your phone call, I was ready to dismiss you entirely." Slowly, he looked me up and down like a piece of meat. "You look... intact."

"I was..." I tried speaking, but something about the old man's intense stare caught me off guard. Noticing this, he pulled the door open and gestured inside his luxurious apartment with one arm.

"Come in!" He cried. "I had my staff confirm you really have done work in the church. I am *fascinated* by what you might have seen."

"I was told you bought Mr Halswell's paintings," I said as he ushered me into a room decorated with gleaming hardwood furniture and beautiful red velvet wallpaper. "A collection at an auction," I stammered. "You spent quite a lot of money on them."

"Yes," he replied while sitting opposite me. "Halswell was touched, you know. Spent his life trying to exorcise the things he saw."

"Err, right," I stammered. "I just wanted to know if you had any information on the mural in the church."

"My boy, you've actually seen it which makes you far more of an expert than I am!" He spoke like he was giving me the greatest compliment. "I never had the nerve to go look. I love my esoteric hobby as much as anyone, but I prefer the occult where it is unlikely to do me harm."

"Well I'm just concerned, I had two friends collapse in there and one of them... well, I can't rightly explain it but, she went missing for a while. The church isn't a lot of help, but they told me to speak to you if I wanted some information about the artist."

"Oh, the Church has no real record of that place. Not properly, anyway."

"What is it?" I asked, growing tired and wanting to cut to the chase. "What did George Halswell paint? I've had two colleagues pass out down there, and now one of them isn't answering my calls. Please, I need answers."

"George didn't paint anything," he said with a shrug. "He was sent down as a handyman and found it hidden behind crates of old rubbish. Whatever he saw, he felt compelled to paint *over* it. An attempt at censorship. He wanted to hide it away. That's why he was charged with vandalism by the old priest, who is long since dead. But George's efforts were in vain. He could not unsee what he'd seen, and it would stick with him forever."

"I don't understand. The mural is..."

He leaned forward and grinned. I could tell he'd been hoping for this.

"Yes yes," he whispered. "Tell me about it."

"It's not just tar on a wall," I said. "It's... more. It has a kind of depth. There are brush strokes all over. Thousands, if not millions. They don't look like they form a pattern, but they do. It sits behind your eyes and burns the sinuses. It's an impression of something. The darkness inside a coffin. It looks featureless, but it isn't. Sometimes it's as if it *crawls*."

"Fascinating. Well, the brush strokes don't surprise me," he said while sitting back with a satisfied grin. "George used his hands. But whatever he tried to hide, it didn't just go away because he painted over it. He didn't erase anything. Merely *changed* it. Gave it a different face to wear."

"But if he didn't make it, who did?"

He shrugged.

"Who knows? Those tunnels are so extensive because there were multiple archaeological dig sites held there throughout the 19th Century. They found mosaics dated to the Romans' first arrival in Britain, along with pots and clay that were even older. Some say the church was built atop it to hide the darkness below, but that was too long ago for anyone to remember. When I called the Archbishop to check if they'd really sent you down there, they seemed under the misconception George had created the mural from scratch. But the painting on that wall predates us all." His shoulder sagged and a look of defeat took over him as he added, "I wish I had the courage to see it. I was afraid. So often, the truth can be frightening. When I heard Halswell's daughter was auctioning off some of his later works, I thought... I thought maybe this could be a chance to catch a glimpse of it. A way of seeing what George Halswell saw, as retold by him through new artistic expression."

I sighed. This visit hadn't really told me a great deal so far. Sensing my disappointment, the old man smiled. "Would you like to see them? His paintings?" Suddenly he was the spry and lively person who'd opened the door to me just a short while ago. He sprang to his feet and clapped happily. "Come come come!" he said in a frantic tone. "Come. They're something special. Whatever George saw down there, it really did a number on him."

He wasn't taking no for an answer. He even reached out and grabbed my hand, pulling me along like an excited child until we arrived at a small room he'd decorated as a gallery. The walls densely packed with paintings and prints worth millions, some of which I recognised as worth millions. But he strolled past them like they meant nothing. When he shoved me eagerly in front of his newest collection, I understood why.

Halswell's paintings were not pure black. Spiritual relatives of the mural, but with just enough light to see things beyond. They were detailed and beautiful, at least in the artistic principles used to make them. The forms and anatomy. The use of colour and space. But it was the contents that gripped me and made me nauseous. There were seven, all showing an array of people in various forms of torture and deprivation. Flaying. Amputation. Drowning. Bright white eyes staring at me from a wretched abyss. But it was two of them in particular that had left me feeling like my heart was about to fall out through my stomach.

They showed Marie and Alec. Thin and starved, weeping and broken. Screaming into the emptiness as some unseen force dragged them into icy black water. It shouldn't be possible. George Halswell had died sixteen years prior. There was no way he could have painted my friends, but there was no mistaking the people in those images. Christ, it even showed Alec's tattoo.

"Whatever was buried down there and found by George," the old man said as he savoured the shock and terror on my face. "Is an open invitation to something no one wants to meet. I would say best of luck to you and your colleagues, but there's no point. You're already done for."

<hr>

"Al! Come on! Let me in!"

I banged on the door for the tenth time without reply. Last time I'd seen Alec was when I'd driven him home from the hospital after he collapsed and that had been three weeks ago. I'd just assumed he'd gone to stay with his parents, like he told me he was going to do. But after I saw those paintings, I had a terrible feeling that something bad had happened to him. I called his parents, hoping he'd be there, but they told me they hadn't heard from him. Didn't even realise anything bad had happened. Half an hour later and I was outside his door doing everything I could to reach him.

"Come on!" I shouted before knocking again. "Marie's missing! Is she with you? Please Al, tell me you're both okay."

Anxious and scared for my friend, I put my ear to the door, hoping I might hear him approaching. There were only faint sounds of movement. Irregular. The slightest suggestion of somebody talking.

"Al?" I cried. "Al, please open up."

Something loud struck the door and made me jump, and that sinking feeling in my chest grew worse. He was alive, at least. But that didn't mean he was okay. Even if it meant pissing him off, I was going to have to get in there and check on him. Thankfully I had a spare key from a long time ago and used it to pop the door open just an inch or two and peer inside.

But there was only darkness.

"Al!" I cried through the small opening and immediately regretted it. Something about the smell of the place. Mildew and damp. It made my skin crawl. And the carpet was soggy, like there'd been a leak no one had bothered to fix. It reminded me of the church basement. Not just the water or the smell. But the shadows. The distant sight of doorways leading into empty spaces wreathed in darkness. I didn't want to announce my presence in that place, but I had to let Alec know I was entering his home. "Alec! It's Mike. Are you in?"

There was a muffled bump way off in the back, so I pushed the door open the rest of the way before propping it in place with a nearby extinguisher. The light that streamed in was feeble, but it offered me slight comfort. Unfortunately, I only took a few steps before the door slammed shut and I was left in total darkness. Desperate, I grabbed my torch and turned it on, and what I saw nearly made me drop it again.

There was someone staring at me from a doorway at the far end of the hall. Sunken eyes and pale skin. Hair thinning so badly I could see the scalp, inflamed and raw. And that expression. A dull but hateful glare. The drooling gaze of a lobotomised killer. I didn't even recognise it as Alec at first. It took a few seconds of being gripped with terror before I realised it was my old friend leering at me from a darkened room.

"A-a-alec?" I stuttered. "Are you okay?"

He said nothing. He simply stepped backward and seemed to dissolve into the very shadows. I summoned what little bravery I had left and took a few careful steps towards the doorway where he'd been, but I still couldn't see anything. Only when I stood so close that I had one hand on the jamb did I manage to get a good look inside. Alec was crouched in the corner near some broken furniture. Naked and pale. Spine jutting out from between distended shoulder blades like a starved survivor. He was muttering quietly to himself, the same phrase again and again. I couldn't be certain, but it sounded like he was saying *it's so dark in here*. I wanted to call out to him, but the words were caught in my throat when I saw his blackened fingertips and the buckets of empty paint.

He had remade the mural. Or perhaps just some version of it. A dark and confusing mess of thick, glassy obsidian brush strokes that covered an entire wall. His TV lay smashed on the floor where he'd pulled it down. His sofa pulled out. The coffee table tossed aside. It was like he'd been in a mad rush to get at the wall. Now everything in that place was broken. Taken to pieces. Worse, even. A lot of it was rotten, turning to filth and mould. It was as if the church basement was crawling out of that black wall. Musty air and stagnant water seeping through the waxy paint to taint everything it touched.

"Al," I said, unable to hide the tremor in my voice. "We need to get out of here now."

He looked back at me with teary, desperate eyes.

"He says if you want us back, you know where to look."

With alarming speed, Al jumped upright and ran towards the wall, where he disappeared into the paint like a rock falling into water.

I thumped down into the water with a splash and immediately scanned the basement. Black water rippled away into the distance as my chalky light swept over old boxes and broken shelves. I tried everything to hold on to that sense of urgency and bravado that had compelled me to come rushing over to the church, but in the face of the aching dark that lingered at the edge of my torchlight, I could already feel it slipping away. I knew I had to go marching into those shadows, deep into the tunnel at the far end of the room that would take me to the mural. I had to save my friends. Every time I thought about leaving them to their fate, I remembered that painting. The look on their faces. Agony and torture written in such despairing eyes. If there was even a chance of reaching them, I had to try. And given Al's words to me in that apartment, there really was no doubt about where to look.

Each step was a struggle. The sound of water drove my paranoia to new heights as I kept stopping, expecting to hear the footsteps of some unseen pursuer. Or perhaps something up ahead. But it wasn't until I reached the room with the piano that I finally heard the sound of someone else down there with me.

Music.

I stopped, not quite sure whether I could trust my senses. Was I really hearing it? Or was my terrified mind just conjuring the worst-case-scenario? But soon enough the background noise died down, and clear-as-day I could hear a dreadful song. A strange, discordant tone. Weak and off-key, played with only the vague memory of real musical talent. Shaking with terror, I dipped my light in a desperate bid to make myself less visible, and approached the doorway.

Marie was sitting there, waiting for me. I recognised her as my friend, but this was not the woman I knew. She had aged decades in the time since I'd last seen her, and grown so thin she didn't even look human anymore. And her eyes. Beady and black, nestled above a manic and sadistic grin that was anything but joyful.

"He's taking his time with you," she said in a lilting singsong before rising to face me, her broken, sagging body on full display with thick, knotted scars. This was not the woman I'd put in that ambulance. Maybe it was her after she'd survived a nuclear war, but no... it simply wasn't possible that she could have changed so radically in so little time. But that was her face, twisted with hate and a kind of hunger. But still *her* face. She looked ready to lunge at me. The tense anticipation of a coming. And I really didn't like the thought of those bitten yellow nails scratching at my face and eyes. But instead of leaping, she simply giggled and slid quietly into the water, disappearing beneath the black surface.

I contemplated leaving and turned to look at the way I came, but some twenty metres away my light caught a glimpse of Marie's frightening face staring at me. I jumped, shocked at how she'd managed to slip past me and all the way over there without me noticing. And now she waited, daring me to try and leave. I wanted to. I wanted to march over there. But Jesus, the look on her face... I decided I had no choice but to move onwards to the mural. Maybe Alec would have come to his senses and could help me. A slim hope, but that was all I had to steel myself. So I walked slowly to the final doorway and stepped over the sandbags and into the room with the mural.

Everything was where we'd left it weeks before. Even the old x-ray machine on its tripod. Slowly, a kind of darkness seeped into my thoughts. And the air grew dense and fluid, filling me up like I was drowning in filth. I tried to keep my mind in order and work out the next course of action, but it was useless. I fell to my knees and started to heave, but the harder I fought for breath, the worse it became. Minutes stretched on as the edges of my vision pulsed red and black, and I realised it was as if I was drowning but could not die. And then a horrible notion started to burn its way into my mind. Slowly, it came to me as a powerful truth that all the time I'd spent outside that room was a lie. Just a kind of dream. All the daylight I'd since seen. The mornings waking in my own bed. The sight of London's skyline, and the sound of a world made of bright and colourful things. Those memories were just thin plastic over a far deeper truth. That room. Alec's collapse. Marie's disappearance. They were the only real things I'd experienced. And the cold and damp and dark were all that remained to me. There was no outside world. All of that was a dream. *His* dream.

The only thing that really existed was the ocean on the other side of that wall, and everything else was dreamt up by something that lay in its depths. I nearly collapsed beneath the weight of these thoughts. Every breath was a struggle. Every moment I tried to recall from my old life was like passing a kidney stone.

And then I heard it. A trickle. Looking towards the wall, I saw water seeping out of the paint like sweat from skin. Slowly at first, but then it grew and grew until the trickles turned to a steady pouring. Leaks springing in a dam that held back waters from another world. Eventually, it gave. All at once, a great and terrifying torrent of black water spewed from the painting. It did not last long. A few seconds at most. But it was enough to quite suddenly fill the room with another foot of water.

And once the foam and crashing waves dispelled, I saw him. Alec, kneeling in front of the mural.

"It's your turn in the dark now," he groaned, and all thoughts of rescue fled my mind as I looked at him. What had I even been thinking going there? What was I going to do against *that*? You couldn't fight it. Couldn't stab it or kill it. And Alec's words had chilled me to the bone.

God no! I thought. *No, I'm not going in there!*

"He wants one of us back in there, and it's only fair it ain't me," Alec cried as he rose to his full height. Whatever he'd been through, he was in a far worse state than Marie. He wasn't just starved. He was falling apart. His torso was covered in great weeping lesions so large and deep that you could see exposed muscle and bone beneath. It was as if he had been coughed up out of some giant's belly, half-digested and barely alive.

"No," I muttered. "No no no."

"We had our turns!" He screamed suddenly. "We went in! It's your turn now!"

I ran. I launched myself over the barricade, and fled screaming down the tunnel.

I moved through the water like I never had before. I wasted no time looking behind me. Didn't even waste energy on thoughts of what was happening. There was only the need to drive one leg forward through the water, like a piston in an engine. The burning in my muscles didn't matter. The thunder of my beating heart, so wild and furious it felt like I might just collapse and die at any second, didn't matter. None of it mattered. All that existed to me in those desperate few minutes of flight was the memory of the world above. Sunlight. Birds. Smiling strangers and delicious food. My home and my bed. A world where things made sense.

I was crying when I finally reached the basement and saw the stairs leading up into the light. My heart quickened as I climbed up them on all fours, and my hand reached out for the final one when the world exploded.

Pain. Red. Something like lightning seemed to shoot out of my mouth, spreading across my face in terrible pulses of agony. I had slipped and smashed my face onto the final stone step, catching the very edge on my bottom teeth, shattering them into shards that now floated freely in my mouth. But that wasn't what brought me out of the shock. No. What brought me back into awareness was the feeling of cold water rising over my shoulders, and a hand clamping onto my ankle with almost machine-like strength.

Alec had caught me at the final moment, and was now dragging my floating body back towards the darkness.

I wasted no time. I immediately thrashed and struggled to find my way back onto my feet as he turned and pummelled me with ape-like blows.

"It's your turn!" He bellowed. "We spent our time in the dark!"

In the frantic struggle, I saw Marie crouched in the corner and sobbing.

"We're all his anyway," she whined like a petulant child. "We all have to take our turn. *One way or another, he has us!*"

She launched herself towards me, and I finally lost all desire to help my friends. I hit her as hard as I could. One solid blow in the face. That scrawny little neck whipped back, and she disappeared beneath the waves. Jesus Christ, I still don't know if I killed her. I only know that from that moment on, it was just Alec trying to drag me back towards the mural.

He'd always been bigger and stronger than me. And while he was a bone-thin ghost of his former self, he still held onto me with a steel grip, using one hand while he rained terrible blows down on my head with the other. Bloody and confused, I ended up using one hand to cover my face while the other groped desperately for anything I could use. Eventually, I found something. Cold and wet and slick. An old piece of wood. I swung it as hard as I could, and it broke across his face like rotten mulch.

He stopped and grinned.

It hadn't even fazed him. But where the old piece of wood had broken, I now clutched a jagged collection of splinters. Gritting my teeth and tapping into what little reserves of anger I had left, I reached forward and drove the few inches of broken wood into the largest open wound in his gut.

This time, he didn't grin. He screamed and let go of me, staring in horror at the filthy wood jutting out of his flesh. I wasted not one second more waiting for him to recover.

I ran up the stairs, up into the open light of the church, and slammed the trapdoor shut with a heavy, final thud.

<hr>

Alec and Marie were found unresponsive in their homes just a few weeks later. Not much was made of the painting on Alec's wall, nor the one Marie had apparently made herself. The police questioned me briefly, but seemed to ask a lot of questions about drugs. I think, based on the state of their homes, the police thought Marie and Alec had been addicts. Flooding. Mould. Decay. I did ask the police to destroy the murals they had made in their homes, but they told me it'd be down to the landlord to deal with repairs. Although they said that both apartments would likely have to be gutted and rebuilt from scratch.

Alec and Marie are both still in hospital to this day. Comatose. It was years before I summoned the strength to visit them, and even then I never went further than the door to Alec's room. I merely lingered there and watched him for a moment, hoping that I might convince myself everything that had happened was just some kind of sick dream.

Hopes that were dashed when Alec briefly came awake and turned to me.

"It's your turn in his belly," he said. "This life or the next, you're going there."

He grinned before collapsing back into unconsciousness, and I left and never returned. Since then I've worked a number of jobs, the sole requirement being I never ever want to work on another painting again. Retail. Construction. Factories. Anything, so long as I don't have to pick up a brush or look at one's work. Alec's words in the hospital have frightened me so deeply that I doubt the fear will ever fade. Each night, I dream I'm back in that basement. Others, I am in a timeless void and something terrible is looming towards me. A mouth bigger than most football stadiums, ringed with teeth several storeys high. But the worst are the ones where I am trapped, suffocating, in total darkness, as some invisible fluid burns my skin. But no matter how much I scream or cry, I can't claw my way to freedom. Instead, the more I thrash, the more those ribbed mucus covered walls seem to compress around me until I can hardly breathe.

These dreams are growing more frequent, and recently I have begun to worry that Alec and Marie were right. *It is my turn in the dark.* It has always been my turn. This life or the next, it's where I'm going.

Or maybe I'm just going mad!?

After all, I woke up this morning to paint all over my hands, and the beginnings of something strange daubed in filthy finger streaks upon my wall.

AN INFINITE EXPANSE OF ARID WHITE C LAY

The desert of Liloppo was an infinite expanse of arid white clay. The peat like soil forming a glassy plane with only rippling currents of air and a blinding reflection for a horizon. Wherever Anx took a step, his foot broke the bleached crust and sank into clay the colour of a grapefruit's flesh. Days before, he had watched the caravan prepare for this crossing with hushed reverence: the strange nomads burning noxious incense while praying in an awful chant. The following morning, mothers prepared their crying children by wrapping them head-to-toe in plain cloth and leashing them to their waists. Able bodied men grabbed swords, spears, and bows, and then taken up strategic positions in the caravan. Anx, thinking he'd be expected to help had reached for one of the curved blades but was stopped by the caravan leader.

"The desert is dangerous," the strange man told him while leading Anx to a spot between an old woman and a fat ox. "Put one foot in front of the other, do nothing else. Liloppo is too dangerous for foreigners, you understand?"

Even now, as Anx plodded along in the otherworldly heat, something about their superstitious mutterings frustrated him. He'd spent the day staring at the distance, hoping to see something unusual on the sea-bed of a dried out ocean, but for hours he was unrewarded. Just as Anx wondered if Liloppo was a featureless, near-eternal, void he finally glimpsed something unusual passing by. It was a half-buried cloak, and at first Anx believed it to be the corpse of some lost traveller, but as each step took him closer he realised with utter horror that the body beneath was still clearly moving.

"Look," Anx cried. "Look! They need help." The old woman behind him slapped his hand hard enough to hurt. "Ow, you miserable hag," he hissed. "Someone out there needs help!"

The old woman went to grab Anx's arm, but he resisted, swore at her, and created a temporary pause in the caravan's movement. The old woman's toothless mouth grunted strange words at him. In an embarrassing turn, Anx tried to push her away but lost his footing and fell over. Spitting salt out of his mouth and swearing under his breath, Anx cursed the strange foreigners who had all stopped to stare at him.

"You stupid old bitch!" he shouted. "Can't you see? They need help!" He pointed to the body that still shuddered and twitched in the oppressive heat.

Frustrated, Anx ignored the cries of the caravan leader, who was begging him to return. The closer he got to the body, he saw that there were no footprints leading to them. Nervously, Anx reached out to pull the robe back when he was suddenly bowled over. The old woman had, for some reason, run over to Anx and shoved him over. Anx was already crying out in anger when he suddenly stopped. Behind her, the strange robe had blown open, revealing a misshapen pile of bone and mottled grey flesh. Whoever it had been, their corpse had become a hollowed-out home to a writhing mass of white marbled ticks that bubbled over one another. Anx cried out in horror and immediately began kicking his legs, trying to push himself further away. Suddenly the old woman began to cry and yell in pain, swatting violently at her face and the air. A few ticks had broken away from the corpse and were making a beeline for her feet, and some had already crawled up her ankles and were now deep inside her robe.

The caravan were shouting in a mass panic, but no one broke formation to help. Stranger still, Anx noticed with great concern, a few of the men had armed their bows and watched the scene suspiciously.

"What's wrong with you!?" Anx screamed. Already the ticks had started to swarm around the old woman's feet. In the hysteria she stood on a few of them but succeeded only in allowing even more to race up her feet. A steady stream of the skittering creatures already stretched from the corpse to the old woman like a river made of stones, and visible lumps had formed beneath her skin.

In only a few minutes, she was covered by them. When she fell to the floor, blood was leaking from her robe and her eyes were glassy and lifeless, but her body still twitched. Anx gave up any hope of helping her and backed away.

He was startled when an arrow whittled through the air and landed by his feet. He turned to find that the nomad leader was standing half-way between him and the caravan. He was grim-faced, and had his sword drawn with several armed men by his side. A few of them even had their bows nocked and ready, aimed squarely at Anx's chest.

"Do not come closer," the leader shouted. The caravan, seemingly unchanged by the spectacle, was already moving on. Anx took a step forward, but another arrow flew past his head. "Do not come closer," the leader screamed. "Were you not warned? Were you not told to stay still? We gave you every chance we could. Now they will follow you wherever you go. They will never ever stop. When they find you, if you are near us, they will spread from person to person, killing everyone until nothing remains."

Anx took another step and this time the arrow passed between his legs, ripping a small hole in his robe. He couldn't say if they had missed him intentionally or if it was just luck on his part.

"Do not take another step!" the man screamed, his face reddening. "Your stupidity has already cost us dearly, and we will do whatever it takes to protect the others."

"What?" Anx shouted. "You can't be serious? You can't honestly expect me to... to what? To stay here and die?"

He took a step forward, and another arrow flew into his robes. This one did not miss, but embedded itself into the fatty side of his calf muscle. Anx fell over immediately and screamed out in pain. Already, the men were walking backwards while the caravan receded into the mirage-like horizon. They were moving quickly and as Anx tried to crawl a step in their direction, he saw one of the men nock another arrow. Tears welling in his eyes, faced with an unspeakable death in a hopeless desert, Anx stopped and watched the last of the caravan disappear behind the shimmering heatwaves.

"No," he cried. "No, no, no, you can't leave me!

This was the nightmare of every traveller who passed through this desert.

Not far from him, the old woman's skin had already begun to turn grey and dry. Even worse, Anx saw that she was being dragged back towards the other corpse by thousands of the swollen, bloated ticks. They moved her like ants moved detritus back to their nest.

Strangely, some of the ticks were running in circles. Anx clutched his leg to soothe the pain and began to pull the arrow out, crying in agony as he inched the shaft out of his flesh a small bit at a time, but was stopped by his own morbid curiosity. The lone ticks, the scouts, he thought, were running in a series of outward spirals until one finally stumbled into a footprint he'd made while falling over. It immediately jumped out and ran back to the swarming body from which it had came. Soon, it ran back out with dozens of other ticks and this time it took them straight to the print it had found. They all went tumbling in, like children into a pool. Slowly, others began to follow the trail and soon a steady stream of ticks were running back and forth between the old woman and Anx's trail.

More scouts emerged from the footprint and ran in a spiral until they found another step in the trail and repeated the process of leading others to their quarry. They were systematically leading each to Anx's prints when one of the ticks came within a metre of Anx he realised the danger he was in. He reached down and tore the arrow out of his flesh, wondering if he'd ever experienced as much pain in his entire life. He quickly pushed himself up, cursing the gods, and began to hobble away.

He quickly found the caravan's trail and became determined to follow it out of the desert. He just hoped that the stream of ticks that connected several of his footprints would be slow enough to let him.

⸻

Anx had tried his best to stay on course, but as the merciless heat took its toll, his mind had started to wander. During the first leg of his journey, he was constantly glancing over his shoulder at the chittering army of ticks that dogged him, and each time he turned his head back he had to take a moment to clear his mind and find the caravan's trail. Eventually, a time had come when he had looked back and found the caravan's trail completely gone. It was impossible to concentrate for long in the heat. Sweat tickled his face, and he wiped it regularly, and dust caught in his throat constantly forcing him to cough until he felt sick. The heat was abominable and there was no shade or break in its unrelenting torture. If he had his wits about him, Anx figured he had a chance at finding the trail again, but as exhaustion set in he struggled to even remember his own name.

Some small gifts had been granted, at least. A few miles into the trek, he'd found several flasks of water, and some flint and driftwood, left behind by the caravan. They'd even left some cloth so that he might bind his leg. This wasn't to help him though, Anx realised, but to keep the ticks occupied chasing him for as long as possible. Now that he was lost, he would do just that, wandering deeper into the desert and taking the ticks further off-course than if he'd died within arm's reach of the caravan's trail.

Eventually night came and he may or may not have dreamed of being lost in the desert, chased by nightmarish insects that buried their way into his flesh. When morning came, he wasn't sure if he'd even slept at all, or if he'd just spent the night dazed, staring at the horizon and ruminating on the past day. The ticks had never been more than a hundred yards behind him, and they were slowly tracing his steps with terrifying patience.

At least he got to see the desert up close. With no caravan to badger him, and no trail to follow, Anx was free to stumble across the blinding desert floor to stare at whatever strange things caught his eye. After a full day's trek, it had started to reveal strange things. There were fossils half buried in the orange clay. Huge glittering ammonite fossils the size of houses, skeletal remains of dragon-like monsters, and mountain ranges made of needle-like volcanic rock that turned the horizon into some kind of hellscape. A few sights even offered a distressing glimpse into mankind's deep history; frightful humanoid shapes with finned legs and distorted bodies. It would have been easy to dismiss the fossils as the remains of peculiar animals, were it not for the fact that a few still clutched spears in their bony, prehistoric claws.

Another time in his life and Anx would have stood in awe of the staggering implications of the find, but now all the secret truths of the universe meant nothing to him.

He carried on, wandering past strange bubble-like ruins buried in the soil. A quick glance through a half-buried doorway—one that was curiously no more than three foot high—showed that there was no hope of taking refuge inside. Even if he could have, the ceilings were obscenely low and clearly these homes were not built for men of a normal stature. Venturing further into the desert, he began to notice more overt signs of aquatic life, including barnacles larger than a palace, the jaws of ancient fish that could swallow men whole, and even distant shipwrecks speared on sharp volcanic formations.

But no matter how fascinating, everything he saw was dead. The strange spear wielding merman, the goliath fish, whoever had built the diminutive homes; they were all dead. The only living thing in the entire desert was Anx and the ticks that relentlessly hounded him.

Looking back at them, Anx was ready to consider whether it was better to die of thirst or to be eaten alive when his foot broke through the desert floor and he fell forwards into terrifying darkness.

He awoke screaming. He batted at his body, crying hysterically. In the few fleeting moments of unconsciousness, he had dreamed of being hollowed out by the nightmarish ticks. It took him a while to catch his breath and realise that it had just been a dream. As his eyes adjusted, he saw that he had fallen through a rickety wooden structure from which sand and salt now poured like a waterfall. It looked as though he had fallen into the cargo hold of an ancient ship. There were wooden beams, crates and barrels stacked to the roof, and nets and fishing gear tossed carelessly onto the floor.

Anx cracked one of the barrels open and was staring at the black tar within, when a strange clicking noise caught his attention. A tick had come charging after him and fallen straight into the ship, landing on the floor with a hollow *click* sound. There was only one at the moment, but Anx knew more would follow. He also noticed, with great distress, that the tick's movements were erratic, faster, and more aggressive than usual. Clearly the fall had disoriented it, and it seemed desperate to find his trail, running in unpredictable patterns.

Just a few short feet away was a stairway leading to a manhole. Anx reached down into the barrel with an empty flask and collected as much of the tar as he could, and then bolted for the stairs. Between him and the exit, the tick ran in manic circles until he came closer and leaped over it. As soon as he came within a metre of it, the tick somehow orientated itself and made a beeline for the very stairs he had landed on.

Anx thundered up the steps, suppressing his fear and slamming into the closed hatch, hoping with every last fibre of his body that some boulder or unseen rock wasn't blocking it. It took some effort, a great heaving force that nearly drained him completely, but he finally managed to move it. Through the slight crack he made, dust began to flood into the room along with blinding light. He forced it open further and then dragged himself through the gap he'd made. There, on the desert floor, he shuffled backwards and then finally stopped, lying there to catch his breath.

He was shaking with terror, his heart sinking as he felt a strange stabbing sensation in his leg. He pulled his robe away and saw that a bloody gash had been torn in the bandage around his calf. A fat white body was jammed into arrow-wound, and fresh blood trickled down his shin. Overcome with revulsion, Anx reached down and immediately grabbed the tick with his hand and began to pull as hard as he could. When it finally came free with a sickening pop, the pain in his leg only grew worse. In his hand there was just the fat grape-like body of the swollen tick. Its head remained embedded firmly in his skin and when he tried to push his thumb into the open wound, nearly passing out from the pain, he saw the black arachnid head bury itself so deep into his skin that it disappeared from sight.

Anx wanted to tear his leg open to find it, but he looked up and saw that the ticks had circumvented the hole leading into the ship and were already approaching the drag marks he'd left as he'd clawed his way free of the cargo hold. He cried out in frustration and pulled himself up, watching as blood pooled onto the floor from his leg. He had no choice but to carry on, his leg dragging behind him as it throbbed and itched. He did his best to ignore it and took out the flask full of tar and began to wonder how, exactly, he was going to use it to set a trap.

———

Anx had spent a long time observing the ticks and figured out that, while they were utterly unstoppable in their pursuit, they could still be slowed down. Now he watched the ticks follow the convoluted spiral he had danced across the dusty clay floor, one he hoped would take at least an hour for them to clear while he prepared the tar. He poured it around him in a circle, wide enough to let him sit and rest while he lit a small fire close to him.

He hoped to turn the ticks' relentlessness against them, wondering if they would follow each step with such blind faith that they would walk straight into the flame one after one until the whole hive was burned to a crisp. They were so dogged, he imagined it just might work.

But the bait had to be good.

Night fell, and against every instinct in his body, Anx sat and waited. He watched the ticks follow his circuitous path and still he didn't move. He counted the steps between him and the ticks, counting them down from fifty to a meagre ten. The bubbling horde was so close now he could hear the sounds they made as they clambered over each other in desperate hunger. His leg itched and burned hot with infection, and he had to resist the urge to tear the rotting tick out of his flesh with his bare hands.

He had to focus.

When there was five steps left between him and the ticks, he lit the fire. He waited anxiously as the first tick ran into the open fire and popped, almost instantly, from the intense heat. Slowly, more and more of the ticks marched forwards into the flame where they were cooked alive, bursting open with terrifying pressure as the bubbling tar set them alight. Even better, Anx found himself cheering as some of the ticks retreated while still alight and ran straight back to the writhing hive. The dry insect bodies, all huddled together, must have made good kindling because it took barely a minute before the whole hive was burning like a bonfire. Anx found himself whooping with joy and crying with mad pleasure as lone ticks tried to flee, only for others to follow, bringing the flame with them. They were driven by an evolutionary instinct that they couldn't escape, a hive mentality that Anx had exploited with glorious results.

Eventually, the movement stopped, and the fire continued raging as the hive popped and crackled like the fires Anx remembered from home. When Anx was finally sure they were all dead, when the charred mass no longer gave off any heat, he collapsed from exhaustion and dreamed of the lakes he swam in as a child.

———

Anx awoke in the sun and smiled slyly as he remembered the great victory of the night before. He lay on his back, slowly staring at the crystal blue sky, when he noticed that, somehow, he seemed to be moving. He tried to sit upright, but his legs were unresponsive, almost as if someone had wrapped them in dozens of thick sheets. He could barely move his arms above his chest and was horrified to see that the skin on his forearms was swollen and lumpy. Panicking, he tore open his robe and saw that his torso had inflated to bizarre proportions. Unable to stand, Anx turned his head side-to-side and began screaming at the nightmarish vision before him.

He was surrounded by an endless sea of white marbled ticks that carried him, like ants ferrying food from a picnic.

VOYEUR

"So that's where the... that's where *she* will be sitting?"

I gestured to the glass wall that made up one side of the room. On the other side was an empty chair lit by a single spot light, like something out of an interrogation scene.

"Yes," the aide answered. "You'll spend three months in here and right over there will be the corpse."

"Will it smell?" I asked, unsure if the question was inappropriate.

"No," he replied. "The room is airtight. Nothing can get in or out."

"That includes flies?"

"There will be no flies," he said. "Just the body which will, as you know and have been told, decompose over time."

"How did you find her?" I asked.

"Mr Brynshaw has his methods."

"I assume you've seen her, then," I said. "Does... did she really look identical to me?"

"I am not allowed to answer that," he replied. "You'll have to judge for yourself once the exhibit begins in earnest."

"How did you guys find her? She's not... she's not actually related to me, is she? This poor dead girl? She's not some long lost twin?"

"Mr Brynshaw is an astonishing man," the aide replied. "Many of his exhibits are organised decades in advance and the considerable wealth at his disposal means there are very few obstacles he cannot overcome. His wealth is second only to his remarkable insight. I wouldn't worry about the *how* of it all. That's for the critics to scratch their heads over. All you need to concern yourself with is staying busy for the duration of the exhibit, and when it's all over, collecting your payment."

I could read between the lines. He was telling me to shut up and take the money.

"Onto the computer," he said, moving swiftly over to the nearby laptop. "It cannot connect to the internet and the only application installed is a custom messenger service that allows you to communicate with a staff member elsewhere in the facility."

"I was told it'd be like having a personal shopper."

"Exactly," he replied with a reptilian smile. "You are encouraged to use the service to acquire whatever comforts, creature or otherwise, you desire. For that reason, the room will be bare except for the laptop and a bed on the first day. I have been instructed to remind you that nothing is off limits. Our staff are creative and enthusiastic. It doesn't matter if you ask for oil paints, a pound of cocaine, or even a human heart, we'll be able to find it for you. "

"I can't imagine I'll need much more than a kindle and netflix," I joked.

"We'll see." He smiled and then pointed to the cameras on each wall. "Quite literally. The livestream begins tomorrow."

The premise of the exhibit was painfully simple, but also frustratingly clever. The kind of thing you hear and immediately wish you'd come up with yourself.

I was going to spend a month in a room sat across from the decaying corpse of my own doppelganger. When it was all done, the footage would be edited into some weird arthouse film. I could spend the four weeks doing coke, or I could spend it learning to play the piano, or just binging tv. It didn't matter. It's all too easy to imagine how anything I did could be twisted into some commentary on my fear of death.

At I figured it'd be easy.

But no one could have prepared me for what it felt like to look at my own dying face. This wasn't a mere resemblance. She was my ghost.

God, I thought, *did they have to leave her eyes open?*

She looked sad. More than anything, that's what surprised me. She was posed upright in the chair and clothed in the same plain outfit as me. Her features were an almost-perfect mirror of my own. She was not a mirror-image, but neither are identical twins. There are always subtle differences, and the effect was eerily uncanny. Out of some morbid curiosity, I pulled up my own chair and placed it opposite her. I sat down and studied every feature of her face in the same way I would with a mirror.

Why is she sad? I wondered, only to feel a little stupid. *She's dead,* I thought before getting up and trying to shake off the goosebumps that were crawling up my back. There was no need to look so closely...

She and I were going to spend enough time together.

A slot on the door opened and a small package came through. It contained the eReader I'd asked for just a few minutes ago.

"Better than Amazon," I grumbled before looking up and catching *her* eyes. I tried not to look her way, but it was hard not to. The room was so bare... so plain. And the human form is naturally attention-grabbing, especially when its cold dead eyes are glaring right at you.

To my surprise, I realised she had a kindle in her hands.

"That's elaborate," I said, then looked at each one of the cameras. I didn't want to look shocked, even though deep down I was pretty damn impressed they'd managed to slip in there and give her a prop without me noticing. I was also a little unsettled, though I swore it didn't really mean anything. *They're playing games,* I thought. *You knew it wouldn't all be spelled out to you. You knew there'd be little surprises along the way.*

"Were you a reader?" I asked the pale figure before I'd even realised I was talking aloud. Of course she didn't answer, but she *looked* like a reader.

"What did you read?" I asked. "Romance? Horror? Historical fiction?"

She didn't answer. Nor did she move, but I felt that she was listening to me anyway. The idea was ridiculous, so I shrugged it off and went off to read a bit of Agatha Christie.

My room was looking a little fuller. I had a bookshelf, a desk, a Switch, and a pretty damn nice desk chair. Duplicates of everything had somehow made their way into the other room when I wasn't looking, which was starting to annoy me. It always happened in the few seconds when my back was turned. But it wasn't like I spent every minute of every day staring at her. If I wasn't sleeping, my head was buried in a book or watching TV.

Would it really be so hard to run in there and shove a book on the table next to her? I told myself it wasn't a big deal, that this was just part of the game being played by the artist. Before the exhibit began I was convinced that the hardest part of this job would be the solitude. But between the cameras and *her* glassy dead eyes, I actually felt claustrophobic, almost suffocated under the weight of so many potential gazes.

I looked up to see if anything about her had changed, and nothing had. It had been twenty minutes, and I'd read the same line six times because my eyes kept darting upwards to catch sight of *her* sitting there, always in the background and out of focus. If I put on headphones and turned away, I knew I'd get a chance of ignoring her, but as the days ticked on it was getting harder and harder to turn my back to her. I had no way to explain the feeling except to say that she didn't feel dead. I'd seen bodies before and I never felt anything around them. They were just meat. They weren't pleasant to be around. Sometimes they made me feel sad. But I never ever felt like I was looking at anything other than an inanimate object.

A person is what goes on inside the head and without that, they're just inert matter.

But with her, it was like she was looking right back at me, and my brain didn't know what to do with that information. I told myself, and I admit this is a pretty morbid thing to think, that the creepiness would probably get better as time went on. The more she rotted, the less she'd look like me, and the sooner the illusion would fall apart. Sure it'd be gross, but at least I wouldn't see my own features reflected back at me like I'd floated on down to attend my own funeral.

Without knowing why, I got up from bed and walked up to the glass. Feeling hopeful, I looked for the first signs of decay, for some subtle change in the fit of her clothes that told me she was starting to bloat. There was nothing, but as I watched a little fly emerge from behind her ear. It flew a few short figures of eight in the air before landing on the glass and slugglishly crawling around. I didn't like it there, didn't like knowing where it had come from. It must have started life as a maggot and I already had a good guess as to what it had feasted on, just out of sight.

I struck out with my hand and hit the glass. I only wanted to scare it off.

Imagine my surprise when it died beneath my palm in a fuzzy splat.

<hr>

I woke up later that night to find the stain on the glass gone. I flicked a switch, and the lights came on with a rising whine. Slowly they brought the rest of her room into focus. The kindle lay on the table (much like mine), the bed covers were ruffled (much like mine), some books were on the mattress (much like mine), but she hadn't moved an inch. There were no scrape marks by her chair. If anything, you could see the first few signs of dust gathering by her feet. I knew that all of that background stuff was just theatre. It had to be! She was hardly climbing into bed and sleeping just like me, but I had this strange pit in my stomach that stopped me from letting it all go.

Quietly, almost stealthily, I got up and approached the glass to study it. I told myself that I was only interested in understanding how that rich bastard had pulled the fly-trick off. But that didn't ring true to me. The fly had come from *her,* quite literally emerging from behind her neck and making its way towards me. It couldn't have magically passed through the glass.

It just couldn't have.

I touched the window and in an instant, my thoughts were filled with images of gossamer wings and writhing maggots. I gasped and pulled away, nearly stumbling over the chair that had slid behind me without me noticing. How it got there without me moving it, I couldn't say. But I hardly noticed it. The images in my mind had felt so vivid it was almost like an attack. I put my hand to my neck just to check nothing was crawling there, but I could feel it. I could feel *something,* some ghostly sensation that persisted and that was when I got the strange idea that the thoughts I'd just seen never actually belonged to me.

They had been *hers.*

"Ridiculous," I muttered aloud, if only to hear my own voice.

I shook it all off and went back to bed, desperate to forget. But from then on the nights got *really* hard. Whether I was painting or reading or watching tv, I could feel her eyes glaring at me through the glass. I felt watched, the same feeling you get from creeps on the bus or train. And worse, it never went away. Every night these thoughts and sensations intensified and that got me wondering if it was just the isolation playing on me. I considered myself a pretty robust person. I don't scare easily, and I took the job *knowing* I could do it and make it out fine.

But you hear all those stories about what happens to inmates in solitary, about cabin fever...

So I started keeping a diary, only it didn't go very well. They delivered it within the hour and the first thing I wrote was *Have I overestimated myself?* I immediately hated such an admission of self-doubt. Anything I made would be part of the exhibit, and the same went for those weak, sad little words. I refused to let that happen, so I tore the page out and what lay beneath was like a punch to the face.

There were words. Hand-written in a fountain pen. The same one I was holding. The ink was still wet. But the writing wasn't mine. And the words... reading them felt like reading my own death sentence.

I'm so cold, they said. *I shouldn't be here. I am meant to be somewhere else. I am meant to be nothing.*

I want to be nothing.

Why do I still have shape?

There are thoughts in this place that are not mine. They crackle like fireworks in the distance. I can see things silhouetted in their light. Tall things.

I am not alone in this place.

———

Her name was Natalie, I typed into the computer. A few seconds passed before I got my reply. Somehow, the digital words seemed nervous.

You were not permitted to research the subject, they said.

It had been a guess, or at least I'd thought it was. I'd woken up one night to find the name echoing in my mind like the passing scream of a motorbike. It had pinged around in my head all day and I was desperate to know if the impossible was true, so I came up with this little gambit to check.

We will investigate your behaviour prior to entering the room and check for signs of misconduct. If we find any evidence, you had prior knowledge of the other woman's identity, we will discontinue the exhibit and payment will be revoked, the computer told me.

I guessed it, I typed. *She looks like a Natalie.*

We will tell you the results of our investigation when it is over, they replied.

———

After a full week, she finally began to rot.

I found myself constantly touching my own face to see if the skin felt puffy or cold. I checked my hair to make sure it wasn't falling out. I pinched my legs, my arms, to see if they were as skinny as the reflection in the glass. Wrinkled skin, lips that pulled back, black gums and unnatural teeth... She was changing and in ways that I didn't expect. Her eyes were like glassy marbles embedded in her skull, grotesque glistening off-white orbs whose surface was a road atlas of blue and crimson veins. She looked wrong. I'm not an expert, but I always thought that bodies lost their shape over time. But she looked as if she was coming together. Her muscles looked hard, her face was more expressive, her finger nails had become sharp and chipped. The look in her eyes... it was the look of a torturer trying to decide where to put the first needle.

I continued to check the diary every day. There was always something new, something harrowing. Most of it was just her talking about the empty aching sadness she felt, the sense of invasion, of her thoughts being shared. But over time, the entries were starting to change.

The pain is unbearable.

The tall things that live here won't leave me alone.

Sometimes I think I dreamed another life but I don't like to think about it. This is reality. The only one that matters. There is only pain and hunger and deprecation, all at their hands.

I shouldn't be here. I was meant to dissolve into this place. But something is giving my thoughts shape. Something is keeping me whole.

The tall things tell me there is another world. Another me. They gloat. They tell me about the comforts she enjoys. Sometimes I catch glimpses of her, legs crossed on a bed while reading a book. The sight of it hurts more than anything I thought possible. Sometimes I feel as if my chest is going to cave in from the heartache, and the tall things laugh and tell me I don't have a chest. Not here. Not in this place.

My connection to the other world intrigues them. Excites them.

They want me to hurt her.

I woke up retching and gagging, barely able to breathe. For a second, I thought the staff were pumping gas into my room, choking me with some toxic vapours. I was sick all over myself before I even got half way to the computer. My eyes burned so fiercely I could hardly see. My nose was bleeding. My mouth ran over with spit and vomit.

It was a smell. I was deep in something, inhaling it. And it didn't take a genius to figure out what. I looked over to *her*, and she was smiling. Of course she would be. This was *her* stench, *her* rotten, rancid grotesque miasma that she had somehow sent after me. I felt like I had my head inside her bloated, slick stomach. This was the odour of a sacked city. Of a mass grave.

I reached the computer and banged out a message on the keyboard while I gagged and heaved my way through each individual breath.

I can smell her!!!! I typed.

Three dots.

Someone was replying.

That's impossible.

I vomited once more and passed out before I could let them know exactly what I thought of their impossible.

The dust was no longer gathering by her feet. It was disturbed, and footprints showed that something had gotten out of her chair and stalked its way into the darkness behind her. Right now, she was still in the chair. Still looking at me. Still grinning. At least the smell was gone, although I'd had to spend all morning cleaning my own vomit. Even worse, the computer was unresponsive to my demands for cleaning supplies. I had to use some dirty bedding to mop it all up.

I thought you said this place was air tight! I wrote in anger. *I could clearly smell her!*

I waited and waited, but no one wrote back.

I sat in my chair and reviewed my supplies. It had been two days, and no one was doing anything for me. I told myself it would be fine, but I didn't feel it. The night before I'd woken up to the frightening sound of wet feet slapping against a tile floor. As I rolled over to look, there was a hurried pitter patter and the sound of a screeching chair. She was back in place by the time I got the lights on. It could have fooled someone else, but not me. I saw the path she had carved through the dust and, even worse, the viscous brown fluid her rotting feet left behind.

I was alone with his thing. They had stopped bringing me food, and I had no way of opening the door.

Unless I wanted to try eating my books, I was going to have to get inventive. I looked around. I remembered the smell and looked upwards. There was a vent, and it was easily as wide as my shoulders. I had no idea where it led, but it would be better than staying here, I decided.

But I figured I'd have one last go and reaching the people outside.

Please help me! I typed.

And then I waited.

And waited.

I didn't want to go for that vent. I wanted this to be part of it. To be part of the exhibit. I wanted them to reveal this was all a big hoax. And I knew a lot of what I'd seen and experienced could be a hoax. I knew that. With enough money, just about anything could be faked.

Please help me! I typed into the computer for the thousandth time. I was crying again. Sometimes I wasn't sure I ever stopped.

Three dots.

My heart leaped. I was so happy I let out a slobbery laugh, the kind where you don't even check if you've let spit run all down your chin. But it quickly all came crashing down.

I'm so cold, the screen replied.

I hate it here

Why won't you let me die?

When I turned to face the window, I saw that she was gone.

The vent came off easily. I'd had to dismantle the computer to find a strip of metal that was thin and sturdy enough to match the flat headed screws. And then I had to turn the desk over and stack it on the bed so that I could reach the ceiling. It took me a good ten minutes of balancing in the air before I got the screws out, but when it was all done, the flimsy bit of cover was sent tumbling to the floor with a loud clatter. Above lay an empty square cut into the metal ceiling. It was freedom, hard earned, but all the better for it. I reached up and momentarily hung off the edges, just to see if they'd hold my weight. They buckled slight, and the metal was sharp and rough enough that it was already starting to cut into my flesh. But the ceiling still held.

I hauled myself up and took a look. The vents reached a long way to my left and right. There were no obstructions, and they clearly went past the boundaries of my room. Hoping they'd be able to hold me, I dragged myself into the vent and made towards the right so that I was moving away from *her* side of the room. The only thing I had for light was a smart watch that monitored my vitals. It wasn't under my control, but if I tapped the screen, it lit up with the time. So that's what I did. I tapped the screen and used whatever meagre light there was to shuffle forward a few feet at a time. I could have done it in the dark, but it was tight and uncomfortable, and my heart was already in my throat. Every voice in my mind was telling me to go back, but I knew that wasn't an option. I'd already eaten what food I had, and if I'd found a way out of the room, then surely with enough time *she* just might find her way in. I couldn't just stay there like some sitting duck.

Thankfully, the vent held up, and I was making slow progress, but it was still progress. I couldn't exactly just turn around and look, but I did manage to sort of angle my head so I could get a sense of how far I'd come. The only source of light was from the open panel, and it glowed behind me by a good distance. That meant I must be past my room and that if I could just find a way back down, I'd be out and about in the main facility.

That was something I was desperate to do. My paranoia was already firing on all cylinders. Whenever I stopped to get the light back up, I'd swear there was a moment where the rhythm of my feet carried on without me. It made me think that something was behind me, stopping and starting to match my own movements. And even worse, I knew deep down that if this was true, it must be catching up with me. Slowly but surely, it was taking its time. Having its fun. I was all alone, trapped in the dark, metal walls compressing me so tight I couldn't even get my hands above my head. I had to inch along with my feet and elbows. Anything coming after me could take its time.

I just needed to reach another vent that I could knock out. But for some reason this duct just kept on going and going. It never turned, it never sloped up or down. It just kept marching on. And the longer it went, the more convinced I became that any second, I'd feel something brush against my ankle, or my heel, before it clamped down and dragged me away. And each time I checked my watch, I saw that the seconds ticked by with agonising slowness. By the time I stopped and let out a desperate, panicked sob, I'd barely been crawling for ten minutes.

"Please," I whined to no one in particular. "Just let me the fuck out of this place."

A smell came wafting out of the darkness. It was the same overpowering odour I'd woken up to on that night. For a few seconds

I remained frozen in place, acutely aware of how vulnerable and exposed I was while holding my breath, desperate to catch some sign of what might be coming my way. But deep down, I already knew what it meant, sign or no sign. She was in there with me. She'd realised what I was doing, and she'd slithered up here to find and take me. As if to confirm my worst fears, I heard the sound of her breathing.

Long, laboured, and wet. It was like someone sucking oxygen through a stoma in their neck. I immediately began to wriggle forward, desperate to make any kind of progress. But the metal walls rang with more than just the sound of my struggles. Somewhere behind me, her nails thrashed against the metal panelling with an excited and manic screech. There was no doubt in my mind now. She was chasing me, and the sounds she made grew so loud, so quickly, they filled me with despair. But I didn't let it overwhelm me. Sobbing and shaking, I kept on inching forward for as long as I could before something in me snapped and I tapped my watch to get a tiny slither of light. I wanted to use it to try to turn and get a look at her coming behind me.

Instead, it lit up her face just inches from my own. Wild angry eyes, half-orbs bulging from her skull, glared at me while a smile twisted her face into a rubbery exaggeration. I went to scream, but it stuck in my throat. I was paralysed, so frightened I felt my heart swell and I wondered if it was possible to die of fright.

More than wondered, actually.

I hoped.

And then the light on my watch died.

A greasy palm smeared against my cheek. She tittered with excitement. I practically dislocated my shoulder so I could wrench one arm over and use it to defend myself. I'm still not sure exactly what happened next, but I think she bit me. There was a feeling of pressure on my forearm. Intense. Sharp. Painful beyond imagination. But I used the leverage to push her away from me. Any distance between us, I figured, would be good. It must have angered her because she stopped giggling and started grunting, and with one hand she awkwardly grabbed my face and began to dig her nails into the skin. It hurt like hell, and I kicked, screamed, and thrashed with everything in my power. She responded by digging her talon-like thumb into the fleshy muscle of my cheek. Using her nail like a shovel, she began to dig and grind her way past the skin. And then, with growing force, she just *kept* on digging and digging until there was a little *pop* and a sudden release of pressure.

And then her thumb was in my mouth. Salty and sour and foul in a way that will haunt me forever, she laughed and used the leverage to pull me forward. I felt her teeth release from my arm, and I knew even in the dark she was opening her mouth wider than was possible while yanking my face and closer and closer to a dislocated jaw full of too-many teeth. Meanwhile, my mind reeled from the alien sensation of her wrinkled leathery skin pressed up against my tongue.

I'm not sure I ever really thought about my next action. Not the reason for it, or even the potential consequences. Something in my mind snapped and did it for me.

I bit down.

I bit down so hard that one of my teeth cracked. But I didn't let up. I didn't stop until I heard a loud snap and felt her hand slip away while something else came loose in my mouth. I spat the thumb out and screamed and with my free hand, I began to rip and claw at anything that might be in front of me. I was so out of it, so enraged and disgusted, that I didn't even feel the air duct start to swing and move. In fact, I wasn't really aware of anything other than hate and malice until something gave with an audible *twang* and the tunnel was flooded with light.

I briefly felt myself falling and then there came a blow so hard it knocked everything out of me all at once.

When I awoke, I was still in the vent, only it had been relocated to the dusty concrete floor of a storage space filled with old boxes. I immediately pulled myself out and looked around for any sign of her, but she was nowhere to be seen. The only thing left of her was a thumb whose foul stink still permeated my mouth and sinuses. As my body crashed, I finally took the time to bend over and heave up what little bile and fluid there was in my stomach. Meanwhile, my skull pounded, and my chest felt like I'd fallen asleep with a boulder on top of it. But in a way, I enjoyed the pain and discomfort. It reminded me I was alive, despite everything I'd been through.

As soon as I was done going through the motions, I straightened myself out and made for the nearest door. I was shocked to find a hallway lit by the thin suggestion of sunlight. Windows, up high, glowed blue and the sight of it made me laugh out loud. But there was something else behind the appearance of escape. Something unpleasant. When I'd arrived, the facility was thriving with people, and electric lights carried a warm amber glow into every nook and cranny of the winding hallways. But from where I stood there was not a single light turned on, nor was there the hum of nearby electronics, or the passing of feet.

It was dead.

Abandoned.

Looking around only confirmed my suspicions, but perhaps not in the way I'd hoped. I found an empty office with a smear of blood across the walls. Papers thrown around the place. A canteen with the fridge turned over, and the tables smashed to pieces. An archive with signs of a fire having raged through the filing cabinets. One room looked like an altar with all kinds of funny symbols drawn on the walls. Whatever its purpose, no one was around to tell me. Something had torn through this place and left no survivors. Didn't take a genius to guess what.

After a while, I found my observation room. Rows and rows of cameras showed every little inch of my room, including the toilet. Given the pay check, maybe I shouldn't have been surprised they had no respect for my privacy. But it pissed me off anyway. Well, they weren't observing me anymore. A greasy trail of bloody footprints that led out of the room and towards a wrenched-open bulkhead let me know that Natalie had gotten out and dealt with the staff. And from the smell, I'd have to say it happened a good few days ago, around the time they'd stopped replying to me. That made sense. I did find myself worrying a little about where their bodies actually were. Maybe they'd fled. Maybe they never got the chance... What Natalie might want with them I couldn't imagine, but if she had taken them away I only hoped they were dead. I'd looked into those eyes and they were filled with a special kind of hatred.

Natalie had at least returned to her room. What motivated her to stop attacking me, I couldn't say. But as I approached the screen that showed her, she turned her head slowly to gaze through the camera and right at me, and I knew she was aware of my watching her. I got the sense that it agitated her. That my mere proximity wound her up like a toy, and the longer I looked the more I risked her sparking into full-blown life and coming for me.

So I turned away and moved on and I eventually managed to make it out of there using a set of keys I found dangling laying in a pool of blood. After a process of elimination, I found the parked car they corresponded to and used it to get the hell out of that place. I was all too happy to leave it behind, of course. To leave it all behind. Escaping with my life was more than enough for me. But a few weeks later a check did arrive That didn't bother me so much. It felt earned, if I'm honest. And I'm glad I got the money. I noticed that Mr Brynshaw had signed it, and even worse, he'd written a little note for me on the back.

My condolences on the loss of your long-lost twin sister.

Along with those faintly mocking words was the diary Natalie and I had somehow come to share. A congealed brown handprint covered one side, and her name was scrawled onto the back. The sight of it made me feel sick.

But that didn't stop me reading the final entry.

———

It was nice meeting you.

Even though you weren't very nice to me. You're lucky you fell asleep. When your thoughts stopped, so did mine. But that's not a permanent solution, is it?

I'm still out here.

Maybe I was a little impatient.

But I won't make the same mistake again.

THE WATER PARK

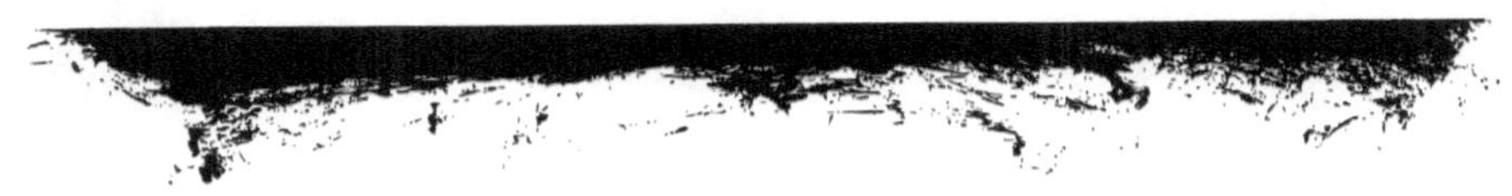

The summer I got a job here I was 17, and it was a good year. Ellen Ditsworth used to work the hotdog stand, and we'd sneak cigarettes under the beams of the Dragon Slayer ride, cringing and giggling as the cars went overhead, dripping water all over us. Wet hands and damp cigarettes... but it was near her station and I think she found it funny to get splashed. It was out of the way, too. It was always quiet and cool down there, even in the summer heat. If any of the ride goers smelled our cigarette smoke as they hurtled overhead, they didn't say anything. One time, when we fumbled around and flirted, I kissed her fingers, and they smelled like an ashtray. I still think about it to this day.

I was twenty-two when they offered me the winter job. Ellen was long gone by then. No more bright red short-shorts and poorly shaven legs that she'd invite me to stroke under the pretense of showing just how bad she was with a razor. There were other girls, but by the time the final summer rolled around, I'd long felt uncomfortable hanging out with new hires. Sometimes I'd stand there listening to them talk, and I'd feel lonelier than I had when I was by myself. I was thinking about my future around this time when the manager told me he had an opportunity for me to make good cash.

They needed someone to stick around and keep the place ticking while everyone went back to the real world. Usual guy had walked, and they needed someone bad. Last day before the park shut for winter was always Halloween and that was only because it had a fireworks show. After that, it turned into a ghost town and I'd be on my own. I'd get a trailer to sleep in, and I could use my own car to get to the closest shop. The park would pay some of my gas. Not all of it. But enough to help out. Only real problem was I'd be alone. Not that the place was a desert island. There were two towns within easy driving distance. And I could have friends around so long as we didn't mess with the rides. But other than that, I'd be the only staff member on hand for the entire four months. Security guard and janitor rolled into one. I agreed, but I told him when the park reopened in March, I'd be done. I figured it was time to move on. Get a degree like some of my friends had. Or maybe my dad could help me out with a job somewhere. World was wide open to me, and I figured I'd sit on my ass all winter, make a shit ton on overtime, and then go onto some new adventure where I'd meet another Ellen Ditsworth or two.

Yesterday I turned 38 and I'm still in the park. Government signs my cheques now. Couldn't tell you when that happened exactly. Probably after the media got wind of Denise Surrey who broke in with her friends and never left. Lotta kids have gone missing here over the years, but she was the one who went mainstream. Her parents were doctors, and she had blue eyes, so she got just enough attention to get the news cameras out. When the fuss died, and the media moved onto its next story, some government guys came and installed 8ft steel palisade fences. Gave me the keys to the only gate and scarpered real quick. Gave me a funny feeling seeing four men in suits, barrel chested with pistols on their hips, climb into an unmarked vehicle and accelerate out the parking lot so fast the back of the car fishtailed. One of them looked over his shoulder at the park and he was so scared it was like he was looking at a mushroom cloud.

I was the one who found Denise. She'd gone crawling head first down the AstroMissile water slide. One of those up and down kind of slides that have you bouncing along on a padded dinghy. Rides like that are usually open top, but this had long sections in a closed tunnel with LED lights to look like stars. Thing is, depending on weight, some people would catch air and hit the top of those tunnels going twenty mph, maybe more. We used to take turns going in there to pull out any teeth that'd got stuck in the roof. Fifteen years later and that tunnel mouth looked like something out of a nightmare. Fairy moss covering the opening. Darkness inside heavier than the night around it. Bone dry and with no obvious way to safety.

Denise died of thirst.

They think she was in there for six days, crawling around in the pitch black looking for an exit that should never have been more than a hundred feet away

There were signs something was wrong with this place back when it was still open. I just didn't register them. There were the injuries and accidents that are common in every water park, but we had a couple hundred serious ones every year. Usually one a day. Tried to mitigate it with safety measures, but half the time they didn't work. Radios would bug out when you'd try sending a warning. Repair guys would get lost, calling up angry saying the road just kept going right forever, and they'd had enough of this shit. Out of order signs would go missing. Sometimes kids would insist some staff member had waved them through on a closed attraction. They'd be so adamant I started to believe them. I think the manager did too. He made it policy to have name tags on us at all times, and if the kids said whoever gave them the go ahead didn't have one on, he'd tell us all to forget it. Like it wasn't even worth trying to figure out who needed a disciplinary.

I had it happen once where I radioed to the guy at the top of one slide and told him to stop any kids coming down. The last one had come out bleeding and looking unresponsive, and I wanted to check on him. I remember pulling him out of the water and looking at this boy all slack and pale as a sheet of paper with blue lips, so fucking cold it hurt just to hold him, and I wondered if I was holding someone dead when out of nowhere another kid slammed into me so hard I went under. Scared me shitless cause for a second or two, it was like I couldn't see the surface of the pool. Almost like there wasn't one. Just blue forever and ever. Before I could start to panic my feet found the floor and I surfaced only to see the kid I'd been holding seconds ago standing there looking worried. He was the picture of good health. Asked if I was okay, said sorry for hitting me when he came out the slide, but really it was my own dumb ass fault for standing there in the first place.

Guy at the top swore on his life he'd never got any radio message from me. I put it all down to the head injury, which was bad enough the owner made someone drive me to the emergency room. Looking back, I'm pretty sure it was the park having its fun with me. Could have been worse. You could say it likes to play tricks, but those tricks are mean as hell and over the years they've only got worse.

Despite all I've told you so far, the first winter alone wasn't as bad as you might think. Creepy as hell walking around all those rides that were usually so busy and full of life. Tarpaulins pulled across all those pools, big and small, moving with gentle susurrations in the icy winds. It wasn't great in the day, overcast and dreary, the air seemingly blue. But at night it was even worse. I made those rounds quickly, stopping sometimes to summon what little bravery I had to shine a light in the pitch-black toilets, or to check one of the changing stalls dotted around the place. Things went missing a lot. Moved around. Once one of the rides came to life at 3am and I woke to the sound of tinny music echoing throughout the park. But winter came and went without any real incident.

First day the park reopened, I went to see the manager and slipped in some water. Broke my left arm and did a number on my back. Owner was so scared of being sued he threw money at me. Told me he'd cover the medical bills and sit me up in my trailer and pay me to do nothing. *Nothing*. What was I gonna do? I'd arranged to start another job on a construction site in a few weeks, and there was no hope of me doing that kind of work with my injuries. I needed money and had no other way of making it. I agreed to stick around until I felt better, but unfortunately I *never* felt better. Winter soon rolled around again, and the same deal as last time was back on the table. He needed someone on-site, and I needed money. I took it thinking another few months in the park wasn't so bad.

I was wrong. Second time round was a lot worse. Part of it was me. 23 years old and with a bad back, drinking most nights and struggling with the prescription painkillers. Spent most days haunted by the strange feeling that my life's honeymoon phase was over. Hardly any friends accepted my invite to come spend a couple weeks, and those that did weren't around long. Couldn't tell you if that was just us growing apart, as friends often do, or the park's strange influence.

Dave came round with his girlfriend for a couple nights. She grouched the whole time. Hated sleeping in the trailer while I stayed in a tent outside. But she hated the park too. Said she felt watched all the time. Trip was cut short when we found her screaming one morning. She was pointing at one of the slides saying something had come out of it and was in the pool swimming around, but when we looked we didn't see nothing. She did have a hell of a bite on her ankle, though. Funny shape to it. Dave looked at it and got real freaked out. They left in a hurry. Another car's tyres screeching as it hauled ass outta here at top speeds. Never did figure out what happened, but if she didn't like the park, well... I guess it didn't like her either.

Not that I was much safer. Found myself getting cut up like crazy doing basic odd jobs. Things broke all the time, even if they'd been fine for years and years. And then one night I came into my trailer to find a drowned possum on the little kitchen table. Poor thing was soaked in chlorine water that dripped onto the floor in a puddle. No marks going to or from it, like it just appeared there out of thin air. It stank like hell, though. It had clearly been dead for days and days. I gingerly dropped it into a garbage bag using a pair of tongs and threw the lot in a dumpster, but I still couldn't spend more than a few seconds in the trailer without gagging, so I slept in the tent instead. Pitched it as close as I could without picking up that smell, but I had a bad feeling the whole time I set it up. Like I was being watched. By the time I was climbing inside, it was midnight, and I was desperate to get to sleep and see the cold night turn to day.

Barely an hour later and I had to climb back out of the tent because the trailer door was banging in the wind. *Okay*, I told myself as I shuffled over in my tighty-whiteys, arms wrapped around my chest for warmth, *that's my own stupid fault for leaving it open.* I closed it in a hurry and went back to the tent, but stopped dead in my tracks when I saw the zipper was pulled shut.

I hadn't left it like that.

I didn't know what to do. My brain went in two directions at the same time. One said I was mistaken. I had closed the tent and just forgotten it. The other said something or someone had crawled inside and was waiting for me. It'd set the whole thing up as a trap, and the best thing to do was to get in my car and drive until the sun rose. But I was already half-cut and knew I shouldn't be driving. The sceptical half of my brain made an appealing case. *The world isn't a nightmare,* it said. *It can look like one sometimes, but it isn't real. If you hear a bump in the night, you go looking and find it was all nothing and you take a deep breath, laugh at yourself for getting scared, and move on.*

Still, it took everything I had just to take a step towards the tent. And I shone my light at it hoping to see some sign of something in there. By the time my hand was on the zipper, I was shaking like a leaf and rethinking my ethical code of not driving drunk. But when emotions get that high, it's like you run on autopilot. Must be a survival thing. I opened the flap without really telling myself to and then I was looking inside my tent and there was nothing there.

I crawled inside quick as I could, pulled the zipper back the other way, and tried to go to sleep.

I settled down for maybe another thirty minutes when something's hand pressed against the tent wall, and that was when I started screaming. The way it came at me. Palm open, fingers spread, tent fabric stretching to near breaking point. Makes my skin crawl just to remember it. Long fingers that tapered to a point. Almost razor sharp. And a palm not much larger than a golf ball, even if the fingers spanned a dinner plate. In the nightmare-reality of the moment I saw it the way I might see a spider. Equal parts disgust and terror. I had to get away, and I backed up so fast I wound up rolling the whole tent like a hamster ball. Lost the zipper in the panic. Didn't find it again until the last scream finally left my lips and I was forced to catch my breath in the silence of an empty night, accepting that whatever was out there was either laughing its ass off at me or waiting patiently. Either way, I was at its mercy. Only thing I could do was collect myself and leave the damn tent.

When I finally climbed free there was no one waiting for me. Only a couple of wet footprints going to the nearest pool. I considered pulling the tarpaulin back and looking, but I was already scared shitless and had no courage remaining. Instead, I ran into the trailer, slammed the door shut, barricaded it with every last piece of furniture that wasn't bolted to the floor, and fell asleep with the smell of rotten meat filling my lungs. Come morning, I was thankful for the sunlight and the feeling that last night's events were just a dream. After that, I locked my trailer door every night, and I never slept in that tent again. No more possums, but it isn't uncommon for me to find scratches and dents in my door each morning. Nothing serious but looks to me like the probing of a curious animal.

Couple days later, something locked me in the boy's bathroom near the East end of the park. I'd only gone in cause one of the faucets was running. I'd just turned it off when the door slammed shut and I couldn't get it open again. Had to kick the lock out, which isn't an easy thing to do. First kick, I nearly broke my ankle. Second time hurt just as bad, and I had to take a breather to cope with the pain. Found myself pacing and occasionally stopping to listen for any sign of someone waiting for me outside. Someone I could shout at, blame it all on. Anything to keep the anger churning and not let it turn to fear. It was a full hour before I got panicked enough to give it my all and finally broke the lock. Burst into the cold air all red faced and flustered, and found the park silent as a graveyard. Just those tarpaulins waving gently in the breeze.

I learned some important lessons that winter. If you feel watched, feel like you're walking into a situation someone planned, it's because you are. When the park reopened I was out of there without a moment's hesitation. Finally got that job on a construction site and it lasted all of three weeks before I hurt my back again. Spent the rest of the summer laid up on my dad's sofa drinking and watching daytime tv. Got a call from the manager around August and he told me it had been a *bad* summer. Not only had the cops been sniffing around like crazy cause some poor kid went missing in the area, but they'd had twice as many injuries as before. Said he'd just spent the day in court hearing testimony from the parents of some kid who'd never walk or feed himself again after he hit his head on one of the rides. He sounded pretty beat up about it. He wasn't the best boss, but it wasn't like we worked for Mr Burns, either. Poor guy was way out of his depth. Anyway, part of the court settlement was he had to have staff members on site 24/7. I'd done it twice before, and he was desperately in need of someone who knew the job. I nearly said no, but he told me it was me or some seventeen-year-old lifeguard who'd shown interest in the job and I didn't like the thought of that.

God help me, I accepted, and when I went back that third time, I took a gun. And this time, I trusted my instincts. If I walked past a changing stall and heard the shower running, I let it run. Hour later, it'd be turned off again. If I saw someone had left the lights on in the staff room, I let them stay on until morning, when I could deal with it in the comfort of daylight. Flushing toilets. Wet footprints. Open doors. I learned to stop sweating the little things and nine times out of ten, they went away on their own. Pretty soon, I found myself laughing at them. A big fat wallet sitting in the middle of a solitary lounger that'd been dragged into the moonlight. A phone ringing from somewhere in the depths of a maintenance hatch. Those kinds of crude tricks weren't going to work on me, I decided. Thought I had it all figured out and there was nothing left for that place to show me.

And then the park ate a drifter.

Or something did, anyway. Did it right in front of me too. I'd found the guy sleeping in one of the brick-and-mortar bathrooms. We gotta keep those things warm enough to stop the pipes bursting, so I guess they make decent enough shelter. He was an agitated old fuck. Called me all sorts as I told him to clear off. He didn't make for the main exit, though. Wasn't like he'd parked a car in the lot was it? Instead, he just made a beeline for the nearby hills. No fences in that part of the park back then, only open fields moving into woodland. His plan was to just walk into the wilderness in the middle of winter, and I wondered if I was actually marching some guy to a cold death. I remember looking at his shoes and seeing the backs of his heels exposed, and I realised I couldn't let him do that. Snow was due to fall that night, and I knew it was gonna get real bad out there.

"Hey," I cried out while slowing to a stop. "Look man, it's late I'm sure..."

My words died out. I didn't really know what to say when he turned to face me. He was angry and tired, and I knew he wasn't ever really gonna be thankful for some randomer's charity, but that didn't mean I shouldn't try. For a moment, the only sound was the tarpaulin of the large pool to our right. Was just about to cough up some more words when his feet went sideways, his body rotated around his centre of mass, and the next part of him to touch solid ground was his head. It made a noise that makes my teeth ache just to think about. A percussive, almost musical note that really shouldn't be made by a human skull.

The blood that sprayed across the tiles reminded me of when I'd go paintballing with my friends. I remember looking down at it and noticing a couple loose teeth. Strange feeling. For a few seconds, everything turned to a kind of white noise as ancient instincts rooted me to the spot with fear. Paralysed me. Million thoughts went through my head.

The guy was dead.
Something had taken him.
That blood used to be inside of him.
I have blood inside of me.
Does my blood look like that?

These thoughts were like the sparks that fly off a loose electrical wire, but I was stuck mired in them until the whistling in my ears faded and I heard something being dragged across the floor.

The guy hadn't even gone that far. He'd flown about eight feet and landed just on the edge of the pool. His legs were in the water, hidden behind the tarpaulin, and only his top half was on dry land. His head was a ruin of blood and matted hair, but he still managed to look at me for just a moment before he slid the rest of the way below the water with a quiet *splunk*. The realisation he was alive kicked my ass into my gear and I ran over to the circuit box and hit the button that pulls back the pool cover. Machine ran loud as it drew the blue heavy sheet back across the water.

Felt like eternity waiting for it. When it was finally over, and I could look down into the water and see clearly there was no one there. Not even a cloud of blood polluting the pool. Nothing. I felt like I was going insane, and I even looked over and double checked that the guy's plastic bag was still where he'd dropped it just so I could be sure I hadn't made the entire thing up. I really didn't know what to do. The only thing in that water were a couple leaves that had made it in there over Fall but that was it.

And then I saw it. I can't explain it easily. It was a sudden overlap of realities, a bit like the hollow cube illusion where it can be two things at once. Without ever taking my eyes off it, that pool became every deep body of water I'd ever seen. All of them, all at once. It was every calm and glassy ocean surface with rays of diffuse light leading into unseen depths, every lake with murky kelp fingers reaching up out of the dark, every flooded basement with black and brackish water. I could smell the stagnant water, could feel the breeze you get standing on the coast, taste the salt. All of it at once. And something moved in those infinite waters, and it was *big*. It was like the first time I saw the Grand Canyon *big*, like when you get on a plane and see the ground pull away so quickly it loses perspective. Whatever was down there was coming right at me and I'm not ashamed to say I pissed my pants. An ocean full of stars was down there, and the thing swimming towards me had a body that obscured entire nebulae. I felt vertigo come over me, and I backed away and I slipped in the blood and then I woke up a few hours later and started screaming.

I had to clean up in the morning. And I had to pull the tarpaulin back across. Machine only goes one way, so I had to do it with a pool stick and it made me feel sick just to go near it. Every time I got close, I started to feel dizzy again. When I finally mustered the courage to look, there was the same old pool it had always been, but I'd never shake the feeling I had when I was looking down in it and saw teeth like tectonic plates. When summer rolled back round, I saw a bunch of kids in that pool and had to go be sick in a bush. The thought of them sharing space with that thing... Jesus.

After that I felt like I belonged to the park, weird as it sounds. Manager didn't have to fight me to get me to stick around for a fourth winter, or a fifth or sixth. The rest of the world didn't feel so real to me anymore. Sitting and eating dinner with my father while he lectured me on my prospects. Getting a beer with an old friend who was passing through. I felt like I'd gone into fucking space and seen the world was flat and now I had to just come on back and pretend like I cared about whether my soda was diet or not.

Not long after that, the park had its last ever Summer. It had gone too far by that point. Government was looking to close it all down on account of the accidents, and the manager was down the station every other day for questioning. Four kids missing that year alone. I found one of them folded up inside a pool filter, but didn't report it on account of not wanting the attention. The rest I don't know about. I was told I'd be paid another month or so after closure until a demolition crew came in, but no one ever arrived. Just me, this place, and a back that's getting worse with each new winter.

I don't patrol at night anymore. Little by little, the park has become something unfamiliar to me. Grass growing up between old tiles. Pool water the colour of cut grass and engine oil. Even in the day, you can see things moving around down there. And the smell of chlorine no longer fills the air. Now it's the heavy stench of rotten algae and dead water, and sometimes the tang of the salty ocean that I've learned to avoid like the plague. Makes me see stars in the corner of my vision and I don't like it. My dreams are bad enough. Drowning in the dark, something huge bearing down on me. I've woken up more than a few times and vomited up saltwater. I can't bring myself to think what any of it means because I just don't want to know.

Last time I went in the park after dark I had a close call. Worst of my life. I've been thinking about leaving ever since, but I worry there's not much else out there for me at this stage. That and I kinda feel guilty I didn't save all those kids with the cameras. Urban explorers they call themselves, and I say *kids,* but really they were college students who record videos for something called tiktok. Anyway, they came prepared. Scouted the park, even scouted *me,* working out my routine and where my trailer is so they could avoid my general line of sight. I had no clue they'd watched me for a whole day. Once they figured I was passed out or asleep, they drove their van close to the fence they found, climbed the top and hopped on over.

For about an hour, they got what they wanted. I've watched the footage a hundred times. Broken down toilets covered in graffiti. Smashed windows and broken glass covering the floor. Old pools full of ancient water covered in thick, brackish scum. You can hear the glee in their voices. That kind of urban decay was their bread and butter. And they were good at it too. They stayed quiet. Didn't shout or break anything. They just filmed. Wasn't until they decided to try rowing out to the castle that things took a turn.

I came too late. What got me out of bed was a scream. Maybe a few of them. It was blurry, and I came to around 3am and still a little tipsy, my head foaming at the edges with a half-remembered dream of a hollow world filled with water. As soon as I saw the van, I realised someone had gotten inside the park and I hadn't just been dreaming the sounds of splashing water and panicked. But by the time I went in there myself, the place was silent.

I really didn't want to search it at night. I hadn't gone in there after dark for a few years and things had only gotten worse. Set something off inside me. A kind of spiritual Geiger counter is how I think of it. An intense primordial warning system that made the shadows around me look almost infinitely deep. More than that, I guess, it felt alien. Sounds stupid, but it really did feel like I wasn't on the same planet anymore. I don't know. That part might just be all in my head, but that's how it felt that night.

I'd pushed myself just about as far as I was willing to go when I heard it. A rhythmic hollow knocking. It was coming from one of the largest pools in the park. A shallow kid-friendly one we called the Castle because it had a giant jungle gym in the centre. A kind of spaghetti mess of platforms and climbing bars and slides that the kids loved. I followed the sound and saw a pile of rucksacks and even a large camera on the very edge of the pool and there, just a couple metres away, was a rowboat.

The idiots had brought it with them. Probably thought they were being smart by avoiding the water below. At least they'd tied it off, so it was easy for me to pull back in. I gave it a cursory inspection, shivering at the mere thought of floating across that nightmare water in something so flimsy, and was ready to leave it until the morning when I heard a quiet splashing. Something had climbed out the water, and my heart dropped as I instinctively flicked the torchlight towards the sound of dripping water and saw a thin shivering shape climb onto the lowest steps of the castle. It looked grey and sickly, and then it started whimpering and I realised I was looking at a girl. College-aged, with stringy hair and an outfit that might have been colourful before she'd gone in the water, but now it was just the colour of ash and moss. At a glance, she almost didn't look human anymore. She looked more like a starving animal. Shell-shocked and shaking. I shouted out to her, but it was as if she couldn't hear me. She dragged herself up onto a dry platform and curled up in a ball in the far corner, knees pulled to her chest, and wide eyes locked into a thousand-yard stare.

And something was in that water. It came close to the surface, displacing small branches and causing the thick pond scum to bulge but never break. From the looks of things, it was circling the castle, and in some parts where the algae wasn't so thick, I got the faintest glimpse of colourless scales the size of my hand and a thick muscular trunk. Sometimes it seemed to bump up against the castle, like it knew the girl was nearby, but it didn't know how to get to her. The whole thing shook, and she'd whimper extra loud, but she still didn't show any signs of becoming lucid.

I'd be lying if I said I didn't think about leaving her until morning. She was unresponsive and looked like she was just gonna stay in the same place. *Wouldn't it be better to just go get her when the sun was up?* I thought. But that was a pretty fucked up thing to think. She wasn't safe there. I wasn't safe just standing in sight of the water, and she was on some old piece of plastic held together with rusting bolts. What if it collapsed? What if something came out of the water? God knows it could happen. Something had touched my tent all those years ago. Who's to say it wouldn't walk on out to take her?

At some point, I made the decision. Don't know exactly what did it, but I think it was the sounds she was making, that and the knowledge she'd been *in* there. God knows what she'd seen. I had to have sympathy. She needed help, and I was the only one around who could give it. So once something deep inside me clicked, I knew I had to move quickly before the fear started to fuck with my head. I grabbed the rope and began to pull the boat towards me. I wasn't sure what would happen. Half-expected something to breach the water like a hungry shark and swallow the boat whole, but instead whatever was circling the castle just slunk into the depths and stayed out of sight. Somehow that was even worse, and I found myself scanning the water obsessively as I worked up the courage to get into the boat.

I tried to keep the momentum, though. I didn't let myself start thinking or doubting myself. I just climbed in awkwardly, one foot at a time, damn near shitting myself when the whole thing wobbled, and I briefly felt like I was gonna lose my balance. But I managed it, and soon I was sitting down and using the oars to pull myself through the water. As I rowed, my brain moved along in different directions. Part of me was almost watching myself, like from above, and asking over and over *what the fuck are you doing?* While another watched that water for the slightest sign of life, and a *third* part of my brain was watching me for signs, I was gonna crumble from the adrenaline and ice-cold fear coursing through my veins. Each time the oars broke the water I kept waiting to see something coming after me, and I was about half-way there when I realised that if it was big enough it could just bowl the whole boat over like a shark knocking a surfer off his board.

It was too far to turn back when I saw the water rise in the distance. Again, it didn't break the surface, but it came close and sent a couple waves rolling across the entire pool where they lapped against the distant edge. They made the whole boat rock side to side like it was just a bit of driftwood. When the bulge in the water appeared again, it was on the other side of the boat, and I made the terrible decision to stop rowing and look over the edge.

There was no bottom to the pool, but whatever was down there wasn't swallowing continents any time soon at least. Hard to pin size down, but based on the steely blue fins that slid by close beneath me, that didn't really matter, it could eat me easy enough and that was all that mattered. Hell, I wasn't even sure if it was a fish or a squid or something else entirely, but I was pretty sure it still had a mouth somewhere in that murk.

It gave the boat a gentle knock. Nothing serious. Not enough to roll it, but enough to let me know it was interested in me. I decided I couldn't just stay there floating in one place forever. I had to move. I grabbed the oars and threw all caution to the wind. The sooner I got off that water, the better. Sure, I'd have to figure out how to get back, but that was a problem for later. Right there and then, all that mattered was the rising terror and disgust that took all my strength to keep from bubbling up into full-blown panic.

As soon as the boat began to move the creature slid out of view again. Didn't know if I ought to be relieved or even more afraid, but I took advantage of the lull in its activity to close the distance and, once close enough, I pulled the boat over to the same steps the girl had climbed. Once there, I secured it with a bit of the rope and hopped onto the first step, cringing at the way the ice-cold water felt slick and slimy against my ankles.

The girl flinched at my touch, but she didn't scream or pull away. I told her it'd be okay, or something like that. Tried my best to sound reassuring. Tried to let her know I was gonna get her somewhere safe. I managed to pull her to her feet when she finally turned and looked right past me. I barely existed to her at that moment. She only had eyes for the water behind me. Something about the look on her face gave me pause, though. She wasn't scanning for danger.

She was looking right at something, and before I had a chance to look for myself, she started screaming.

When I saw it, I wanted to scream too.

I'd never seen anything like it. Or since. A head like seaweed. A face like a scallop. It watched us with an almost casual interest that frightened me more than any predatory scowl. The look of a child about to pull a spider's legs off. The thought of it still makes my skin scrawl. It was so still, so alien, I couldn't help but pause and wonder if I was looking at something real or if it was just bad special effects. And yet the moment stretched on and on, until something in that unknowable mind made a decision and the creature disappeared back beneath the water.

I made a decision too, and I dragged the young woman to the nearby boat where she started to fight me the moment she saw it. Can't say I blame her. Last time she was on it she'd nearly died, but there was no third option. It was stay and die or take our chances getting to safety. Unfortunately, we had barely gotten within a metre of the thing when the whole boat was blown sky high with tremendous force. For a few seconds I stood there dumbstruck, the girl crying, and water falling from the sky like a momentary rainstorm. When the boat finally returned to Earth, it was a couple hundred metres away and hit dry land with a great crash.

My stomach sank. How the hell were we gonna get off the castle now?

Not a moment later and the entire structure began to shake. By now, the girl was close to hysterics, and I wasn't far behind. I took her hand and began to look for some high ground as that thing began to shake and batter the flimsy plastic supports that held the platform up. We were forced to climb up towards the plastic roof of the tallest tower, which wasn't exactly all that high up, but it was the best we could do. The bars leading to it weren't easy to navigate, and at one point I slipped and fell backwards, striking my chin painfully and looking up to see the girl going ahead without me.

For a moment I nearly gave up, but then there was the sound of something snapping and the entire castle began to slide on one side. I looked down and saw black water rising up to meet me. The thought of sinking into that filth ignited something inside me, and I scrambled up the last few rungs and perched on top of the smooth plastic cover of the castle's highest turret. It was barely large enough for us both to sit on, but it was all we had. Looking back, I can't help but laugh. I make it sound like a great tower, but it was barely twelve feet off the ground. As soon as I was up there looking down, water quickly bubbling towards us, I realised just how badly we were fucked. We'd delayed our inevitable death by mere seconds at most. By the time the bright red piece of plastic we clung to hit the water, the castle had broken apart so all its little pieces went floating in different directions. Ours was the last to go in, and it went down beneath our collective weight until the water reached our waists.

And then it came back up. Buoyant and hollow.

It was no boat, but it came damn close.

"Paddle!" I cried at the girl, and she did. And we pulled ourselves through the water to the nearest edge. Pretty soon, the makeshift raft bumped up against the tiled wall and we were dragging ourselves up onto dry land, where she rolled onto her back. I continued to crawl for another few metres until I felt like I was far away enough from the water. Only once I felt safe, I let myself collapse and lay crying and laughing for what felt like hours.

But the girl only cried. At first a whimper, then a sob, and then a howl. A painful, gut-wrenching scream that made my own joy wilt until I could do nothing except listen to the raw grief in her voice. When I sat up to see if she was okay, she was sitting upright and staring at the thing that was rising out of the water. Again, no malice. Not really. At least I don't think so. It'd be like looking for a recognisable expression on an oyster. But it did watch us calmly as it ate what I can only assume was one of her friends. A man, I think. Hard to remember details. He didn't cry, but he did look at us for help that we couldn't give.

I'm not sure I could even tell you how it ate him, but it looked painful, and slow. Reminiscent of a starfish, I think. At some point, the girl passed out, and not long after, so did I. I doubt she ever made a full recovery. The only thing she managed to say, even hours later after the paramedics had sedated her and I'd finished giving my (less than truthful) statement to police, were the words *the stars* over and over. I think a lot about how changed I was when I first looked down into that water and saw the abyss below, but that poor girl was actually *in* it. She'd swam in those waters. Submerged. I don't even know how she came back from an ocean that doesn't have a surface, but she did and somehow, I don't think she'll ever be the same.

But it's got me thinking about myself. About what I've lost to it. Jesus Christ, I'll be forty before I know it and what then? Just gonna wait here forever and ever? There's a number on the back of my paychecks, and I wanna try calling it to find out more. Like, what would they do if I tried going somewhere else? Would they let me?

Because it's gone. The days of Ellen Ditsworth are gone. The days of a good back and strong legs are gone. The person I was before I saw that drifter die is gone. *Yesterday is gone.* The past is a shared hallucination. Only the present is real. I need to get out of here before I lose more of myself. I'm never gonna understand this place. I realise that now. I can only accept that it exists and try to move on, which I should've done the day I saw those stars. Because there *is* an abyss, and it doesn't flow through time like we do. Doesn't occupy space like we do. But it's there, and it's full of gods the way a koi pond is full of fish. And I'm worried the more I think about it, the worse the park gets, and the closer I get to falling into waters that have no up or down, and which never *ever* end.

In my dreams, I am choking in the acidic bile of a creature that swallowed me whole. I'm worried that if I stay here much longer, I'll forget how to wake up.

STALKER

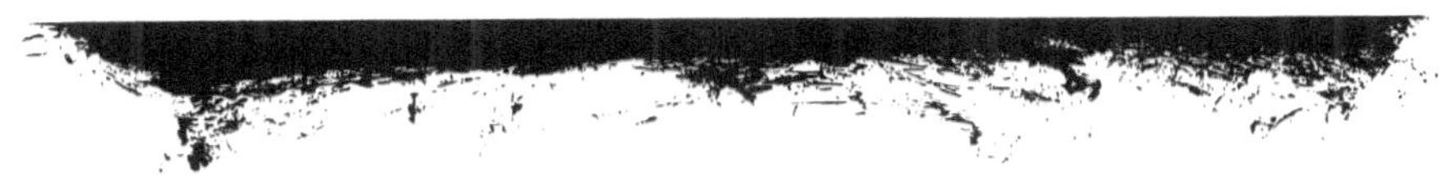

L et's get the obvious out of the way.

  Being a PI sucks. It's not what you think. It's pretty much harassing women. Men hire PIs to go harass their wives and girlfriends and once in a blue moon you get asked to find a missing dog, or to harass a man instead. But that's it, really. Sometimes I'm looking for hard evidence of infidelity, but a lot of the time my clients just want to rattle the soon-to-be-ex. To make them paranoid and jittery and less reliable in a courtroom, or less likely to pay attention to small print agreements that stiff them out of the holiday home. So that's my job. I'm a pawn and it is almost always on behalf of the kind of men who think women reading a book in public are secretly looking for male attention.

  I don't have an office. I did for a short while. But things are tough, as I'm sure many of you know, and PI work isn't exactly lucrative. I don't know why I'm still doing this job, except to say I'm my own boss, and it's not easy out there. I went into this with vastly different expectations. If anyone wants to hire someone who was convicted of insurance fraud while training to be a police officer, let me know. Otherwise I'm on my own, following people in cars and sleeping in dingy motels. So when someone reached out looking for a guy to stalk them, I just figured it was a fetish thing. I got a nephew who went to art school and makes big bucks painting cartoon characters doing fucked up stuff. He ain't painting the Sistine Chapel, but he pays the bills and looks after his family. I figure if that work is good enough for him, it's good enough for me.

So I met the woman and was surprised at how normal she looked. It was in a public place, a park with a nice bench. And even though it was starting to rain a little, we didn't let it bother either of us. We sat there, two tape recorders running, and hashed it out. She said she liked me. If she hadn't, she wouldn't have gotten out of her car. That was flattering coming from her. Good looking woman. Professional. I didn't know at the time, but I'd quickly figure out she was a forensic accountant.

Anyway, we got talking. She never gave me her motivation, but I would later come to understand her as an amateur narcissist. She was new at loving herself. She was smart, accomplished, and actually rather beautiful provided you didn't spend a great deal of time agonising over things like symmetry or eyebrows, and instead paid attention to how a smile reaches the eyes, or how laughter sounds when it catches someone by surprise. But she grew up dirt poor and spent her teen years unable to visit the dentist, or access a gym, or even just eat home cooked food that wasn't microwaved. Plump frame, blotchy skin, hair she kept short with a pair of scissors because her and her mother relied on the shampoo and soap they stole from the motel where they shared cleaning shifts. When she fumbled awkward questions at some of the better-looking boys in her class, she rarely met with success. That's not to say she was an outcast, either. She had a social life. It's just poor kids have to grow up early. Prom's a luxury. Eating isn't. If you know, *you know*. Otherwise, you might be surprised by just how fucking tough it can be for some kids in this country. Anyway, she got out of that hole, fought tooth and nail, got an education, a good job, and by the time she finished her victory lap and took stock of her life she was thirty-five years old and a thousand miles from the trailer she was raised in.

And she looked *good*. The woman in the mirror was a stranger that she wanted to get to know. I think hiring me was an act of self-love. I think if she could have, she would have sat in a car and watched herself get a cup of coffee, spying closely at the professional-looking woman doing a little half-run half-skip to get out of the rain. The way she stood in line rocking back and forth on her heels to the music in her airpods thinking no one'd notice. She wanted to admire herself, but unable to time travel or clone herself, she instead resorted to hiring me as a kind of proxy.

I had my own boundaries, of course. They covered anything that was gonna get me in trouble. The gist of the contract, after a nice week spent meeting after work and talking, was that I was to follow her as often as I could and just... *observe* her. Photos. Videos. Secret recordings. Occasionally a little bit more. Nothing physical. For example, one time I inventoried her handbag after she left it in a taxi by accident. I'm not a photographer, but something about all those knick knacks laid out on a motel bed snapped with a black and white polaroid, it looked good. Like something you'd see in a fancy gallery. *Avant garde* my nephew would say. She loved it. Paid me a bonus for it and everything.

Anyway, this carried on like this for about six months. They were... interesting times. Tailing her across train stations, racing across open parking lots to install a tracker on her car, standing on a bridge and dropping an air tag in her bag as she walked past. It was a little bit like being a spy. She even paid for me to buy high end equipment. Crazy stuff. One camera, I could sit on my balcony and read the texts on her phone from a block away. Occasionally, there were days where I couldn't or wouldn't keep up the required intensity. Stalking requires a lot of cardio. When that happened, when I didn't feel like following her into a crowded place, or sprinting half-way around town following her car, I'd do research. I'd investigate who this woman had once been. I created fake Facebook profiles and tracked down old school friends, spoke to former teachers, lovers, all of that. The whole job was a matter of mapping her out, like she was a country, you know? And a country isn't just hills and rivers and borders. Countries have history.

She was happy with my initiative. The text she sent me when I showed her the research folder was a glowing commendation. First one I'd had in a long time. It was nice, someone telling me *good job*. She had a real way of making me feel like a kid getting a gold star. I didn't realise at the time, but I was putty in her hands. Head over heels, bless my stupid heart. Of course, I didn't know what I was getting into, but I'd had just enough time to grow over confident. I made the mistake of thinking that I wasn't gonna find anything in her past that'd give me trouble sleeping.

Boy, did I get that one fucking wrong.

Her mother. That's where things took an odd turn. Now I knew from news reports the mother died in their trailer while her daughter was off staying at some boyfriend's place for a few days. Natural causes, it read. I wanted to know a little more about what natural causes they were. Figured if there was a congenital thing, it seemed like maybe I ought to know. You'd think the way the trailer park owner reacted to me asking about it, I'd tried asking the Russian government for proof of a democratic election. Thin reedy little woman who gave me hell the moment I mentioned a name. *What do you wanna know that for? Who's asking? Who's paying you? Why you wanna dig this shit up?*

Oh, she ripped me to pieces. I put it down to the natural sprinkling of crazies in the standard population and took a different tact. Started calling up the older folks in the park. Residents. Every single one of them put the phone down on me the second I mentioned her name.

Well, all of them except one.

Some people wanna talk and this old bastard was one of them. He had a lot to say about everything from the president to social media, and I let him ramble on before starting to press my point. Told him at the start I was a historian looking into the local area, that made it so it wasn't too suspicious when I began asking about this and that. Slowly making my way to the death of a fifty-three-year-old woman a couple trailers down from him some years ago.

Again, soon as I mentioned her name, there was a change in the air, even over the phone. For a second, I thought this old guy was gonna hang up just like the others. Could hear him smacking his dry lips as he mulled it over.

"Francine didn't deserve what happened to her," he said after a while. "She wasn't a good woman. Didn't treat her daughter too good neither. But didn't deserve what happened. Maybe if they'd found her earlier, some of those fellas in white coats could've got more evidence, put that little wretch of hers away. But from what I understand, weren't much left of her at all."

Then he hung up, leaving me with a whole lot of questions.

This frustrated me. I had, until now, had a fair bit of luck at this new profession of mine. They say be careful what you get good at. Sad truth was, I was getting good at stalking, and this was my first real roadblock. I remembered the way I felt when she told me *good job* and it bothered me I couldn't really say much about this critical part of her life. That and, well, maybe I still got a chip on my shoulder about being a failed policeman. If you give me a problem, I can sometimes drive myself crazy looking for a fix.

So I hopped in my car and drove to the trailer park, damn near on the other side of the country. Don't know what I was hoping to find. No way the trailer was still there, and it wasn't. But what I found odd was the lot hadn't been replaced. There was a hole in the ground, about the right size, and nothing else. Just an empty spot where the trailer had once stood. And the trailers on either side weren't occupied either. I could tell by politely and legally looking through the windows. Most of them were cleared out, but a few weren't. They still had plates and other knick knacks left hanging around, like the owners had left without bothering to pack.

"You shouldn't hang around there, mister."

The girl who appeared stood a good twenty feet away, shouting over the wind so as to be heard.

"Smell can make you awful sick."

I wrinkled my nose, aware of the odour she was talking about. Had been since I approached the empty lot. A faint musty smell that made me think of an exotic pet shop.

"What do you mean?"

"Smell makes you sick," she said, like it was self-explanatory. "Woman who died there left behind an awful stench. Made the neighbours sick. And the neighbour's neighbours, and so on for a couple trailers in a row. No one likes to live there now. Still can't. Had a couple move in a year or two back and they got sick too. Daddy says it's a bad one. Not even rats go near that hole."

The smell wasn't pretty, but this trailer park looked like the kinda place where hubcaps went missing regularly. Figured they would've been used to bad smells. What made this one so special?

I looked over at the girl.

"Where *is* your dad?"

Few minutes later and I was stood outside a trailer waiting pensively. The little girl had disappeared inside to fetch her father and since then I'd been sat listening to the quietest trailer park in the whole world. Crickets and silence. Traffic on a distant highway. Place was dying, that much was clear.

When the father finally did make an appearance, he said nothing for the first few minutes. Lit a cigarette, offered me one. I refused on account of having quit some time back.

After a while, he spoke up.

"I'd invite you in, but if you been hanging around that old lot, not sure I want you inside my home. No offence."

"None taken," I replied.

"Sally says you're a historian."

The man wasn't terribly old. Mid-thirties, at a guess, but he looked me up and down like I was a teenager caught throwing eggs at his house.

"What're you really?"

"PI," I replied.

"Ha, now that makes sense. Some relative looking for answers? Heard the Hendersons had a sister with money."

"That's exactly it," I lied. "She didn't buy the official story."

"Nor should she," he replied. "Henderson was fit as a fiddle day he moved in. Weren't no justice in what happened to those who got sick. And poor Francine… They say she died of natural causes. Man, even back then I knew it was shit, and I was just a lil kid. The smell alone. Think it's bad now but at the time, before they came in with a crane to lift the trailer up whole and move it to the dump. Shit, it was something awful. There was talk of moving the whole park. Course no one gave enough of a shit about us to go ahead and actually do it."

"What *did* she die of?"

"Don't know. Only thing I am sure of is that that girl of Francine's lied. Said her mother was live and well when she left before the weekend and they was all on good terms, but that was bullshit. We heard 'em fighting for weeks before, for one. And of course the body, state that was in, ain't no way it'd been rotting for just a few days."

He offered me another cigarette. I refused. He lit it up instead. Second one in what felt like just a few minutes. Made me itchy just to see. I wanted to say something, anything, to get a little bit more. But I'd told a big lie pretending to be there on someone else's behalf, and didn't want to catch myself out, so I just sat and listened to the quiet buzz of his little patio light.

After the second cigarette was done, he reached into his back pocket and took out an old photo.

"I hope you find justice for Henderson and the rest of them," he said. "Only real bit of proof I ever had something fishy went on."

He handed me the picture. Wasn't easy to see what I was looking at. Pile of old leaves, maybe. Mulch. I squinted at it for a few good seconds but couldn't make heads or tails of it.

"What...?"

"Took that the day they arrived to get rid of the trailer. Had to stand on my friend's shoulders just to reach."

"What is it?" I asked, my skin starting to crawl as I picked out details. Whatever I was looking at, it was slumped on a sofa with floral wallpaper in the background. It was about the size of a man, but riddled with holes and cavities the size of golf balls. In my whole life, I'd never seen something that looked like that.

"Why that's Francine," he said. "Or at least what was left of her."

He let me keep the photo. At a guess, that was the only interesting thing that'd ever happened to that man, and he'd been waiting to share it with someone. All I had to do was give him an excuse. He seemed to take some pleasure in passing it on. Certainly found my reaction to it amusing. I must've gone pale as I grappled with thoughts of what had happened to make a body go bad like that. Back in the hotel, under a good light, I checked that picture again and again. Something about it made me deeply uncomfortable. Knowing a woman was under all that... all those holes and crevices must've been made in her flesh. And what'd happened to her skin that'd turned it such a funny texture? Looked furry, like the kinda thing that grows on top of a long-forgotten cup of coffee.

A part of me considered asking my client about this, but I knew that wasn't the way to go. First, she probably wouldn't tell me *good job* if I had to ask. She hired me to do a certain thing, and that didn't involve politely requesting information right from the source. Second, well... I'd read the police reports, what was publicly available, anyway. And she'd made it clear she'd left on the Friday and came home on the Monday and...

Well, what if that guy was right? Did she really leave her mother alive and well? I mean, people kill. Not just psychos. People like you and me. We do it every day and sometimes we even pull it off. Only half of US murders get solved. That's a fact. If anyone could be in the right half of that equation, it'd be her. She was smart as hell, my client. Even at seventeen, she would've been a clever one. Clever enough that she might easily have been able to cover her tracks. Gone over to some boyfriend, twisted his arm into giving her an alibi. Sure, I could see that.

I just needed to figure out what the fuck was going on with that crime scene in the trailer. Thankfully I got some friends still on the force, one of which I even have a bit of leverage on. At first he couldn't find much on the actual mother, but then I asked him to see if he could take the photo I had, show it around, and see if anyone had seen something like it before. That proved a lot more fruitful. Few days later he came back with a strange one, but straight away I saw the connection.

I'll spare the details. Old man was found in a tub, all sorts of fucked up, in some old apartment building. It had since been condemned on account of the body, which is fairly weird since bodies don't usually cause that much fuss, but less weird when you realise that said body was in such a bad state it made three people sick and caused long-lasting structural damage. Whatever happened to this guy, it ate through the tub he'd been lying in and seeped into the floors and walls below. Turned plasterboard to shit and apparently even caused some trouble for the sturdier elements like steel and concrete. I don't know how that works exactly, but that's what the file said and going by the photos, I didn't feel like anyone was lying.

As for the pictures? What can I say? Made my fucking skin crawl. No blurry little polaroid snapped by a kid. These were pro-fessional crime scene pictures that showed something in a bathtub that didn't register as human until my eyes went looking for details. He looked like a hairy paper-wasp's nest, only there were fingers and nipples and other little things that made it clear it had been built using a person as the framework. No face though. Just a head like a pile of used paper plates. Looking at those photos made me learn a new word just to describe how I felt. Trypophobia.

Wasn't just the one guy either. Building was linked to the disappearance of the ground floor tenant. Some computer geek. I didn't worry about him too much. But what did catch my eye was there was only one woman living in the whole place. Second-floor apartment. The registered name was... *somewhat* familiar. Close enough to a certain someone's that it raised the hairs on my neck. Police at the scene managed to get a photo of her and sure enough, there she was. My client going by a different name. Clearly something fishy was going on or else why the pseudonym? I figured it possible she'd maybe offed her own mother. Parents and spouses make the most common victims. But what connection was there to that second corpse, and what about the missing guy?

It was like a horror movie was following her around, and she was just blissfully unaware. Condemned buildings and festering trailers made for a far cry from the professional accountant who enjoyed oat milk lattes and used sweetener instead of sugar to spare her teeth. But there was no denying she was the connection. There was photographic proof she'd lived in that building. If I wanted to get ahead of this, to really understand what was going on, I had to figure out what had happened to those bodies. I'd pretty much exhausted my favours with the police and truth was they didn't know any more than I did. But it turned out the building was still standing. Condemned, but they hadn't demolished it, partly because no one wanted to take responsibility, but I reckon it might have had something to do with the biohazard warnings slapped on every single window and door.

Good thing I'd brought a gas mask. I waited for sunset, geared up, and entered through the unlocked door. First thing that hit me as the door swung open was the smell. Similar to the trailer park, but full pelt and hot as hell. Made me think of lizards and poorly kept terrariums. Strong enough to make my eyes water even through the mask. One thing was clear as I took a look around the hallway—the building was diseased. Not just rundown or decrepit like the usual urban decay. This was something else. Looked like the inside of a clogged pipe. You know how limescale fills it up? It was a bit like that. This oily rust coloured fluid had seeped down the walls and left them glistening and soft. Ropey stalactites of the stuff hung down from the ceiling like old party banners, and I edged around them afraid of what might happen if one touched me.

Best guess was that stuff was digesting the place. Anything soft or organic was going or gone. Old umbrella frames were left standing in one corner, the fabric burnt or dissolved away. The carpet was reduced to just a few patches no bigger than my hand. And a bunch of old cardboard boxes piled up under the stairs had turned squat and half-liquid, almost flowing down and around each other. The worst came when I took a look in the back room. More of a broom closet, I guess. Wouldn't have gone in but something caught my eye. A well-worn shoe that wasn't covered in that oily shit. Sign of recent activity. That and the way the door was ajar just raised my suspicions, so I took a look.

Even now the timeline eludes me, but someone, a vagrant most likely given the way they were dressed, died a nasty death in there. Chemical burns come to mind. They were balled up in one corner, eyeless, looking up at me as I pushed the door open to take a closer look. Pink flesh threaded with red blood vessels, yellow bones poking through here and there. From the looks of things, they'd been trying to work the door open. You could see a history of their escape attempts left by bleeding hands. Rust coloured finger streaks ran all along the door's edges, special attention paid to the hinges. And he'd broken the only window and tried hauling himself up there, only to realise it was barred from the other side. The jagged glass that still clung to the frame was covered in old blood. His palms must have looked like grated cheese. Eventually he'd given up and lain down in that shit and the thought of it made my chest feel heavy and tight. I'd only been in the building a few minutes and that shit was already eating through my shoes. I could hear the thick rubber soles sizzle and pop with each step. But that guy had been forced to sit down in an inch deep puddle of the stuff, likely because exhaustion had left him no choice but to tough it out. So how long had he tried staying up right?

Hours? Days? Weeks?

Him getting stuck in there had to be deliberate. I was sure of it. A feeling in my gut. Someone had locked the door behind him and left him to die slowly. God only knows why, but did that mean they were still hanging around and waiting for a chance to get to me? Looking around, I sure didn't feel safe or alone. The shadows seemed too deep and the steady *drip drip drip* of that rancid oil oozing out of every surface was too monotonous. Someone or something lived in that filth and chances were they'd been responsible for that poor vagrant's agonising death.

That meant getting out of that shithole was a priority, so I made for the stairs and started the climb. If there were any answers in that place, it'd be in the apartment where that old man died. The crime scene tape was still hanging off the door frame when I found it, and the TV and sofa, or what remained of them, stood in the same place as in the photos. Back in the day the old man had been a hoarder, and I was surprised crime scene hadn't cleared all his shit out. It was all still there, only what had once been a chest high maze of papers and magazines was now just a kind of hardened pulp, almost like magma dried mid-flow. Whole fucking place was covered in the stuff like a coral reef, growing up the walls and even patches of the ceiling. Looked a hell of a lot like a wasp's nest, and it looked to be the source of that oily looking fluid. You could see it sweating out of every crease and fold in that strange hive. It was almost hypnotic to look at. Glistening amber beads oozing out of papery sheets that flowed like rock striata. There was a gentle, barely perceptible rhythm. Hypnotic.

I don't know why, but I reached out and ran the tip of my finger as gently as I could along the surface. It felt like the underside of a mushroom. All those papery gills. Gossamer thin. Soft and inviting. I wore no gloves, and the brief moment of contact had deposited a single bead of that strange syrup on my fingertip. It caused a tingling sensation that was not entirely unpleasant. Even the blood that trickled down my knuckle felt warm and wet, like testing a hot bath with your hand. I liked it. I liked it and I wanted more.

I went to reach out and push my arm into the nest when a hand burst out of the nest and gripped my wrist. I was so surprised I didn't even make a noise, but instead wordlessly fell back as the hand pushed me away from the nest. A very nearly skinless forearm followed and soon after a face emerged from the papery nest like a grime covered nightmare. Black eyes and a lipless mouth. It was a man that could have passed for a corpse, like a half-digested piece of meat. Terrified, I struggled to my feet and realised that this person had broken damn near every bone in my wrist with that single grip.

"Your meat smells raw," he growled before heaving himself out of the nest in a disgusting parody of childbirth.

My sanity flickered and the next thing I knew I was on the ground floor with bleeding eyes and both hands frantically pulling at the door handle. My mind returned in pieces. I blinked red tears away but didn't stop trying to open the door. I felt it, that urgent need to leave, like a suffocating man feels the need to breathe. But I'd fucked up bad. I'd sniffed out the closet and saw the trap laid there, but hadn't seen the larger one set for me. There was only one way in and out of that building and I hadn't jammed the door open! Now it was shut and nothing I did could get it open. With more time, maybe I could've pried the jamb or even kicked it down, but my heart was racing and my vision blurring. I wanted out of that place. A hot primal need to get the hell out. The air was too hot. My mask too stifling. Sweat condensed on the inner plastic and made it damn near impossible to see. And the pain in my wrist was a throbbing explosion that made sensible thought impossible. I'd realised early on into my little foray that I was underprepared, but the scale of what that meant eluded me until I was there wrestling with thoughts of exposure and contagion and disease, fumbling at a greasy doorknob with a broken hand while suppressing thoughts of what might be crawling up my leg or back or neck. Panic threatened to consume me. The world and all the normality it represented was right fucking *there*. I could hear it. The distant hum of traffic. The amber glow of streetlights that lit up the biohazard posters. Not thirty minutes ago I'd been there. Safe and far away from this waking nightmare.

I was being reduced to a prey animal. Even in the moment, I could sense it happening to me. Being made into something lesser, but it was like my actions were no longer my own. When I finally gave up on the front door, I turned around and saw the shadows way back at the hallway begin to shift as something descended the stairwell. There was no other way out. No door. No window. Just me, a long corridor, and a nightmare coming right at me.

Something inside me gave up. I don't know how to describe it. I'm still not sure if it was that building and that strange fluid that seemed to warp my own thoughts, or maybe there's just too much one person can go through. But I could practically hear the thin membrane of my sanity tear as I fell backwards into the door and slid down onto my ass, breathlessly awaiting my terrible fate. I almost contemplated turning off my light, but by then it was too late. I could see him coming towards me. He was legless. Nothing from the waist down except blackened viscera trailing up the stairs behind him. He pulled himself towards hand over hand with hungry eyes. Before I knew it, he was on top of me, one hand gripping my mouth with a salty palm, the other stroking my hair.

And then in an instant, his demeanour changed. He pulled back with a terrified cry and scrambled away like I'd just stuck him with a blade.

"No no no no no," he muttered. "No no you should have said you should have said I didn't know I thought you were another one I didn't know I thought you were here for me I didn't know you were hers."

He cowered away, pedalling on both hands backwards while keeping his eyes fixed on me.

"Tell her I did not know you were hers I could not smell until I was close very close if I hurt you I am sorry tell her I am sorry I did not mean to hurt you it is just I do not get to eat often and am always hungry."

With a rapid gesture, he threw the key for the door at me. It skittered across the floor and fell just short of my feet.

"Tell her I did not know."

"W-w-w-what are you?" I stammered.

He looked at me curiously, stopping his retreat only briefly to gauge my expression.

"She likes to be seen, but I looked without asking and I got what I deserve."

"Who are you talking about?" I asked.

He very nearly laughed, but with such deformities, it was mostly a drooling guffaw.

"You know!" he gasped. "Don't be stupid. You're in love with her. Just like me. But different. You got permission. I didn't. But she was good. She left me an old nest to live in. And I have permission to eat anything I kill or trap myself. Hard now that people know to stay away, but sometimes I get lucky."

His eyes flicked to the closet with sickening hunger.

"What has this got to do with her?" I asked.

"What colour are her eyes?" he replied, almost manic with excitement. "Answer. Answer. Tell me. Tell me. What colour are her eyes?"

"G–"

I stopped. The word felt wrong in my mouth.

"Bl–

"Bro–"

"No no," he chittered. "None of those."

Seemingly excited but afraid, he raced forward momentarily and gripped my lapels with twisted glee.

"*Compound,*" he hissed with such forbidden pleasure. "Her eyes are *compound*. She's jealous of us, you know?

"Jealous we get to love her."

And then he disappeared into the darkness and something inside me gave way entirely and I passed out.

I don't know much of what came after, exactly. I was found a few hours later in my car, idling at a traffic light. I'd made some effort at getting away on my own, but didn't get very far. No surprise here, but I got sick as a dog going in that place. A deep chest infection. The kind that scares everyone at least once in their life. Only fair given how fucking stupid I was. But forgive me, I hadn't anticipated nightmares beyond human comprehension. I challenge anybody to think that fucking far ahead. You think junkies. You think flies. Squatters. But that guy... that man slipping out of the nest and barrelling towards me on two hands. My mind going *sizzle pop* along with the soles on my boots. In real life, shit like that always sneaks up on you.

So I paid the price. Six months. Jesus. Six *long* months. I got every fever you can think of. Sepsis. Kidney failure. Liver failure. Month after month drowning in my own fluids, coughing up shit that made the nurses gag and leave. I asked the doctor what the long-term effects will be, and he winced before reading a list of things that didn't leave much hope for a happy retirement. And if it was hard on my body, it was even worse on my mind. Those fever dreams... doctors say what I remember in that building, that was all just part of the sickness. Say I spent a good three days in a coma and strange dreams are the norm. Which I might accept if it weren't the fucking skin graft still healing on my right hand. No one can explain that.

My client visited. Just the once. There are universally sad moments in life and one of them is realising someone you have a lot of affection for doesn't have it back. They have some. Just not the same amount. It was always one way though, wasn't it? I saw her every single day, but if I was doing my job right, she only saw me once a month for our meetings. Our arrangement ended not long after, so I hope anyway. She left like it was nothing but me... ah Jesus, it felt like someone excavated my heart right out. Even after what she told me why she was there, even after what I did, I could barely stand up straight. I was so heartbroken. There were times after that I wished the sickness would just take me. Maybe that defeatism is why it got so bad. Who knows?

She came to me looking for a recommendation, of all things. She wasn't cold. Far from it. But there was a sense of disappointment as she sat beside me and eyed me up.

"I liked the initiative," she said after a while. "But the results leave me unimpressed."

"What the fuck happened in that place?" I asked, and even though I could barely hear my own voice, she seemed like she heard every word. For a moment, the way she contemplated it, I thought I was gonna get a straight answer.

"You know, my mother said men don't see ugly women. They know they exist, but they just *poof* them right outta their mind. Like a magic trick. She said we worked better being a little plain. Good enough to take home for a night. Any more and we'd start to leave problems everywhere we go. That guy was a problem. She was trying to warn me about the dangers of attention but silly me, I went and got addicted. I hoped with you there might be a degree of... separation. Infatuation on a contractual basis."

She took a deep breath like she'd had a long, hard day.

"I don't know. Maybe Mom was right. It's ridiculous, I suppose. The fly shouldn't admire the spider. It either sees it and fears it, or doesn't know what's coming until it's too late. I think Mom was telling me to go for the latter. It's no fun being invisible, though. You spent all that time looking at me. Following me. What did you see?"

I looked at her until my eyes watered and something throbbed in my skull.

"I don't know," I tried to lie.

"Be honest."

She looked right at me and something in the air changed. I don't know what. Hot. Jesus, it was hot. Like looking at the sun. I remember the heart rate monitor going nuts and then... then I remember gossamer wings and serrated chitin. A tick on the inside of your cheek. A leech on your tongue. A horsehair worm that won't leave the skin. And then an instant later my eyes refocused and there was just a normal woman in front of me.

"Someone I could have loved," I answered, unable to stop the words spilling like vomit. "Someone who I thought deserved love."

"See," she said. "Who wouldn't like your version better?"

I was crying again. Heart racing. World like butter, going soft at the edges. Whatever she did, it was like undergoing brain surgery in real time.

"I'd like a recommendation," she said after another minute or two of silence. "I'd like to see myself. I look in the mirror and I don't see what you do. I'd like an artist to paint me. A version of me, at least. It won't be easy on them. All this time you've probably looked directly at me for no more than five, ten minutes in total. Just didn't realise it. Always the back of my head or my hair obscuring just *so*. That won't do. I want a portrait. I want to know what you see."

"What will you do to them?"

"I won't do anything. Not intentionally. But if you ask someone to paint the sun, expect them to go blind. Whoever paints me will be painting the sun in their living room. Going blind is the least of their problems. Now, fess up. You know someone. You mentioned them once in passing. A cousin, maybe. An artist in need of cash. I'm sure of it."

"Why would I tell you anything?"

"Because you love me," she said. "And because despite everything, you will get better and you will come back to me. Year or two, I think. You are adamant I have no hold on you, and you will think that for a long time. And this period of freedom, you'll enjoy it only by my good grace and mercy. You did a *good job*. Better than any before. I've read your notes and reports over and over and seen details of myself I didn't even know were there. It's a thing of beauty, what you did. And one day soon you'll come back to me with some excuse for why you want the contract to continue."

I tried to spit the word *never* but managed, at best, a weak shake of the head. Something that put a most peculiar smile on her face.

"It doesn't work like that. It'd be like trying to brute force your way through Alzheimer's. You'll be back. Even now you're mine. All mine. I'm just being gentle. And you're going to give me the name and number of this artist because even though you know I could no more love you than a spider loves the fly, you are desperate to please me. Because when I broke the man in that apartment building. When I tore him in two and told him that he would live for as long as I desired, writhing without air for years and years, drowning in sickly fluids and trapped helplessly in a hive he is determined to maintain even though I wouldn't be caught dead going back there. *He was grateful.* And, with time, you'll be grateful too."

She put the pen in my hand. She smiled, mouthed the word *good boy*, and God help me...

I gave her my nephew's number.

CROSSWORD

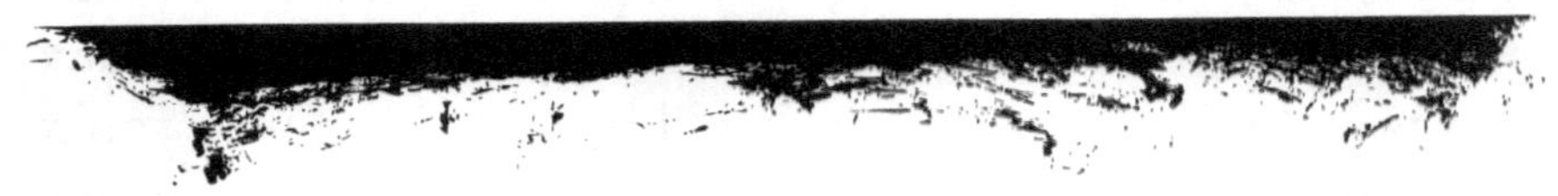

I latch onto specific problems and when I do, everything else around me diminishes into nothingness until I complete the task at hand. I line these problems up and solve them, one-by-one, and I find updating the task list awfully difficult. If I am on my way to do a job, breaking off to attend to something else is almost impossible. I once finished buttering my toast before putting out a fire by the stove. I once lost a girlfriend after she trapped her fingers in a food processor, and I quietly went over to the fridge and put the milk away before turning to help her. She couldn't believe that I hadn't rushed over straight away, but of course, it wasn't really like that. I was unable to review or address my priorities until my mind had freed itself from the current task.

I have to manage these tendencies. And I learned at an early age that it helps to focus on discrete tasks that, if things get really bad, I can remind myself don't matter. That, at least, limits the anxiety of abandoning them. I have my work and that gets me through the day, but outside of those hours, I need other things to pull me through. I can paint and read and they're involving, for sure, but they don't tend to have the sense of completion that I get from a simple puzzle. Jigsaws, sudoku, word searches, videogames; these all make up part of it but oddly enough it's crosswords that have taken over my mind. It started because they weren't too taxing and if I was pushed to cheat, then it didn't really matter. They let me say things like,

"Right, I'll do 9 across while on the toilet and that's it."

Like most things I put my mind to, I quickly turned the hobby into an obsessive pursuit of completion. The harder they were, the better. If I had to watch a film, read a book, or even visit a real-life location to get an answer, I would. And I credited it all with pushing me out of my comfort zone in order to experience new things. I would have never watched Breakfast at Tiffanies, read Little Women, or visited the London Museum of Natural History without needing to get answers from them. And they were all new experiences for me, some better than others, but I enjoyed the feeling of expanding my little bubble with each new puzzle.

Crosswords, like everything, have communities surrounding them and I even found a few friends online. For some, the compulsion to get obscure answers was a vital lifeline to the outside world, and you'd be surprised at some of the cultures lurking at the fringe. A good crossword is more than just a puzzle, it's a curated string of experiences picked to evoke a deliberate journey. A common example might be the kind of thing some tourists could use to guide them around a city:

Below the Phoenix of a Blinded Saint, 8 down.

Resurgam—the answer can be found carved on a stone beneath a statue of a phoenix at St Paul's Cathedral. But what about something like the following:

The final song of a thunderous singer, 5 across.

The answer was Toxic, the final song lip-synced by a Drag Queen (Daytona Thunder) at a popular club in Manchester. I went a long way for that one and had a surprisingly good night, albeit one a little outside my wheelhouse. But still, I got the answer, and it wasn't like I'd find it just by reading the forums (posting answers is a big no-no if you want to get into the best clubs). The creator was a well-known Queer academic working out of London who has a popular following in the community. I appreciated their work, but perhaps not as much as those by one anonymous Berliner.

A companion's lips tasted through the looking glass, 6 across.

Her name was Alice, and she was an escort for an agency called *Intimate Companions.* She was wearing Cherry lip gloss, something I found through a process of elimination.

Over the last few years, I've discovered more about myself than I ever would have at home. I have learned that I can lie very well, that when I know who I am meant to be, who others want me to be, I can be confident and even charming. I have learned that I am not a jealous person, that I am not a vain person, and that there are times when I can be as reckless and adventurous as anyone else. I just need a reason to, a job to complete with routes to success I understand.

The name of a one-eyed watchmen's gun, 12 across.

There was a policeman—with two eyes, I might add, but the unfortunate Christian name of Dick—and the answer was the serial number of his gun, converted to letters. That was an odd one, but absolutely invigorating. The crossword had been made with clearly defined geographical boundaries, which helped (many of us attended it as a communal event although I largely acted alone), and for a moment I almost thought the policeman was in on the game. Right up until he tried to shoot me.

Like I said, the experiences can be *invigorating.*

But the good ones, the really good ones, they can be a struggle to find. You have to be accepted into the right groups. Often you'll be vetted, even tested, but the reward can be worth it. I'll never forget the day I had a hand-delivered envelope deposited at my doorstep and the anticipation I felt opening it, unknotting the brown twine so delicately tied around the heft. God, some of them even had wax seals. I liked those the most. I found the violet and crimson seals delicious to look at.

But they were so, *so* much more than simple puzzles.

A principled affair, 5 down.

The headmaster of the local school was having an affair with her sister-in-law, Sarah. It was hard to find that out. It wasn't exactly public knowledge. Frankly, I had to resort to stalking, and it wasn't a good look, but it was a new experience nonetheless and the few times I nearly got caught were quite exhilarating. But what was truly amazing was that this was at the school just a few blocks from my house! You have to understand, it wasn't just a template handed out to everyone. I still don't know how big any of these communities really are, but I imagine they're quite small and involve people from all over the world. It was truly remarkable to think someone had laboured over a tailor-made puzzle just for me.

There are quite a few groups I belong to now. Some aren't even organised online, instead requiring that you ferret them out, sometimes as clues in other puzzles, sometimes as their own elaborate games. But there are always more to be found and in the best circumstances, they find you, choosing you out of all the people in the world to rise to the challenge at hand. The right ones will push you to do things you never thought possible.

A baker's jewels, 7 down.

Harriet Baker, who died in 2012 at the age of 86 and was buried with an emerald necklace in the local graveyard. I still have it, kept away somewhere in a special drawer along with news clippings of the crime. It even has some of the soil from the grave still muddying its shimmering gems, and admittedly they do still smell a bit. But I bet that I know something most people don't, and that's what happens to little old Grandma five years after being sealed up in a box beneath the Earth. Not just the abstract, either. I know the specifics, I know *exactly* what she looks like, smells like, and even what her cold lumpen flesh feels like. I spent years as a child wondering what happened to the many relatives of mine who passed away, but it was as an adult I finally found the answer.

People have lived their whole lives looking down on me. Teachers assumed I was slow at learning, my parents mourned that I cared more about organising my wargaming miniatures than I ever did about girls or friends, everyone around me treated me like I was a timid mouse in a world of thundering giants. But I've lived a more exciting life than they could ever imagine, and it hasn't been in spite of who I am. Only someone like me could pursue these clues to such dogged ends, and I gladly take the bad with the good.

The colour of the tea plates served by the Biellier Historical Society, 9 up.

Don't let the name fool you. The Society is a private organisation for some rather unusual gentlemen who serve tea *after* their annual conference is finished. Crazy bastards, I can see why they need a drink once they're finished and I'm not surprised half of them didn't take a seat during refreshments. I'm just not sure I'll ever look be able to look a farm animal in the eye again.

Oh, and *turquoise*, by the way. That was the answer.

I know things very few people know. That's a rare privilege and, like I said, it comes with a price. It would be ridiculous to think one might look upon the fraying edges of our world without having to face some uncomfortable sights. And you might think the worst of it is a leather-bound orgy in a dungeon or perversions you can safely find on Wikipedia, but there are other lingering truths buried in the Earth, and I am one of the few who have seen them. There is always more to learn, always another word to find, another puzzle to complete. And I have come a long way in my education since I first received that letter on my doorstep years ago.

The inheritor of Maeson's oldest home, 6 down.

Albert. Albert was the named inheritor of the first house built and designed by obscure architect Harold Maeson. It was not, as almost everyone first expected, the current owner's first-born son named Alexander, but instead the old man's male sexual interest Albert, who was a rather unwilling 17-year-old. Perhaps the old man thought it made up for his actions towards the boy he had kept around as a family friend for years, disguising his abuse as mentorship. Either way, no one could have possibly known what Harold had planned. The will was written up in total secrecy, something I spent considerable resources finding out.

Credit where it's due, Harold put up a fight, but his death was the only way I could get my answer. After that, Albert's face was all over the papers, along with details of the coming legal challenge by Harold's children. I can't speak for others, but I found the experience quite a revelation. I felt as if I'd learned profound hidden knowledge, a truth about reality found in the glassy bloodshot eyes of a man violently dying. There's something in there, you know, something that lies just beneath our own reality. I saw a glimmer of it that night, just like I had so many others before it. It's quite beautiful, a confusing, glittering mess of contradictions and unknowable madness. It is by definition beyond our ability to every truly know, but you can still see facets of it, one bit at a time.

It's beautiful. But... well, it's not always so painless.

The missing piglet counted right to left, 5 up.

Eight. That was the answer. I spent all night researching fairy tales and children's rhymes only to fall asleep at my desk sometime around 2 in the morning. When I awoke, I had been moved to the sofa and my left foot was raised on the armrest and bandaged heavily. The whole tingled from anaesthesia and it wouldn't be until noon before I could walk on it again. Anxiously, I undid the white swaddle of blood-tinged gauze and winced at the sight of my mutilated foot. The middle toe on my left foot had been amputated cleanly, the wound sewn up neatly like a cross-stitched grin. Counting right to left, I noticed it was the eighth toe missing and I have to admit, I pumped my fist in the air and rejoiced at having the answer.

But the experience caught me off guard, and it might not surprise you to know that I have since looked into slowing down and maybe even taking a short break from this hobby. Somone had amputated my toe, and the lengths they went to were deeply concerning. But there have been some difficulties in applying the brakes to this fixation of mine. For one thing, they won't stop sending new puzzles, and it's all but impossible for me to ignore them. And there's another thing; the clues are becoming increasingly pointed.

A sea of white and flakes of gold to flood a castle of ivory, 6 down.

I thought the answer was *cereal* right up until I discovered a needle hidden in my cornflakes. That, it turned out, was the correct answer and I was lucky to catch it before it wound up anywhere near my mouth. The thought of that thing sliding down my throat or catching in the roof of my mouth produced some intense anxiety. Clubs have pushed things in the past, boundaries take a backseat when it comes to pursuing the absolute limit of knowledge. But it felt like such an odd inclusion for the latest puzzle, one that didn't necessarily teach me anything. If I had the ability to trace it to a single group, I might have a better sense of what it was meant to mean, but then again, anonymity was always kind of the point.

The currency of a strategic withdrawal, 3 up.

I initially thought of the military, but in fact the answer was Yen, and it turned out that around £50,000 worth of them had been withdrawn from my account (by myself, somehow) at the bank. God knows how that was possible, but it happened and there's not a lot I could really do about it. I've written to some of the groups but as far as I can tell, they're playing coy.

I am sorry, one replied. *But our puzzles are sent out as part of a weekly newsletter via e-mail. We're not sure we've ever offered bespoke crosswords, but we'd be fascinated to hear more if there's anyone out there who does. It'd interest quite a few of our members, myself included.*

I received similar variations to this message from just about every organisation I had listed in my ledger, and frankly I found the suggestion ridiculous. I'd always assumed those newsletters were part of a front, making it appear as though the focus was on banal little puzzles about obscure military defeats while secretly directing us to brothels and illegal casinos. It made sense, perhaps, that they would maintain the ruse, but an acquaintance I called wasn't exactly reassuring.

"Well of course they're a front," he said. "Don't you get the packages? I've had a few seedy adventures with those!"

"Oh that's good!" I laughed while breathing a deep sigh of relief. "I was beginning to think... well, I'm not sure what I was thinking."

"Oh yes, the packages are very real," he replied. "The Spring edition was quite a naughty affair, don't you think?"

"Invigorating," I smiled. "I didn't even know where to buy a burlap sa—"

"Strawberry!? Can you imagine? The Mrs and I had a delight trying out the different flavours."

"What?"

"Oh come now man, no need to be shy. It's quite normal to use... *lubricant,*" he whispered it like a dirty secret. "Agnes suggested we try it on toast!" I hung up with his laughter still bellowing down the other line. My Spring edition of our shared club was not anything like his. I told myself that it made sense it wouldn't, they were *meant* to be custom made for each participant, but it alarmed me to hear that his activities were so dreadfully banal. Most of the clues in that edition had directed me to the consumption of a range of meats, including something I scraped off the side of a suspension bridge.

Nothing my friend had said to me rang true. Rightly, I should have stopped there. But... but the thing is... it was never really an option, not then and not now. I'm sure you think it's a silly compulsion or anxiety, but it's not. I can't do it. It's simply not in my nature, especially not now I know that God-knows-what could be lurking around the corner. I've explained this to myself and others before—I am task focused. I needed to finish the job at hand.

PO Box 19777, open it from within, 9 down.

I found the box with ease, but there was no key nor any means to open it from within. Whatever the rationale was behind the puzzle, I thought at the time that the whole affair was beginning to frustrate me. I didn't see any significant challenge to tracing the address, aside from finding the key which, it would turn out, was very much part of the clue. In fact, I'm still not entirely sure how they did it. I awoke to a sort of gagging sensation one night, dreaming that I had swallowed a tangle of wet hair. Only the terrible retching sensation wasn't entirely dreamed up. Tied to my canine was a line of floss that I painfully had to pull up from my stomach. It was unnecessarily long, spooling out of my throat in a bloody tangle for a good few metres while I vomited and cried from the struggle. It took nearly half an hour to inch it out, but eventually I regurgitated the key, collapsing afterwards to the floor to heave and sob as I recovered.

There was a teddy bear in the locker, and I didn't find it particularly amusing. And, yes, okay, there was a mild satisfaction to getting the answer, but the rest of me was filled with that growing distress. I felt like the punchline to a joke that wasn't funny.

A starry orchid's window of choice, 7 down.

The answer was eyeball, and to find that answer I had to consume a poisonous flower causes bloody secretions from the tear ducts, not to mention renal failure. The price for that answer may one day be dialysis. The doctors couldn't say for sure what the chances were. At the very least, I got to spend a few days in hospital, and I hoped that would give me a kind of break, but if anything, it made things worse. I was not prepared to be incapacitated for so long with the knowledge that the puzzle was just one clue from completion.

I was itching furiously for the last few hours. There would be no rest for me until I had finished the puzzle, and I swore to myself, swore blind on my mother's grave, that it would be the last. When I arrived home it was with the kind of relief I never thought possible. I am forever learning more about myself and those first few steps through the front door made it clear to me I was in the thrall of some kind of addiction. No matter what the price was, I told myself over and over again that I would pay it and move on. I would change addresses if I had to or pay someone to physically slap the damn pencil out of my hand if I went to complete another crossword! God knows I have the money.

I will climb this final hurdle, I told myself, *and see it through.*

The final clue was waiting for me and it's... it's something else. I half-expect there to be some ghoulish double-entendre hiding in the words, but for the life of me I cannot see one. It seems more like a hideous joke—one I don't really understand. I have a possible word choice, and it certainly fits but... It's been weeks and I can't bring myself to write it in. This is the final clue! The final step at the end of this increasingly desperate adventure and I can't figure it out. I'm half-tempted to say that I won't see another answer because I don't want to finish it. That might be it, surely? I'm an addict. I'll admit that all too readily and this wouldn't be the first time I took things too far. It's just...

The hand that has written these clues and led you down this path, 4 down.

I keep expecting to find a severed hand by my door, or to wake up one day missing most of my fingers. It's a strange thing, but I have come to find myself ruminating often on the look in the old man's eyes. For while I am sure that I saw something terrible and beautiful deep within the popping veins of those suffocating retinas, it had not occurred to me until now that something was looking back.

And it's waiting for me to write in the final answer, though God knows it must be wrong for it simply cannot be possible that the answer is '*mine*'.

WRIT COIN

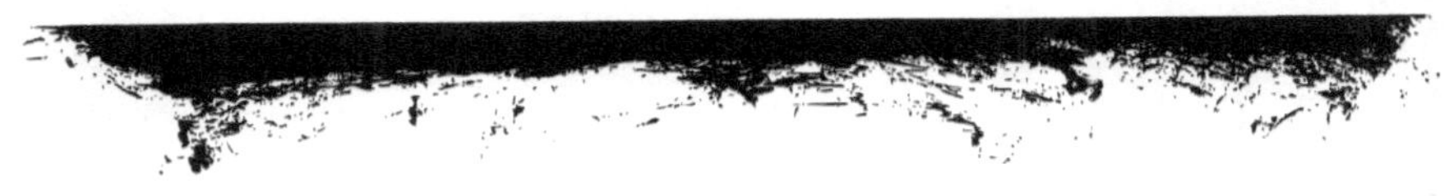

The screen, the same one that had lit the young man's face a pallid blue, painting his tortured features like a bad Halloween decoration, showed only a column of numbers that ran down the left-hand side. The rows started on 318.23, and ended on 83,290.86, each entry increasing by small but seemingly random increments. At the bottom was an old-school block cursor flashing over and over. I was still trying to make sense of it when the techs turned the lights on and began to work while Jack, my partner, approached. He made a despondent sigh as he swung the desk chair around and got a good look at our victim.

"Jesus Christ!" he cried.

"Be careful where you stand," I said, gesturing to the piles of old tissues and tied up plastic bags, their contents leaking carelessly over the floor. Jack nudged one of the sodden lumps with his foot before looking to me for confirmation.

"Diapers," I said.

"Why?" he asked.

"Nature called?" I shrugged.

"What happed to this poor guy?"

I pointed to the legs. A trypophobe's nightmare. A pen had been used to punch holes in the fleshy muscle of his thighs. There could've been a thousand holes in each leg, enough to render a sponge-like effect. They were clean the closer you got to his crotch, and so gangrenous by the knee I was surprised nothing had fallen off.

"Any idea who did this to him?" Jack asked.

"Him, probably. He's still holding the pen."

My partner checked and quickly looked away with a grimace.

"Could someone have made him? Gun against the head, that kind of thing?"

"Why not?" I said. "But there's nothing to say there was anyone else here. Besides, there's worse hanging around. I'd stay away from the kitchen if you ever wanna look at a microwave the same way. And those diapers have all sorts of funny stuff in 'em. Nearly got pricked by a needle earlier. All of it suggests self-inflicted injuries. I think that if someone made him do this, it was through the computer. He lived on it. Few years ago he dropped out of college to stream some game, got caught up in crypto investing and then lost so much money his parents had to re-mortgage. Eventually, his downward spiral led him here."

The apartment was one room, and too small to even be called a studio. It was a run-down shithole with peeling wallpaper and a sagging ceiling.

"I understood very little of that explanation," Jack said. "But I think I got the gist. He lost out, went recluse?"

I nodded.

"Fancied himself some kind of mathematician, I think." I flipped through one of the kid's notebooks. "One dollar equals thirty-eight seconds," I muttered. "Whatever that fucking means."

"So was he nuts? Or was he coerced?" he asked.

"Maybe both," I said. "But you gotta figure he was in that chair for a reason. The caller—his sister, by the way—said it all started after he got into something new about a year ago. A package from a friend he'd been excited for. I'm guessing it's got something to do with this." I bent down to the tower and pulled out an off-white USB. The screen immediately turned black.

"Huh," Jack grunted, and I could see that he was perking up a little now that we had a lead. "What's on the drive?"

"Let's find out."

"They weren't happy, but they did it, they made a copy," I said, placing two cups of coffee down on Jack's desk. "They said it was a silicon brick. No firmware. No OS. And when they cracked it open, they complained it was full of wires that connected to nothing, and it was all riddled with bits of soldered metal made into random shapes. You shoulda seen their faces when they put it back together, plugged it in, and the forensic program just sprung to life and started copying. They looked spooked."

"Well it was plugged in at the scene and doing... *something,*" Jack said. "Something important must be on it."

"Hopefully they'll find where it came from. They've got the original, but this copy," I held up a new drive, "is ours to take."

Without asking, I spun Jack's laptop around, made a point of closing his thirty-eight open tabs, and plugged the drive in.

"Some of those pages were research," Jack said, hiding his smile with a quick sip of coffee.

I was about to say something, some minor upkeep of this running joke we'd been sharing for years, when the computer beeped and reset with a startling *thunk*. You could hear the hard drive go dead with a little click, and then after a few seconds, the screen came to life.

WritCoin

Each letter was typed out one at a time, the font huge and green like a bad vision of the future from the eighties. After a few seconds, the words were erased and something new was written.

Let your wealth be writ upon your flesh

And then again, on a new screen:

Enter bank details below

There were several underlined spaces asking for input, and I noticed they were just enough for a bank account.

"I'll get a card from forensics," I said. "Something that scammers—"

"Ah fuck that," Jack said, grabbing the laptop and typing away with one finger on each hand. "Anyone wants to ruin my credit score? They're free to try."

He punched in his details and, after a few seconds of tiny whirring motors, something new flashed up on the screen.

1914.45

"Well," Jack cried, genuinely surprised. "That's my balance. I checked it this morning and there it is. Start of the first world war, with the end of the second for change."

"They shouldn't be able to get that from an account number," I said. "Maybe it's just a coincidence."

Jack looked at me like I was an idiot.

"Ain't no coincidence. I've been hacked." He said that last word like it was both dirty and hilarious. "I've heard what people can do on the internet, stealing identities. So... now what?" he asked. "They gonna drain my account and use it to retire early? I heard there are some real nice super yachts going for just under two grand."

I tapped the keyboard. Nothing happened.

"I don't know," I said. "I don't know what's next."

Jack scratched his head and reached over for his coffee. He took a sip and we were both surprised when the screen changed.

1921.72

"It just went up!" he cried.

"I saw," I said. "But I don't understand. It's... what, free money? Maybe it's a crypto mining thing?" I asked. "Hijacks the computer, uses it to mine and then deposits a small fee back into the user's account?"

"Like another language," Jack mused as he took another sip of his coffee. Once again, the number went up again.

1911.96

Wordlessly, I slid my glass of water over and he took a sip. Nothing changed. He tried the coffee once more, wincing at the heat, and there it was, the number jumped up again.

Jack realised first. He always was a little better at seeing things through another's eyes. Without saying another word, he held his hand over the cheap linoleum floor and slowly poured what was left of the coffee over his skin. He hissed at first, but through sheer will kept his hand there until the last dregs of coffee had drained.

Before I could shout at him, he nodded towards the screen.

1913.03

"It's pain," he said, drying his hand on his shirt. "The balance increases with pain. That's why he was hurting himself so bad. Every poke with that pen was another deposit. You need to go to forensics ASAP and get them to check the kid's account, and then mine. I wanna know if something's actually being deposited.

"It'd be a fucker of a joke if it turned out this was just numbers on a screen."

"Huh," Chris said, staring at the screen as Jack plucked a hair and the tally went up. "Will you look at that."

It had been an arduous few hours convincing the computer forensics guy we weren't messing with him. Bank statements were pulled out for both Jack and our victim, and we formatted three whole laptops before he was finally willing to even consider that the stick was the real deal. Jack accepted the premise the easiest because he knew the least. All computers were magical to him. I knew enough to be sceptical, but Chris, our resident expert, was completely baffled by the whole thing.

"I just don't understand where it's coming from," he said.

"We've got accountants on that," I replied.

"But why?" he cried. "Let's accept the cash is there. It's real. Why would anyone pay for... for what? Pain?"

"Maybe it's like proof of work, right?" I asked, leveraging my night's research into crypto in the hope of offering some insight. "Maybe they don't want computational work to prove the new blockchain is authentic. Maybe they want pain?"

"No... sure, whatever," Chris said, throwing his hands up in the air. "But that still doesn't answer how. This machine is a brick as far as internet is concerned. No webcam. No wifi. Can you do it again?" He turned to Jack for the last part and mimed pulling out another hair.

"I don't have an unlimited supply," Jack groaned before yanking an eyebrow hair free. Sure enough, the computer's tally went up once again.

Chris stared at the screen for so long that Jack wandered off and began poking at the vivisected computers that lay all around us.

"Alright guys," Chris said, suddenly sounding unusually helpful. "Leave it with me. I'll have to see what I can dig up."

Something inside me tensed up at Chris's suggestion. I wanted to instinctively say he couldn't have it, but that was ridiculous. How could he help without keeping hold of it for at least a few days? One look from Jack told me he hadn't registered anything strange about the request, so I decided to just let it go.

"We'll leave you to it," Jack said. "See ya Chris." But Chris didn't even look at us as we left. He was already wheeling the usb drive from one laptop to another while muttering quietly to himself.

"What's eating you?" Jack asked as we waited in the elevator.

"Did you know Chris gets migraines?" I asked.

"What of it?"

"I don't know." I shrugged. "But he gets 'em damn near daily. Spends hours each night in pain."

"Huh."

"You don't think...?" I asked.

"I doubt it," Jack replied. "Chris is a smart guy. Long way from poking holes in his leg and jury rigging his microwave to cook with the door open."

"Yeah, but sometimes the darkest pits have gentle slopes. That gamer kid, I reckon he started off small before he got all..."

"Creative?"

"Yeah." I nodded. "Creative."

I couldn't escape that feeling of dread building up in my gut. What if Chris started out just letting his migraines do the heavy lifting? That'd be something. Hell, it'd be a force for good. Guy was in pain anyway, might as well make money. But the pay outs were small. Anyone could see that. That kid hadn't earned billions. He'd sold his health and his sanity for what seemed like a pittance in comparison to the suffering he went through. And yet the potential of earning cash for pain... the idea stayed with you. Every ache in your gut and every twinge in your spine could have a dollar value attached to it and who wouldn't want that?

I knew I would.

But would the average person just sit back and let it just tick upwards day-to-day, content to live on whatever meagre pay out it threw their way? I told myself that's what I'd do. I'd be smart. But I also knew you could go through a lot of pain and heal up just fine. Wouldn't it be better to take some time and figure out what the usb stick really wanted? Once you knew what sorta injuries gave the biggest pay out, then you could plan a safe way to make as much money as the body could physically handle.

And it was probably that kind of thinking that led that kid to start experimenting with sharp things. He hadn't even made a withdrawal. He just kept letting the money pile up. Something about that struck me as truly insane.

I could tell the implications hadn't completely escaped Jack because he pursed his lips for a few seconds and finally offered an opinion.

"Remind me to check up on him tomorrow."

———

"It's mine!"

A gunshot rang out, and everyone ducked around the barricade. Even the paramedic being wheeled into an ambulance flinched and he was doped up on painkillers. He'd been shot just fifteen minutes ago, but he was still a lucky man. Whoever was up there had fired blindly around a corner and clipped his leg. Could've easily been a lot worse.

Above us, a pale-looking head stuck out of the window and screamed,

"It's mine! It's mine! My flesh! It's written on *my* flesh!"

I noticed Jack's hand on his holster. He'd never fire, of course. Way too dangerous. But damn if it wasn't tempting. That ratty-looking bastard had spent the last few hours taking pot shots at cops and doctors after wounding the first response team. They'd been on their way up there, reporting to neighbour's complaints of a missing person and an awful smell, when he first opened fire on the very people supposed to help him.

"Any news on the infra-red?" Jack asked.

I looked towards the special response team. A large man in a black visor gave me a thumb's up.

"He's alone," I said. "No hostages. They want to take the shot."

"I'd like it if we could keep him alive, could they disarm him?"

"How the fuck are they gonna do that?" I asked, but before Jack could reply, the officers around us began to cry out and our attention was back on the shooter above.

"Didn't take him for a jumper," Jack said as we watched his skinny torso wriggle its way out of the tight confines of the open window.

"You think it's like the last one?" I asked as I gestured with one hand for the clean-up crews to get ready. "He's been yammering on about wealth written on flesh."

"I don't know," he said. "Can't really get a pay out if you're dead. Just doesn't make any kind of se—"

The perp finally pushed himself past the point of no return and his body entered freefall. My memories of it, in hindsight, are turgid and stuffed with too much detail. I can close my eyes, even now, and imagine the look on his face and the neon lights of our patrol cars flashing against his back, none of which I would've been able to actually see. Still, the memory is very ingrained in my mind, and I suspect most of the vital and lively details have been layered on fresh with each new recollection. What I do remember for sure is thinking to myself,

What the fuck is in his mouth?

Half-a-second later, I found out. It was a bit of rope that he'd been slowly feeding himself for a few days. I don't know how that works exactly, but the techs assured me it's something the body can easily do. Bit of training with your gag reflex and just about anything can pass your gullet. And then, if it's long enough, it goes right out the other end.

It was that end he'd tied to the fridge just before he jumped.

"How are they?" Jack asked, and it was a grave sign of how bad things were that he, of all people, would be asking after the clean-up crew.

"Angry," I said. "Not, like, *angry* angry. Just... not very happy."

Jack walked over to the window and looked outside.

"Yeah I get that," he said. "Anything off the doctors looking at the guy?"

"Uh yeah," I replied. "Confusion, for sure. No postmortem, obviously, although they're adamant it's coming. Guy can't possibly survive those injuries for much longer. Still, they did as we asked and looked for prior injuries. We've got what looks like a lot of broken bones, many partially healed. Just one break piled on top of another. It's a miracle he could walk, let alone do that."

I gestured to the fridge that had been dragged away from the wall before it was used as an anchor. Although at least some of that distance had been the result of his dead weight hitting a snag in the rope.

I shuddered at the thought and let my eyes roam the walls. They were covered with hundreds of thousands of the same simple equation repeated in a brown greasy scrawl, each one slightly different.

$1.12 = 35 seconds
$1.14 = 39 seconds
$0.87 = 26 seconds

I tried to focus on the numbers, tried to make sense of the clues while recalling the ancient history of entry level stats. Normal distributions were part of the general scrawl in some parts, along with what looked like some kind of Bayesian equation. But none of it stuck for long in my mind. My eyes, no matter how hard I tried to keep them in one place, kept coming back to the glowing CRT monitor on the ageing kitchen table.

252,038.13
252,038.76
252,039.09

It was still rising, but for all that he'd gone through, the shooter had barely earned 250k. Scrolling up, I found his grand finale. It netted him just over a few grand. It was so little it felt like a deliberate act of humiliation, and my ire began to rise. I took some satisfaction in watching the numbers disappear when I yanked the thumb drive out. Then, when that wasn't enough, I started kicking the shit out of the tower.

"Woah woah woah," Jack cried while stepping over. "Calm the fuck down."

"This is bad," I said. "Whoever made this knew what they were doing. Right now, it's just two guys, but if it gets big... The desperate, the greedy, and the plain ol' fucking stupid will line up around the block to play with this thing. *How the fuck do they even know!?*" I cried and I could hear the anger in my voice. "How does anyone even know the guy on the other end is hurting himself!?"

I didn't usually find myself fraying at the ends like this, not in front of Jack, who had a good fifteen years on me and was the kinda guy who you always wanted to see you at your toughest. But after what we'd just seen, there was a helplessness building up inside my chest that felt like being buried alive.

"Calm down," Jack said. "I'll finish up here. You go home and get into bed. Get your head straight."

"I'm gonna hear that noise every single night for the rest of my life."

"Yeah well... you're not alone," he replied, and I'm not sure if he meant to or not, but he found the one thing that managed to comfort me.

———

It was 11am, and I'd been in bed for six days using up my annual leave when the phone rang and Jack's name lit up on the screen.

"Jack?" I groaned, surprised at just how bad my voice sounded.

"It's me," he said. "I need you to come in."

"I'm not doing that," I said. "Not until someone threatens to fire me. Tell me when someone who gets paid more takes this case off our hands."

"Did you know Chris has been working from home all this time?"

My heart sank.

"No."

"Yeah, well he got permission from the day after we saw him last, y'know? The day we gave him the stick with WritCoin on it.

Then three days ago, at about lunchtime, he stopped responding to all emails and stopped answering his phone. His friends are talking about him like he might be ill but..."

Jack didn't have to finish his thought.

"How long's he been home?" I asked.

"Three weeks."

"Fuck. Okay. I'm coming in."

"Chris?"

A few heavy knocks and we heard nothing in return. We weren't exactly light touches either. Jack's hand boomed against the wood so hard I thought the door would bow inwards.

"Chris!" I cried again, but there was still no answer.

"No surprise there," Jack grumbled as he stepped around the stony front garden and tried to peer into the open windows. "Who's he live with?"

"Parents," I said. "Originally, anyway. They passed away a few years ago, so I'd have to guess the place is all his now."

"No wife?"

"Nope." I shook my head.

"Doesn't look like there's anyone else living in there," Jack replied, stepping back from the grimy pane. "Back way in?"

"Let's look," I answered while moving towards a rusted side gate that led to a small and stony garden. Surrounding the house were decrepit apartment blocks that towered above, lending the garden a feeling of urban mysticism, like this one overgrown patch of brambles and greenery was the city's dirty little secret. We soon found a concrete flight of stairs that led down to a cellar door, the steps covered in old broken bottles tossed from up high, probably by some jealous neighbours. Jack and I kicked them aside as we descended to find the door open.

"Jack," I said as we took our first steps inside. The basement was quiet and filled with old junk, curtains drawn across most of it to try and hide as much as possible from prying eyes. Slowly, we made our way through it while my heart took to tap dancing in my chest. "When are we going to go to someone else with this?"

"With what?"

"The case."

"Oh," he grunted. "We'll have to see. Maybe it goes big, viral, like you said. In which case we won't have to do a damned thing. It'll be out of our hands in no time. But so far, these guys, they've all had some kinda connection. Prints show those two drives were handled by the same person at some point. I was working on IDing them when I heard the news. Maybe whoever left those prints, maybe they're the source. If so, we could stop it before it gets bad."

"I couldn't do it."

The voice was startling enough that I went for a gun I didn't have. God bless Jack, he hadn't let me come armed. I hated to be someone he couldn't count on, but it turned out to be the right choice because I would've fired into the source of that voice without hesitation. It was one of those Microsoft Sam jobs, robotic enough to almost be funny, but loud enough it damn near made me shit my pants when I first heard it.

"What the fuck...?" I muttered.

"Nick, Jack, I hope you find this," the voice said without intonation. At this stage, Jack drew his gun, albeit in a safer and more sensible way than I could have, and he stalked quietly over to a small nook covered with a red curtain. He peeked inside and let out a soul draining sigh. Slowly, he pulled the curtain aside for me to see.

We found our head of computer forensics slumped in a desk chair, facing two screens. One was a text document, the other was WritCoin. A muddy splash of brown and red across one of Chris's shoulder spoke of a fatal bleed out, one that must've occurred days before. It soaked his clothes, the chair, and the floor, draining him so thoroughly he looked like something dragged out of a lake. I had to assume it was rigor mortis that kept him upright, but his pose was unnervingly natural.

The robotic voice spoke up once more.

"I'm on borrowed time," it said.

"It's the text file," I said, pointing to the other screen. "A note, set to read out loud. A letter, I think. It must be on loop."

"I miscalculated."

Jack bent down and picked up a kitchen knife covered in rusty blood.

"Suicide?" he asked me.

"I have wanted to die for so very long," the voice said, almost in answer to Jack's question. *"But I was scared. When I saw WritCoin I thought the money might balance out the pain. I left instructions for it all to go to charity. If my death could help people, I thought it would make it easier. I have tried before but never could go through with it. I always thought of the bad I'd be leaving behind. I thought WritCoin would change it. Make it easier knowing some good would come of my suffering.*

"At first I tried pills. But it did not work. So I took more, and it still did not work. I tried to hang myself, but I stayed there, alive, for two days before the light fixture broke. I tried my wrists. I tried electrocution. In the end, I used the knife. I thought it would be definitive, opening my neck up ear-to-ear. I was wrong. I have been bleeding out for two days and am still not dead. Something is slowing it down. And the numbers keep rising. I am alive even as my body shuts down. Soon I will have no blood, no oxygen to work the cells to move my muscles. I hope that will be the end, but if it was so simple, I should have died days ago. At least I have had time to think. And I have a theory.

"WritCoin – I think the money is secondary. It is just a way to get you started."

I had been stood, rooted to the spot, as the weight of Chris's words sank in. He had killed himself and we'd given him the tool that pushed him past the threshold. The thought of it all left me dazed. Even Jack, not a man often given to flights of sympathy, was shocked into silence by the thought of this man's death.

"It is giving us time," the voice continued. *"Pain in exchange for time added on to your life. The money is just a lure. The real pay out is time. The worse the pain, the longer you'll get added onto your life. And if you hurt yourself bad enough, the pay becomes self-sustaining even as the injury kills you. More suffering means more time. More time means more suffering. My only hope is that if the program is interrupted, the cycle can be stopped.*

"If you find me, Nick or Jack, or anyone, please pull the drive. I'm still aware, somehow. I should have died days ago, but I can see the numbers still going up bit by bit. In the end, I think it will leave me in here, stuck in a rotting shell. Whatever this thing harvests, it isn't just physical pain. It's leading to something darker. I think something is out there and it is..."

The document ended, the final statement left unfinished.

Both Jack and I looked at the WritCoin screen.

"You don't think he's actually in there do you?" I asked.

Somehow, the tally was still increasing. Without saying another word, Jack bent down and pulled the drive out with an angry grunt. Just like that, the monitor went dark and a heavy silence filled the cellar. I don't know exactly what prompted the following—maybe it was a shift in temperature caused by us opening the door, or maybe just a build up of gasses—but as soon as the clicking of the computer had stopped, Chris's body fell forward out of the chair. He hit the keyboard face first and there was a blurt of computerised consonants spoken before his body awkwardly gave into gravity and landed on the floor with a wet thud.

Jack dropped the drive and stamped it into pieces on the floor.

"Tell me he wasn't still in there?" I cried. "That all that shit about having extra time was just his brain running out of oxygen and he was rambling?"

"It was gasses, or some post-mortem twitch or some shit. Just a coincidence he fell," he replied, but I don't think even he believed that. Maybe he had or hadn't realised at this point, but it was firmly in my mind that the jumper we'd seen just a week before had died in hospital hours later while we were still in his apartment. Had that happened at the same time I'd pulled the USB drive? I told myself it was impossible, but everything we'd seen so far was impossible.

"Call this in," he said. "We've got work to do."

"They shoulda burned this place down years ago."

The Evergreen high rise was notorious for its squatters. It was a place where a certain kinda person went, and the city preferred them behind closed doors rather than out on the very public and visible streets. Before being condemned, the people who lived there were tenants. Now they were called squatters. To Jack and I, the Evergreen high rise was the hiding place of our supposed distributor. It had taken days to get an ID due to the partial print match, only to find out the owner's listed address was no longer accurate. After that we had to work our usual contacts and informants and they helped, but they could only get so far. Rumours and hearsay was what we had to go with, leading to a list of several squalid shitholes we'd been forced to traipse through one-by-one.

Evergreen was by far the worst.

"Wanna take the elevator?"

Jack smirked as he asked, both of us stopping to look at the wrenched open metal doors and the black water flooding the shaft. I tried looking for the car but saw only my reflection cast in inky ripples.

"They said eleventh floor, right?" I asked.

Above me, somewhere, a door slammed shut. We both waited for sounds of footsteps, but none came. After a few more silent seconds, Jack spoke up again in a hushed voice that still sounded far too loud in the derelict lobby.

"Let's get going."

I found the climb up easier than Jack, who huffed and puffed after just a few short flights. I considered asking him if he wanted a break, but I didn't fancy the idea of hanging around in that graffiti-riddle stairwell. It would've been bad enough if we were alone in that concrete tomb, but we weren't. The sounds of fleeing feet and locking doors told us that the inhabitants of Evergreen were well aware of our presence, and most likely watching us. So far we could be thankful they were staying out of our way, but I wondered if it was just because they hadn't figured out what they wanted to do with us yet.

When we reached our floor, we both waited by the open door for any signs of an ambush before venturing into the dark, torches raised.

"Over here."

Jack walked over to a closed door and put his ear close to the jamb. He was listening to something, and as I got closer, I heard it too. There was a gentle thrumming behind the door, and an occasional blurt of bright and colourful electronic music. Gun drawn, Jack tried the handle and found it open. He took point as we entered and found a bare apartment with the carpet ripped up. The only sign of habitation was a computer station set up in one corner, its five multi-sized monitors lighting the room up in an array of neon blues and pinks. A screensaver was looping over and over as a little pixelated cat chased mice, bursting into joyful song each time it caught one.

"Nick."

"I see it," I said.

I'd seen it the second I entered. A patch of shadow that seemed to eat the light from our torches. It had been a person, once. Some part of my rational mind told me this had to be true. Two arms. Two legs. A pair of crusty old jeans tied around the waist with string. Thinking of the first case and the needles he'd swallowed, and passed, I checked this victim's hand. Sure enough, there were several shards of glass clutched in their first. That explained the distended belly that hung toad-like below a bony ribcage. A classic sign of pica.

"How long has he been here?" Jack asked.

"A while," I answered, as I paid attention to the festering mess of scar tissue and coagulated blood that coated everything above the neck and shoulders. The face was inhuman, lipless and skinless, the features warped from what must have been an endless cycle of injury and healing. No soft tissue was spared. If it could be peeled, pierced, or tenderised, it had been. One injury laid on top of another for what must have been several months or even years. Even the eyes were lidless and had dilated to such an extreme they looked all black with no iris or sclera. I wanted to be professional, but it made my stomach knot and my heart race just to look at.

"Jack?"

"Yeah?"

"I can't stop thinking about what Chris wrote."

"Yeah," he said with a weary sigh, "me neither. Whether it's true or not, there's something... I don't know, spooky, about this whole thing. But we need to fix it no matter what."

Over by the computer, he nudged the mouse, and the screen-saver faded to reveal a standard windows desktop on all but one screen. That one turned black with green text. We'd found it again – another row of numbers starting small and getting bigger.

"Well, there we go," Jack said. "What did our lucky contestant win?"

He thumbed the down arrow key, and the text scrolled for what felt like an obscene amount of time. Knowing that each row of numbers was another injury made the wait for the bottom very uncomfortable.

"There we go," he said when he finally found the bottom. "He got to just under nine million. Jesus, you think he'd retire after like, what, three?"

"Probably saving up for plastic surgery," I replied, and Jack gave a tired laugh, the kind you only do with your nose.

8,879,332.79, the screen read.

And then, soundlessly, it ticked over again.

8,879,335.26

Jack's hand reached for his gun.

8,879,338.95

I nearly said something, but stopped myself. My mind stuttered like a flooded car engine, and I tried a few different explanations for what I was seeing, but it all came down to what Chris had already told us. The tally was rising because whoever was on that floor, they were somehow still in pain.

Quietly, we both waited for some sign of life. When it finally happened, it was fast... lightning fast. Whoever or whatever it was lunged for us with childish giggles that left no doubt as to this thing's state of mind. It wanted to hurt us. Broken legs trailed behind it as it shuffled forward in a blaze of shaking lights and terrified cries that I would later realise were mine. The sight of that thing coming at us froze me to the spot, but Jack stepped up. Gun drawn, he aimed and fired (and fired, and fired and fired) before it could close even half the distance. When the gunshots finally stopped, it came as a relief. All motion and sound ceased as if the normality of gunpowder cancelled out the madness we were seeing.

Lead and fire versus pain and greed. Jack and I were left standing there in breathless quiet. The tension was so immense that when it finally broke, it did so with a chuckle, and it was Jack who went first.

"Guess he wasn't dead," he said after a nervous laugh. "But uh, he is now."

And how couldn't he be? Half the monster's skull had been pulverised. Its head looked more like a houseplant than it did a piece of human anatomy. Just like that, all notion of extended lives were washed away, and I felt as if an enormous weight had been taken away.

"Yeah," I laughed with him. "Maybe I've just let this one get to me. All said and done, that bullet did the trick. He isn't getti—"

The creature sat up.

Slowly, its flower bulb head turned towards us, and it spoke.

"Would you like to live forever?" It hissed, its words shaped by flaps of skin and muscle that I'm not sure ever began their life as part of the mouth. Jack lifted his gun, but I stopped him.

"The computer," I whispered.

"You can skirt oblivion," it tittered. "You do not have to wait to see hell to start paying your dues."

"Shoot the fucking computer," I hissed at Jack.

"No need." The thing held out its hand as a gesture to stop us. Misshapen fingers splayed outwards at stomach-churning angles. "I knew you were coming. There is not a soul in this building who hasn't shared in this gift. Do you think you would have made it this far if I hadn't wanted you to? So take the drive and know that the promise of an extended life is real. Am I not proof enough?"

The creature used a hand to flick back a strand of... *something* that had fallen across the few inches of meat and bone that remained above its jawline.

"Not only of the coin, but of other, higher powers. Death is not the end," it hissed. "And you can hold it back, for a little while, and earn the amusement of what waits to collect us on the other side."

"That sounds like a bad fucking deal," I said as I ran towards the computer and pulled the stick. Only when I turned back the monster was still sat there and somehow, even without a face or most of a head, I could tell it was smiling.

"Mine is elsewhere," it giggled. "I told you. That one is meant for you, detectives."

I turned to the screen and saw it hadn't changed. Frustrated, I kicked the computer and found out it was a decoy. Just an old tower with nothing inside. The monitors must have been wired up to something else. With more time, I could have found it, but with every fibre in my body begging me to leave, there was no chance I was going to stick around just to ferret that thing out.

"But you are right," it cooed. "It *is* a bad deal. But take it from someone who *knows* what is on the other side. I advise you to suffer now and delay the next world. Take your time and think up novel torments. Nothing you come up with will compare to an eternity spent with *them*."

Carefully, it dragged itself across the floor to give us access to the door.

"But they do so enjoy watching us try."

———

Outside, sat on the hood of our car, Jack and I smoked.

"Whatever's up there," I said while pointing to the high rise, "did you believe anything it said? It painted a pretty grim picture of the afterlife."

"I don't know," he replied. Nothing else, just another puff of smoke.

"What do you want to do now?" I asked.

"That thing... its legs they were..."

"Out of action," I told him.

Disgruntled, he stood up and walked to the back of the car. When he came back, he was speaking.

"How easy do you think those stairs would be for it? Let's say, if it was in a hurry."

"I don't know," I shrugged. "Not easy at all."

I finally saw what Jack had fetched from his trunk and, despite everything, I smiled.

It was a gas can and a box of matches.

"Let's see how they cope when all their computers are melted plastic."

THE LIBRARY

Whoever had carved the door relished in the anatomy of suffering.

It was a two-storey tall slab of copper set directly into a cavern wall. Its surface carved with a vast and complex bas-relief that worried the eye. A cloying, confusing mix of human bodies sprawling upwards in a mound of naked flesh, many glancing horrified over their shoulders while fleeing something out of frame and out of sight. Thousands of them. Starved and wretched with gaunt faces and sunken eyes. Jutting ribs and distended bellies.

There were rumours that they moved, but only when you weren't looking.

Less than a week after its discovery, they brought it down with explosives. We didn't really know what we'd found at that point, although I'm sure a few of us, particularly the religious, had their suspicions. The door was *wrong*. All wrong. It just shouldn't have been there. Natural caverns don't go that deep in Britain. Not a thousand metres. As scientists we should have been excited, but we all agreed the door was repulsive. Staring at it too long induced a powerful urge to flee. An ancestral memory, maybe. The same way our bodies know to avoid things that crawl and slither. Things that rot and buzz and stink of death and decay.

They never told us how or why they found it, nor why the project was classified. Only that we had to figure out what was on the other side. When the charges finally blew, they went off like giant firecrackers. A string of them that ran around the gateway. One by one. Deafening booms that shook the entire cavern. I was left blinking dust out of my eyes as great machines lowered the door, now free of its couplings, to the ground.

Looking back, some details come easier than others. The air that wafted out was hot and dry, and I was not surprised. That seemed intuitively correct. Whether I'd admitted it to myself or not, the fact was I'd been thinking of the door as a gateway to hell pretty much since I'd first laid eyes on it. And my mental image of hell was oddly medieval. I expected great big stone walls, something reminiscent of an ancient castle. Rattling chains. The wailing of the damned. The stench of sulphur. God, even little red devils with horns and pointy tails.

But I hadn't expected shelves and books. That was the first real thing we saw. Shelves lining the walls that had been dug directly into the same rock as the cavern. Shelves that rose far above our lights so that when we looked up there was only darkness and dust, but no limits to the endless row and row of shelving. Every last inch covered in books. There were no gaps. Just dust and tattered spines of random sizes. Leather. Fabric. Paperback. Faded pastels and gold leaf letters in alphabets both familiar and strange. And it wasn't just the walls. The floor was littered with random head-high piles of books all stacked up like some tired librarian had gotten fed up of finding room for them. They made a labyrinth of the place, obscuring corners and doors. And the forward team, myself included, progressed carefully along the stone passageway, listening and looking carefully for some signs that would make sense of the place. There must have been thousands of books, and that was just in the first hallway we explored. Whenever we took one out, we found paper so thin it was nearly translucent, and often inked with strange shapes and letters I couldn't recognise. Otherwise, it was gibberish.

Not that we studied them too long on that first day. Whenever I took one, I returned it quickly. Lifting them up, I always had the strangest sensation that I was doing something wrong. Inappropriate. And I didn't like the space they left behind on the shelves. A gap like a missing tooth, the darkness within swirling like deep waters. Safety in that place felt like an illusion, and touching the books was at risk of shattering it. I don't know how else to put it except I didn't want to do anything that might draw attention to me. It was as if we were extremely conspicuous. There were no sounds but those we made. Our own breath. Our own footfalls. The shuffle and scuffle of our every movement. We could even hear each other's heartbeats. The discordant *bu-bump* of several people's chests beating like a broken drum set. And every now and again... a *racing*. A steady increase in the beat's cadence as we turned a blind corner, or lifted a book just to see what it contained, or looked up at the shadows above us. Each of us kept having false starts because there was always this expectation that you were *going* to see something. Soon. Any second now. Squeezed between two books, or dangling overhead...

It took six more hours before that corridor opened up, and when it did, we were dumbfounded. We emerged onto a vast and terrifying mezzanine made of ancient rock, overlooking a chasm with no visible bottom. Just floor after floor filled with shelves filled with books. Millions. Billions. And all along those distant walls and storeys were little openings that led to more corridors like the one we'd just emerged from. So many that it was like staring at a roughshod beehive. To look up or down or anywhere was to be faced with more books than anyone could read in their entire lifetime.

We took our first break on that mezzanine. While radios didn't go very far in that place, we'd had the sense to carry enough wire to allow for a hard connection and using that we contacted the main research site and updated them on the situation. We were to keep going for another six hours and turn around. A day, no more, was the plan. Even that felt like too long. I wanted to leave. I wanted to confirm that somewhere was a doorway that would lead back to reality because ever since I'd entered that place, it felt like I'd entered a nightmare. A place where reality was plastic. I told myself it was simply the scale of it all. The *weirdness*. But it was more than that. The very air down there felt thin.

There were six of us. Three scientists and three soldiers. The soldiers responded to the situation with silence and an alertness that bordered on paranoia. Constantly scanning the dark with their rifle mounted lights. Flicking the beam from one high up shelf to another. Fidgeting. Exchanging dark looks. In a way, I was thankful, but it put me on edge too, and I couldn't relax at all for the first half of our little break. I guess it was natural that the scientists got talking. This was partly to fill the quiet. But also partly to try and convince ourselves we were excited about the *implications* of this find, whatever those may be. Rewriting history. Archaeology on a new level. That kind of thing. It didn't take long before we convinced ourselves to take a closer look at those books. I'll admit it didn't come easy, but we did a pretty good job of convincing ourselves that we weren't really afraid. We started slowly, taking one book down, opening and then quickly replacing it. But then, with false bravery, we took more and more down until each of us were sat cross-legged with several books stacked up on either side, waiting to be read. I remember at some point I must have grown tired and looked up from my own pile because I noticed Dr Aisling muttering quietly as she traced some words with her fingers.

"What have you found?"

"It's Latin alphabet," she said. "First one I actually recognise the letters for. German, maybe?"

None of us were linguists, so we were simply doing our best. But upon hearing Bea mention German, one of the soldiers came over and looked at the open page.

"Germanic, but not German," he said.

"You speak it?"

He nodded.

"My father is German, and I don't know what that is, but it isn't German."

"Is any of it familiar?" Bea asked while handing the book to him. After a brief nod from his CO, Lt Meikle, he took it and began flicking through the pages.

"I think this is the word for death. A sort of rough misspelling, maybe. This one is... I guess it's a bit like wanting. Desiring? I don't know. Not all of the words seem like they're in the right context either."

"So they're in a variety of languages and alphabets, but as of yet nothing we can make sense of. What about you? Any luck?" Bea asked me, and I looked down at the book currently open in my hands.

"Some kind of Cyrillic, maybe?" I shrugged. "I'm no linguist. We definitely need Dr Sellers on the next expedition. I'm sure he could offer some insight. What about you, Dr Rosenstein?"

The third scientist in our group, a little bald man, had been sitting quietly the entire time we spoke, frowning at one of several books that lay open before him. I assumed he was just curious, like Bea and I.

"Grant," I said, trying to get his attention. "Hey Grant! Have you found anything?"

His silence unnerved me. He wasn't just captivated. Sweat was prickling his forehead, and veins bulged along his temple. He had gone pale, and his eyes were wide, and his lips cracked and dry. The soldiers, picking up on the same strange signals I had, stood a little more upright.

"Dr Rosenstein?" One of them asked nervously. "Doctor? Can you hear us?"

The nearest soldier reached out and placed a hand on Grant's shoulder and the little man looked up at us like he hadn't even realised we existed until that moment. At first I thought he was relieved, the way he stared at each of us with a dumb grin on his face, but I soon realised something wasn't quite right.

"Oh!" He said with an anxious laugh. "Oh. Right. Of course." His eyes darted between us. "Of course. Sorry. I didn't mean to alarm you."

"Right," I said. "Well... we were just talking about the books. Bea thinks hers might be in a kind of German or Germanic language."

He nodded like this made perfect sense.

"Yes, I imagine so," he replied while looking around the shelves that towered over us. "Lots of languages, I'd say." And then, without really missing a beat, he added:

"They're sins."

The group fell into silence as each of us tried to make sense of what he'd just said. In the meantime, he stood up and stretched. Like it was the most natural thing in the world.

"What are you on about?" I said once it became clear he wasn't going to elaborate.

"It's fairly obvious where we are," he said while leaning forward and eyeing us darkly. "And these books are a list of all our sins. One for each of us. So there will be books in German, both contemporary and historic German, like the one you found Dr Aisling. But there'll also be books in Russian and French and Arabic and Chinese. Not just contemporary tongues either. Ancient Egyptian. Phoenician. Babylonian. Arameic. Latin. And of course, lost languages. Ones that we never found but existed anyway. All of them. All the transgressions of the world are right here, recorded in the sinner's original tongue."

By now the soldiers had stepped a little closer, and Bea and I were sharing deeply worried looks. Grant seemed to be in the middle of a breakdown, speaking frantically and anxiously, convinced of his own meaning while not really saying anything of sense.

"Grant, I think we need to go ba..."

"The real fun is that I think you'll find books in languages that don't exist yet," he blurted. "This isn't just a record of sins in the past. But all of them. Every last one. Even the ones we haven't committed yet."

"Grant, I'm going to have one of the men go back with you. If that's okay? I think you might not…"

"These are mine," he said, while gesturing to the book in his hand. "All of them." He laughed. "Not just the things I *did*. Petty transgressions all recorded with names and places and even little diagrams. But there are even sins I only ever *thought*. Things I… *wanted* to do. And," he added while giggling hysterically, "Sins I've *yet* to commit."

He flicked through the pages at random and giggled manically at something only he could see.

"Although there aren't many!" he cackled as he turned to the final page, tears welling in his eyes. "Just one, actually. *The last one!* The last sin I'll ever commit."

"Grant," I said, "I think you–"

Before any of us could react, he dropped the book and took a running leap over the nearest ledge.

"This is the way we came, right?"

Bea stood at the threshold of a corridor, her light tracking a wire that snaked into the darkness.

"That's the cable we carried in here with us," one of the soldiers said. "But…" The young man looked over to his CO, Lt Meikle, who had a compass in hand and didn't look happy.

"It's not the direction we came," the older man said. "We came South, so we need to head North. That would be this doorway." He nodded at a second corridor embedded in the rock wall.

"*This* has to be the way," Bea said. "I trust this cable a hell of a lot more than I do a compass. Anything could be interfering with that thing. Besides, we *know* the cable leads to HQ because it's still working. We spoke to them only a few minutes ago *via* this wire. It has to lead out of here."

"That makes sense," I added, "But I marked the way we left with a piece of chalk. And *that* mark is over here."

I pointed to a third doorway.

"Fuck," Meikle muttered.

"Regardless, I vote wire," Bea said. "I trust it the most. It's a physical connection."

"I guess I vote wire too," Meikle added.

"Me too. But what do we do if we're wrong?" I asked. "What does that even mean? Did something move the wire? Or the door?"

We all went silent for a few moments as we contemplated this. When nobody offered up an answer, I eventually grabbed my backpack and hauled it up.

"I guess we don't have much of a choice either way," I said.

"Do you think there's really a book in here for everyone?" Bea asked, and it was the first any of us had spoken in a few hours. So far we had all been walking, fixated on the gloom ahead and behind us, watching carefully for some sign that our fevered imaginations were right to suspect something lurking in the dark.

"Grant seemed to think so," I said.

"Then what are the odds he picked his own book out? I mean, if he's right there are, what? A hundred billion books or so?"

"More," I replied. "If he's right about the library containing future sins as well as past."

"Pretty slim odds then," she added.

"What are you thinking?"

"If he did find it here, I don't think it was a coincidence," she said.

Up ahead, one of the soldiers came to a sudden stop. Fist raised, he muttered something to the others, who knelt and lifted their rifles, aiming at the dark.

"What is it?" I asked.

"Don't you hear it?" Meikle called back.

All of us stopped and listened carefully, straining to pick out some meaningful sound from the white noise of blood rushing through our ears and the thumping of our own hearts. Sure enough, it was there. A gentle rustling. Without speaking, all of us moved as quietly as we could along the corridor until we came to the source of the strange noise. A door–one that hadn't been there on our way in–left ever so slightly ajar. Rifle raised, one of the soldiers used his barrel to nudge it open a little farther.

"Oh shit," he said, his voice loud enough to send echoes down the hall.

The sound came as a shock and Meikle pulled him back, ready to admonish, when we all saw what had been waiting on the other side.

Another corridor, only this one had shelves lined not with books but severed heads. Desiccated, pale, and gaunt. Row after row. All sitting neatly next to one another, evenly spaced. Their skin paper white in the harsh glare of our lights. And all of them with cloudy eyes.

And they were speaking.

Sotto voce. Little whispers. They muttered in a discord of wet lips. No breath. No lungs. Only the action of rubbery jaws to sound out syllables and consonants that were lost in the rustling cacophony. The sound was horrific. Wet and dry and deeply un-settling, it worked its way under my skin until I felt the strangest urge to lash out at the heads. But curiosity overrode disgust, and I approached one, wincing briefly when it fixed me with its cloudy eyes, but I didn't stop. I got close enough to see every detail of its flaking skin, its rheumy eyes glaring at me with such strange emotion. For my own sanity, I reached out and picked it up, noting with disgust how the stump of its neck left mottled brown fluid on the shelf behind. I guess I just wanted to know if it was fake, but its skin was cold, and its brow furrowed with anger at my touch. And as soon as it was in the air, every other head stopped their muttering and fixed me with such foul expressions I quickly put it back down again, relieved when the murmuring resumed.

Still, its eyes did not leave me.

"What the fuck...?" Bea whispered.

"What is this?" Meikle asked as he scanned the upper shelves with his torch. On and on and they went, as far as we could see. "What the actual *fuck* is this?"

Slowly, a strange thought began to form in my mind.

"Blink if you can understand me," I said while kneeling down to look at the head I'd picked up. Everyone else in the group suddenly stopped what they were doing and turned to see the result of my little experiment.

Blink.

"Okay. Okay. Okay." I repeated while trying to calm myself down. "Right... Once for no. Twice for yes. Do you understand?"

Blink. Blink.

"Right. Okay. Uhhh..." I looked to the others for suggestions when Bea piped up instead.

"Are these books a list of all our sins?"

Blink. Blink.

"One book for one person?"

Blink. Blink.

"So what are you?" she asked, and this elicited a scathing look from the severed head.

"Yes or no questions," I told her.

One of the soldiers, the youngest one, the one who'd helped translate the German, stepped up and spoke.

"Is this hell?" he asked.

Blink. Blink.

"Is this your punishment?" he added.

Blink.

"If this isn't the punishment," he said. "What is?"

All the heads stopped their muttering and began to emit the strangest noise. Their faces twisting upwards and warping into grotesque parodies of joy, while their mouths moved up and down in a peculiar sort of rhythm. When I realised what they were doing,

I felt a terrible sensation of cold dread creeping down my entire body.

They were laughing at us.

There was no door.

The wire slipped through a tiny hole at the base of a wall that blocked off the corridor.

All of us were stunned into silence for minutes until at last, Lt Meikle shook himself free from the shock and issued an order.

"Davies, get HQ on the line."

One of the soldiers knelt down and began to remove the communication set from his backpack. Within a few seconds, it was set up and he was speaking into the handset.

"HQ can you read me? Over."

"Err, I can read you."

"Well, I guess the wire still leads to HQ," I said.

"Try checking the wall for seams," Meikle told me. "See if it moves. Hidden hinges or... something. I don't know." Then, turning back to the soldier with the handset: "Tell them we've encountered an obstacle, and we want them to send another team in to get us. Oh, and tell them to bring explosives."

"If this thing opens," I said while running my hand along the edges, "I can't see how. It's pretty solid." Unlike every other wall we'd seen so far, this one was made of red bricks, but that didn't mean it was somehow mobile either. It seemed as sturdy as any brick wall I'd come across.

"Well it came from somewhere!" Bea cried while trying to peer through the hole the wire disappeared through. "Damn it, I can't see anything."

"HQ," the soldier said. "We're gonna need some assistance. There is a... uh... an obstacle. Over."

"Roger that. What's the obstacle?"

"Err, a wall," he replied. "Tell the next team to bring explosives. Over."

"A wall?"

"Just send the team ASAP," the soldier cried. "Our way out is blocked. Over."

"Well, I can confirm we are en route to your position. Just one question," HQ replied.

"What's that? Over," the young man replied.

"Why do you keep saying *over*?" Suddenly, the voice changed. It began to titter and giggle, at first quietly but then louder and louder, like a mean kid laughing at a prank. The cruelty in its high-pitched voice made my skin crawl, and I was about to snatch the handset myself and begin demanding answers when there was the strangest sound. A heavy grinding, like stone turning against stone.

Before I could even ask what it was, Bea fell backwards from where she crouched and quickly leaped up into a standing position and ran off into the dark like a maniac. The effect on the group was chilling. And I stared back at the wall, desperately trying to understand what I'd seen.

"Williams, go get her!" He barked at one of the soldiers before turning to me and crying, "What the fuck is her problem?"

"I-I-I don't know," I stammered.

"Christ," Meikle hissed before snatching the handset off the confused young soldier. "Listen," he growled into it, "I don't know who you really are, but you need to get someone in charge right–"

That sound again. Loud and heavy. The grinding of heavy rocks being moved, and tiny stones came raining down in a cloud of dust. Something up there had disturbed them, and we all stood in silence as they plinked off our helmets.

"Is it just me," Meikle said while looking towards the wall. "Or is it somehow closer?"

"Hard to say," I replied. "I don't–"

The wall moved. A sudden and terrifying lurch forwards, one that startled us all and made me trip over my own feet. Terrified, I scrambled backwards from it as fast as I could while the handset continued to radiate that malicious laughter.

"I think we need to go," I said in as calm a voice as I could manage.

The wall moved again, and this time it did not stop.

The young soldier with the handset did not react enough fast enough. It came forward so quickly that it had him within seconds and knocked him to the floor with a heavy *thump*. And then it rolled over him and it was... well, if you're anything like me, as a child you might have wondered what happened to someone who got caught in an escalator. At the very top. I'm sure you know what I mean. Light was poor so I still don't really understand what happened. Only that there was a lot of blood, and while it was quick, it was not quick *enough* because when the wall was about half-way up his spine, I could still see the pain registering in his eyes. And that was the last impression I had before Meikle grabbed me by the collar and practically threw me back the way we came.

And then we ran.

Running. Plodding. One foot after another. I don't know how long it went on for, but it was as if time seemed to stretch on in the way that only pain and tedium can induce. There were moments where, as I struggled to force one foot in front of the other, I wondered if I'd actually been running for days, not hours. There was no real way to mark the passage of time. Only monotony. Books went by in a blur. The floor was featureless stone. The rhythmic sound of my feet lost all meaning. And behind me, the wall. Ever advancing with the horrible sound of grinding rocks, promising pain and nothing else.

The only thing I could actually focus on was the exhaustion, and that was self-defeating. More than a few times, I wondered if I should just give up. And to this day, I still have nightmares where I am being chased down that corridor. It wasn't a quick pace, but it was quick enough and there were no other routes except forward and therein lay the torture of it. Behind me was death moving at a brisk jog. And ahead of me was nothing. Just darkness broken by the erratic motion of a torch. And the entire time, which I would later realise was a good two hours, the only thing I could think was *when am I going to lose this fight? When am I going to collapse? Or give up?*

Imagine my relief when, up ahead, I heard a familiar voice cry out,

"What is your problem lady!?"

And then I saw them. The young man held Bea by her shoulders while she tried to drag him through an open door. That was when I remembered the little corridor with the severed heads. Not exactly the kind of salvation I was hoping for, but it'd have to do. Together, Meikle and I grabbed both of them and threw us all through the opening. Seconds later, far too close for comfort, the entire corridor we'd been running through went pitch black. The wall overtook our positions, and we were left panting and exhausted on the floor, where thousands of severed heads looked at us in annoyance.

When we looked back the way we came, we saw that nothing but pulsating flesh. A wall of it. Hot and sticky and threaded with sickly blue veins. I don't know what that wall was, but something about the meat behind the stone made me think of hungry coral.

"It was a fucking trap," Meikle hissed as he inspected the horrible mass. "I don't know how, but we were led down the wrong path. It... it swapped the cables. Or something. I don't know. But we were *lured* down there like rats."

"Where's Davies?" the other soldier asked.

"He's... gone," Meikle said.

"What?"

The older man gestured to the wall of meat behind us.

"Whatever the *fuck* that thing is got him. It looked like a wall but it... It could move and it just steamrolled him. Thanks for the warning, by the way," he growled at Bea, but she showed no sign of understanding him. Instead, she was sat on the floor and shaking, clearly in a state of shock.

"Where now, sir?" the remaining soldier asked, and Meikle grimaced.

"Where do you *think*?" he spat before gesturing at the route forward. "The only direction that's available."

The heads made for strange companions. They followed us with their eyes, but did not stop their muttering. It was grating, to say the least. A noise you could ignore for maybe an hour or so, but pretty soon the papery rustle of their ancient lips was the only thing you could focus on no matter how hard you tried to push it out of your head.

At least navigation was simple.

Forward. Only the one way to go. We walked for about six hours before we took our first break. The corridor was wide, but we stayed away from the heads and slept in a row, head to feet, while two of us stayed on watch. Six hours each. I decided to stay up along with Meikle as Bea and the other soldier tried to rest. Bea had barely come of out of shock during the journey, speaking a little towards the very end. She told us, in a broken way, what she'd seen while kneeling by the wall.

"Teeth," she said. "And a face." Although she wouldn't, or couldn't, elaborate on those two statements. I was left with the sense that she had seen something that had come damn close to leaving her completely insane. Even as it was, I doubted she had a full recovery in her. She almost looked like a different woman. Baggy eyed. Thinning hair. Or maybe it was just the conditions down there. Meikle didn't look great either, and I had to assume I looked pretty rough too. Especially after that run.

It had exhausted me. Broken me. Not just the physical exertion, but the nightmare of it. The reason I'd elected to stay on watch first was because I didn't want to sleep. A part of me was worried I'd just dream about being back in that hallway, running from the moving wall, and I didn't want to revisit that place ever again. Not even as a dream. There were moments where I came so close to just giving up. I don't think I'd ever really experienced despair like that before. Not the kind where you feel your knees buckling and your neck turn to rubber as your head bows. It must be what people stranded at sea feel when they lose the strength to keep treading water.

So instead, I stayed up and tried to ignore the muttering of the heads. Even tried talking to Meikle but he didn't have much to say. I could tell losing Davies back in the corridor had bothered him. Hell, it bothered me and I hadn't even known the guy. But I swear to this day I can still see the look on his face as rock met flesh and his legs and hips just... disappeared.

In the end, I had only these kinds of thoughts for company.

And lots of lots of time.

So it probably shouldn't come as too much of a surprise that I eventually fell asleep. It wasn't for long. Ten minutes at most.

But it was enough time for me to wake up and see something drag the sleeping soldier's body into the darkness of the nearest shelf, his neck lolling unnaturally to one side. The movement was gentle. Quiet. But clumsy too. Like a child pulling a rag doll stealthily out of a toy box. I looked over to Meikle and saw he'd fallen asleep as well, so I nudged him with my foot, and he woke up with a sort of lazy start. Only when he looked at me, confused for a few short seconds before slowly registering the look of terror on my face, did he seem to realise what was happening. I'm not sure what I expected him to do, really. But he was the leader and well armed, and I didn't want to be the one who had to figure out what to do next. Possibly because there was a part of me tempted to just sneak off. To leave the young man to his fate. Maybe even Bea, if it just meant I could survive a little bit longer.

In truth, I was relieved when Meikle leapt into action immediately. I didn't want to be a coward. He jumped up and grabbed the young man's foot, and I ran over and grabbed the other leg and together we tried to pull him back. I didn't mention it to Meikle, but the way the soldier's body felt when I grabbed it... the muscles were too relaxed. Too heavy. I don't know how to explain it, but if you ever end up in the unfortunate situation of moving a corpse you might know what I mean. A living body supports itself. A dead one. It's just meat and water and somehow feels so much heavier for it.

He was dead. Still, we fought on. At some point Bea must have woken up, realised what was happening, and joined in. I remember her trying to reach into the shelf to grab a hold of the dead man's arm when she suddenly flew backwards, landing with a hefty thud against the shelf behind her and rocking a few of the severed heads on their little stumps.

Whatever was in the dark was clearly frustrated. It wanted its next meal, and it wasn't going to let us stop it. Slowly, a long inhuman arm reached out and took a hold of the body's groin. Its strange hand had fingers that split at the knuckle, one, two, three times. A terrifying effect, especially given how each one moved on its own. A dinner plate monster of a hand attached to a lithe and muscular forearm devoid of hair. The second I saw it reach out in my general direction, I let go of the leg and fell backwards. Meikle continued struggling for a while, even taking out a pistol and firing a few shots into the dark, but in doing so he left only a hand to cling onto his comrade's corpse and lost his grip. With almost no effort, the body disappeared into shadow, and we were suddenly down to three.

"What the fuck? What the fuck!? *What the fuck!!?*" he screamed.

I wanted to say something. Maybe even something to comfort him. Or maybe an apology for falling asleep, but then again, he'd fallen asleep too. I didn't know what I was meant to do. I was in shock. And it was settling deep into me when Bea said something from where she remained on the floor. Her voice quiet but oddly insistent.

"It isn't over."

That hand reemerged. Carefully. Deliberately, it placed itself on the floor, revealing more of the pale flesh that powered it. And then came another. And another. And then its head emerged slowly from the dark and fixed me with eyes both black, bulbous, and far too numerous for anything that can be called human. And its mouth... A beard made of dirty fingers. Grey and bluish. Long rancid nails. Hundreds of them squirming like the mandibles of a hungry spider.

Meikle opened fire, but he might as well have been shooting hay for all the effect it had. The bullets struck with a wet *thwap*, but no actual damage. The creature knocked him aside with pure contempt and pulled the rest of itself out into the corridor where I saw it had no legs, but instead relied on several long arms to suspend itself between the walls of the corridor like a kind of spider. One of these arms reached out and grabbed Bea and by the time she started screaming, it was already too late. Blood trickled from her ears and there was a sound like a branch snapping. Her entire body went limp, and the monster dropped her where she fell to the ground, her grotesque, misshapen face glaring at me with accusatory eyes.

The lieutenant screamed as he fired yet again, but then that thing seized him like he was nothing but a doll and lifted him, squeezing so tightly he dropped everything he held. His gun and torch hitting the ground with a loud rattle.

"Help me!" he screamed while reaching out for me to grab him. "Jesus Christ! Shoot the fucking thing!"

I ran forward, crouching down in the hope of avoiding its many arms. Already, Meikle was being squeezed so tight that blood spurted from his mouth, and I could tell that the monster was having fun, revelling in his torment. I reached out to pick the gun up from the floor as Meikle let out yet another desperate wet cry for help, but for some reason my hand stopped mere inches away.

I hesitated. Meikle's blood was dripping down. I could hear the crunching of his ribs.

In my most shameful moment, I grabbed the torch and ran.

And Meikle's cries followed me. Screaming. Screeching. Whimpering. Sounds of breaking bones and tearing paper.

Sounds of torture and torment that somehow seemed to last forever.

I emerged from the corridor alone.

It took me a few seconds of stumbling on my failing legs to realise that the monster had given up on the pursuit, and then a few seconds more for me to recognise I was back on the mezzanine. Terrified and exhausted, and contemplating if it was worth trying to escape if it meant having to spend another second alive in that place, I fell to the floor and began to sob. Maybe, I thought, it was time to take a dive off that ledge just like Grant had.

"What on Earth are you doing here?"

I whipped around to see an old man in robes staring at me like an impolite intruder. Without meaning to, I began to laugh. My sanity, it was fair to say, was on its final legs.

"Hmph," he said, while leaning aside to get a look down the long corridor behind. "Now why did you go down *there*?"

I wanted to answer, but couldn't quite bring myself to do anything except laugh and gasp for air.

"I think you really ought to go home," he said like a teacher admonishing a child.

"This place is hell," I cried, while rocking back and forth on my knees.

"Yes." He nodded. "Yes. *Good for you.* This is a small part of hell, one that has a slight overlap with Earth, if I remember? I'm assuming that's how you got down here. The door. What happened to your friends anyway?" He added.

I looked back the way I came and pointed.

"Ohhhh," he sighed. "You know, I left your books out specifically, so you'd find them and figure it out. And I know that bald fellow worked it out. So once you knew this place was hell, why did you waste another second sticking around?"

I shrugged, not quite sure what I was meant to say to that kind of thing.

"We got waylaid," I gasped. "Misled."

"Fair enough," he replied. "Probably should have done more to make sure you got home safely. That's partly my fault. Although I won't apologise. You entered this place. Didn't you see the door? What part of *that* was inviting? You have to take some of the blame."

I wanted to mount a defence, but I didn't really have one. When it became clear the only thing I could do was sob and mutter, the old man's body language softened, and he reached a hand out.

"Come on, I'll take you back."

"What about the demons?" I asked.

The old man frowned.

"Those weren't demons," he snapped. "This place is defunct. Mortal souls were meant to demonstrate repentance by wandering the near eternal halls in search of their book. Only when they found it were they allowed to move on. Whole thing didn't quite work out. 86 quadrillion books. Takes a tad *too* long for the average person to find theirs. So this entire wing was abandoned and now there are only sinners left behind."

"That *thing* was never human," I cried while pointing at the corridor I'd emerged from.

"Nobody's soul looks human," he said, like it was the most obvious thing in the world. "Least of all the sort of person who gets sent to hell. This isn't a place for people who eat meat on a Friday or covet their neighbour's ox. It's for the cruel and the malicious. Cowards and opportunists. A lot of people in this place have souls that have more in common with anglerfish and trapdoor spiders than their fellow man. And it's not a condition that gets better after several thousand years either. The soul changes, twists, and so do their physical forms."

"And what about you?" I said, as I reached up and took his hand. "Why do you look so normal?"

"Oh," he said as he helped me up. "That's because I built this place."

And the last thing I can remember as he gripped me by the shoulder was the sudden and painful sensation of heat.

We woke up in our respective quarters.

We.

All six of us.

I still don't fully understand the mechanics. I tried asking the others how they made it back, but... they weren't in a state to answer questions. Bea was catatonic. Screaming and clutching her head in the hospital, like she still remembered the way that thing crushed her skull like a grapefruit. The soldier who fell to the wall was left paraplegic even though medical tests couldn't identify a single reason why. Psychological, they said. The other soldier, the one who'd been dragged into the shelves, was comatose. I don't know if he recovered, but he was alive. And Grant was left in a permanent psychotic state, compelled to write on any surface he could over and over again. Sin after sin, desperately trying to rewrite the very book that had driven him to madness in the first place.

Meikle tried very hard to kill me.

He had clear memories of being left to die in the dark. I'm glad they caught him before he managed to wring the life out of me with his bare hands. I never found out what happened to him after several men managed to pry his hands from around my throat. Despite everything, I hope he managed some kind of recovery.

The door disappeared, thankfully with no one on the other side. I know they were planning future expeditions. It is for the best that kind of thing can't happen again. They have no idea what's waiting for them.

In a way, I probably could have convinced myself the expedition never happened. Some days, even now, that's what I sincerely hope can happen. There was no physical evidence. Nothing. We appeared in our beds completely naked save for a note stuck to my chest. And it's this final little touch that stood out to me as stern confirmation of everything I'd experienced.

Return to sender,

Six mortals. Five were damaged in transit. Bodies were repaired to the best of my ability, but I never was any good at that kind of thing. Minds are another matter entirely.

Could not help myself in one case. Left fellow mortal to die in the dark. Didn't seem very sporting. Don't let anyone say I lack a sense of humour.

Otherwise, no harm no foul.

Best wishes,

Me!

My heart sank when I heard them read it to me. It confirmed my deepest worries. No one had been very honest with me since I'd arrived at the hospital. They'd kept me bandaged up, so it wasn't easy to tell, but after I heard that note, I finally found the courage to reach up and remove the thick wads of fabric.

Then, with shaking fingers, I finally touched my eyes.

Or rather, the empty sockets where they used to be.

THE DREAMSCAPE

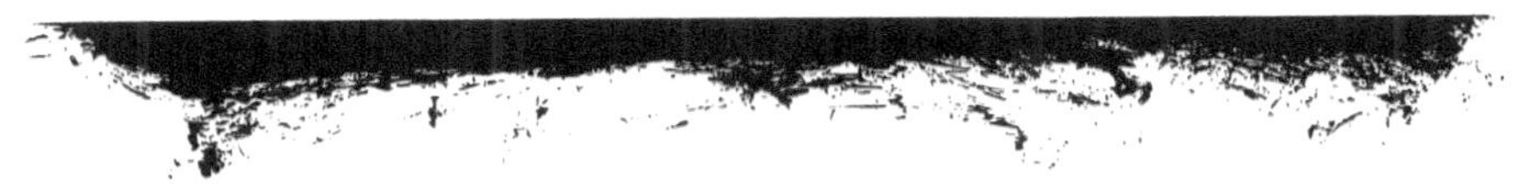

"I'm not listening to another lecture on Jung. There have been three in the last six weeks."

"Don't then," I said with a shrug as I stirred sugar into my coffee. "But Dr Newman attended your talk on inductive bias."

"Nobody made him."

"Yeah but he knew it'd be rude not to show up to a colleague's presentation," I replied. I didn't want to hammer my point home. No one *had* to do anything.

"Are you going?" she asked.

"Oh God no," I said. "There have been three lectures on Jung in the last six weeks. But Dr Newman isn't a colleague. He's my staff."

"One rule for me, another for thee?"

"Not at all," I said. "If you happen to find a mysterious old computer hidden deep in the basement of a university campus, running an unexplained algorithm that could revolutionise our understanding of not only human consciousness, but the laws of physics as well, then you too can have your own staff and make them follow all sorts of rules."

"Do you know where another one of these computers might be?" she asked.

"Funnily enough, after I found the first one, I stopped looking."

"I guess I'll go to the lecture," she whined. "Oh God, I'll go and listen to it all again. But when it's my turn, I'm bringing out my slides on stochastic gradient descent."

"You'll frighten us psychologists."

She flashed a tired smile.

"You sure you're not gonna come?" she asked.

"No, I've got to track the algorithm's output for tonight."

"Like hell you do," she scoffed. "That's an intern's job. And if I tried working the hours you did, I'd be kicked out in a week. None of the time limitations seem to apply to you. And I'm pretty sure I've caught you napping at your desk more than once."

The last time an intern had fallen asleep in the facility, they'd woken up numb from the waist down. They swore on their mother's grave they'd been paralysed since a car accident in their teens, and that they'd only dreamed they could walk. When we showed them the video footage of them strolling into the lab that morning, they became hysterical and had to be hospitalised. They fell into a coma just a few days later and died quickly after that, killed by what our physicists thought might be some kind of exotic radiation poisoning.

We used the coroner's photographs to spook new hires into following the rules.

It was profoundly effective.

"The algorithm likes me," I joked. "You know, if you're feeling up for it, you can come back to the lab and we'll have some drinks in the observation chamber."

"I thought alcohol's not allowed in the facility?" she asked.

"Ah, but as you just pointed out, none of the rules apply to me."

A shoe on a slide, the playground behind it visible, but out of focus, I wrote. I was sat at a random desk with my feet up on someone else's stuff, a notepad propped up on my lap. I was working on my second whiskey and could already feel a gentle buzz take me over. The screen went black, and the room was thrown into darkness and I waited patiently for the next image. The monitor came to life with an audible clunk, followed by the sound of static and a rising whine. I watched as another scene appeared.

A stair well with spidery graffiti on the walls. Symbols appear to belong to standard alphabet, but upon closer inspection are gibberish. Likely location is the tower.

"I hate that one."

I turned awkwardly to look at Kim standing in the door.

"How was the talk?" I asked.

"Same thing as always. Something about a collective unconscious with external pseudolocations that we all visit in our sleep via dreams. The algorithm is somehow capable of visiting these places, they draw from shared experiences but may possibly originate from elsewhere as well... so on and so on. As much as I hate to admit it, sometimes I think you psychologists are the only ones even close to figuring this thing out."

I shrugged.

The screen went dark, then white, and then a new scene appeared.

Dutch angle of a railyard. In the foreground, we see a caboose with a sliding door partially opened. Two pale fingers clutch at the door, holding it closed. The fingers look human, possibly a child's.

When I finished scribbling, I saw that Kim had pulled up another chair to sit beside me.

"You know, the second I found this thing, I knew what it was showing me," I said. "Everyone knows because somehow, whether we admit it or not, the things it shows us are familiar. And whether it's quantum mechanics or the collective unconscious, we're just trying to describe what we already know to be true—this thing is a window into our dreams. No single group of researchers has more insight into how that's possible, it's just that some of us came prepared with the right vocabulary."

"Is this you trying to make me feel better?" she asked as she reached down to her bag and pulled out a beer. She cracked it just in time for the screen to go dark. When it came back, she winced from the glare and averted her eyes. I looked straight at the bright light and waited for the newest image.

A man holds a mug bound in human skin. It has a face. The eye sockets are empty. No scene is visible in the background. I stopped writing and stared at my notes before adding a small addendum. *I think this is one of mine. Will check dream journal at home and update.*

"Squinting at that tiny screen is killing me," Kim said as the screen went dark with another clunk. "Do we have to sit in the dark?"

I considered turning the lights on when I saw the old projector sitting on Dr Allman's desk. He'd brought it in weeks ago for a presentation and clearly forgotten to take it home.

"Hmm, there might be another option," I said.

"Is it me or is the resolution better?"

Kim was right. The image, now blown up, was not blurry or out of focus at all. It had scaled up perfectly, and what had once been a few grey pixels on the old display were transformed into new and vivid details. This was the kind of image 'enhancement' usually reserved for cheese crime procedurals.

"Sharper than any photograph I've ever seen," she said. "How expensive is that damned projector?"

"It's not the projector," I replied. "It can't be. The images this thing outputs are usually 800 x 600. There's no way it could be this sharp."

"Just another mystery to add to the pile? New display, new images?"

"You know I wanted to try this years ago, but everyone threw a tantrum that it might interfere with the algorithm," I said. "I think they forgot I had six weeks alone with the computer when I first found it and would regularly switch up displays. Never tried a projector, though."

I sat back down in my chair with an audible *oomph* and took up my notepad to quickly wrote down what was on the screen.

A children's play centre is visible, ball pit to the right, climbing frame to the left. Everything else is darkness.

I squinted at the life-sized image and leaned forward in my chair.

A child's face is visible in the ball pits, I added. *They look afraid and are staring into the distance.*

The screen went dark, and I was left with a strange feeling in my stomach, like I'd just left someone to die. I shook it off just as a new image appeared. It was a long-dilapidated hallway with broken down doors and peeling wallpaper. Water damaged carpet swelled along the floor, grossly discoloured from years of mould and decay. You could practically smell the rank odour of damp wood and crumbling masonry. I immediately felt my stomach curl up in reaction to the sight.

The tower, I wrote. *Severely run-down residential location, similar to apartment block. Small section of interior apartment visible through broken down door. Corner of cabinet or possibly some other form of furniture can be seen within.*

"I hate the tower," Kim said.

"You've been there?" I asked. She nodded. "Most of us have," I added. "We think it only appears to people who work in this facility.

Or at least, if there are references to it in wider culture, we haven't worked them out."

"I'll remember that the next time I'm having a nightmare and I'm hiding under a motel bed."

I nodded sympathetically. Something about the tower engendered a specific type of nightmare, the kind that felt as if it lasted all night and was so lucid as to be real. There was an internal consistency that defied the usual dream logic so that the dream never transitioned into a dinner with your late aunt Margaret. You were stuck there all night, finding relief only when you woke up soaked head to toe in sweat with a scream trapped in your throat. As a nightmare, it was infamous for sending more than a few elderly researchers to hospital with cardiac arrest. Details of the location varied from person to person so that sometimes the tower was a hotel, sometimes it was an apartment block, once it was even a multistorey carpark. But it was always an infinitely tall building through which the dreamer would be chased upwards by some invisible presence, the surrounding walls on the verge of collapse as the impossible skyscraper wobbled side-to-side in hurricane winds.

It was particularly rough on those with a fear of heights, amplifying our anxiety so severely that many would struggle to ever step foot in an elevator again.

I was lost in concentration when the light flickered and Kim cried out.

"What the fuck was that?" she snapped.

"What was what?" I asked.

"A shadow passed over the camera!" she cried. "As if someone had blocked its light source."

I looked back at the hallway and watched carefully for signs of motion. Maybe it was my imagination, or just the vivid clarity of the realistic display, but I could almost smell the festering plaster and airborne dust. The longer I stared, the more I became convinced that the image was somehow three-dimensional. I'd visited the tower thousands of times in my own dreams, but could only ever recall patchy glimpses of its layout and vague notions of suffering and threat. But seeing that hallway displayed in life-like proportions brought all those suppressed details back from my subconscious. I was struck by memories of cowering under dressers and in wardrobes while listening to the distant roar of apocalyptic winds pouring through exposed rebar and shattered glass. I remembered sneaking on my hands and knees as my palms dug into broken down bricks and splintered furniture, terrified that I would make too much noise and attract outside attention. And when I inevitably did slip up, I could remember the pulse-pounding terror of pursuit through spiralling stairwells and curving corridors, my heart racing as my mind dared to contemplate the horror of my capture at the hands of...

"Is it me, or did you just feel a breeze?"

It was Kim who spoke.

My mind split in two as it processed what she said. A part of me knew instinctively that she was wrong, or hallucinating, or I'd fallen asleep and this whole thing was just a convoluted dream. But another part told me that she was right, that the screen had taken on an impossible level of depth and reality, and that I had been feeling a stiff but persistent breeze for as long as I'd been looking at that screen. Something that was simply impossible.

But it was real, and I could feel it and I could hear it, and I could even smell it.

"I think you're right," I whispered.

Kim went to speak, but was interrupted by the sound of falling stonework. When it dawned on me that the sound had come from behind us *in the room*, something inside my chest swelled so tight I thought my heart was going to explore.

Something breathed in the shadows just as the screen cut out and the room was sent plunging into darkness. The image had changed, and with it went all the sights and sounds and smells. Kim immediately burst into tears, and I'm pretty sure I was crying too.

But I didn't think about that. Instead, I lunged forward and unplugged the projector before it could open up another nightmare.

———————

"You called me down here to tell me you met none of your targets?"

"Did you really expect me to have screenshots of Putin's dreams?" I asked.

"That was what you quite literally promised us when you secured military funding," the colonel replied. He appeared deadly serious, but I knew him well enough to pick out the remnants of a dry sense of humour buried in his wording.

We were stood in the observation room that had now been cleared out of almost all its furniture. As requested, the colonel had brought a small escort. They were just six men, but they were armed with some kind of assault rifle, and whether it made any sense or not, the sight of those guns gave me great comfort.

"Ah yes," I said as I stepped up and began fiddling with the projector. "Well, back then we thought we had a window into the dreamscape, through which all minds are connected."

"And you're telling me that you don't?"

"I'm telling you it's not a window," I said as I turned the display on and the room lit up. The machine had been quietly cycling the whole time and was ready to show us what it had been working on. It did not disappoint.

I now stood in front of what appeared to be a stairwell in the tower.

"As you know, we've always had a few members of the team dedicated to mapping out the 'dreamscape'," I said, even going so far as to use little air quotes just to ease everybody in. The colonel nodded readily, having heard it all before, but the soldier seemed less convinced. "Given recent events, we have upgraded those members of the team and extended their budget and the personnel available. Work is progressing quickly, but not quickly enough. The dreamscape is enormous, possibly even infinite. We have the tower," I gestured to the glowing wall behind me, "but there are other locations, too. There is also The Resort, The Commune, The Tunnels, The Manor, The Office, The Library, The Lab—"

"I read the report you sent over," the colonel said. "What exactly are you getting at?"

I laughed nervously and finally turned to face the screen. This time, the tower looked a little more corporate. The stairway was carpeted in a baby blue, and a broken frame held a faded poster of a calming mountain. It was easy to see how it would have once been a clean and cool location, the kind of sterile stairwell that connected lawyer offices to marketing offices to HR offices in some towering skyscraper in the centre of New York. Time, or whatever governed the dreamscape, had worn that once-clean steel handrail into something dirty and old, and the baby blue carpet had been pulled up in places to reveal a patchwork plaster floor. It was what would happen to any office in Time Square if the world ended tomorrow and scavengers passed through, and I had to avoid a shiver at the thought of how easily that kind of rot and decay could creep into the corners of our own real world.

For a second, I faltered. I'd been avoiding looking at it for a damn good reason. The tower had been a childhood night terror of mine, one I had never even guessed was shared by others until it popped up in the algorithm and other people recognised it. And now I was standing in front of a doorway to the literal stuff of nightmares. It was as if I carried a lifetime of repressed memories I could not access, but which I still *felt* deep inside my bones. I wanted so badly to flee, but there were bigger things at stake, so I swallowed that terror and forced myself to do the one thing I knew would convince the men behind me. There could be no room for doubt, or else we would never get the proper support.

Effortlessly, almost as though it didn't take every ounce of strength in my body, I walked up to the screen, reached through, and grabbed a loose floor tile. It stank of fetid damp, and I noted with interest that the stench filled the room only once it was on the other side of the doorway. Not wanting to hold onto it for too long, I threw it at the colonel who failed to catch it (given the man was quite an athlete, that may have even been a first for him). It just hit him square in the chest and fell to the floor while he gazed, wide-eyed, at the buzzing portal behind me.

For a moment, I forgot my own fear and began to laugh. In the early days, my work had been hot property, but that had been a long time ago. I'd spent a long time having all interest in my little miracle wane until it was just a shadow of what it had once been. It was nice to finally have some tangible progress to show off.

"It's a door!" I cried, almost manic with laughter. "A door we can just walk right on through!"

Instead of awe, one of the soldiers gasped and the other five immediately raised their rifles to their shoulders. Even the colonel managed to draw a small pistol so quickly that his hand was a blur. All three barrels were pointing in my direction, but not quite *at* me. The implication finally sank in and I turned to face the doorway with an almost-certain premonition of my own death.

A pale arachnid-like finger had curled up out of the darkness and grasped one of the railing's vertical bars. One-by-one, a dozen thick-knuckled fingers joined it. I wasn't even sure if it was a fist or some nightmarish spider until another one appeared and this one did not stop to grasp the railing, instead reaching out to reveal a slender wrist.

When the hand breached the doorway, the soldiers opened fire, and it was deafening. Shocked by the sound and the sudden violence, I dropped to the floor and watched as missed rounds pinged dust off of walls on either side of the portal. Still, the hand kept coming, its wrist no thicker than a hose pipe and getting thinner as it went further towards us. It was a basket-ball sized fist made of nothing but wiry fingers, and the soldiers could not easily hit it. Worse, as the distance closed, I noticed their accuracy became worse, not better, until six feet turned to three, then two, then one.

I crab-walked as fast as I could until my back hit the farthest wall and watched as the hand groped clumsily at the space where I'd been just seconds before. Now the soldiers were really going at it. One even grabbed a desk and pushed it aside like some kind of barricade. The hand, however, kept up that dreadful gliding motion, even as the flesh of its arm thinned out to almost hairlike proportions.

The colonel began to give orders, speaking quickly and with authority. He told the others to leave before turning to me and demanding to know how he could stop the screen. I managed a quaky jab in the direction of the projector that was, thankfully, near to the door. He nodded with calm stoicism and for a brief moment I thought everything was going to be okay.

The hand moved suddenly, switching from a teasing ethereal swim to the darting ferocity of a breaching shark. No one had time to speak, not even the young man whose head it clamped around and whipped back into the portal at lightning speed. He hit the same desk he'd thrown down just seconds ago and I remember the whip crack of breaking bone. He was moving at highway speeds, I'm sure of it. Snatched out of reality and into a literal nightmare.

As soon as he was through, the screen went dark, but not before I'd managed a glimpse of the thing's face, lurking just beneath the railing at the edge of the stairs. There was only the very top of its head to see, but even that had been of nightmarish proportions. Its eyes were no larger than a penny, but they were spaced almost two feet apart. Its smooth head had seemed featureless, but those eyes were filled with unbridled joy.

<hr>

The colonel's reaction had been unanticipated.

We did not have the sudden inpouring of funding I'd hoped for. Instead, he personally threatened to shoot me. Perhaps, in hindsight, I should have been a little more careful with my presentation. But this was all new, and I explained as much. Even then, we faced the very real risk that the colonel would smash the computer to pieces and shut the whole project down.

When I first realised that wasn't his intention, I was overjoyed.

When I later discovered what he actually wanted to do, I found myself wishing he'd just shoot me instead.

"Are you ready?" he asked.

"No," I replied. "What do we do if the image changes?"

"We find our way back," he said.

"The engineers have it covered," Kim said from behind me. I'm sure she thought she was helping. She wasn't. "They're pretty certain they can slow the display down for long enough to mount some kind of rescue attempt. 120 minutes is the average of all their latest efforts, but one lasted over three hours."

"Oh goodie! A whole three hours?" I cried, only to realise that the armed men around me didn't find my sarcasm all that amusing.

Briefly I considered the choice before me. Enter the doorway or get shot fleeing. I knew with certainty I had to go with them, of course. But as the screen came alive, and I saw a broken window frame overlooking sickly roiling clouds, my knees went weak and all blood rushed straight to my head. I had to suppress the urge to turn and run, surprised to find that part of me hoped they really would shoot.

The colonel grabbed my arm as if sensing my thoughts.

"Here we go," I said as he dragged me through.

We stood in an empty hotel room, half of us staring at the doorway leading back—a perfect rectangular hole carved into another world—and the other half gawking at the open window. We could see nothing of the Earth below, only a rolling sea of turbulent clouds that occasionally lit up from within with silent lightning.

"What is down there, exactly?" asked one of the soldiers.

"Who knows?" I said. "We're not sure the tower is a real physical location, more like an interpretation of a place. It could be something from our shared history as a species, or maybe even a glimpse into another reality. It's almost as if it's defined by something you just feel." At least two of the soldiers blew raspberries at that, but I kept going. "the tower is a locus of aspiration brought low by tragedy and horror. Don't you feel it?" I asked, and that put a stop to the quiet laughter. "You do, don't you? This place was beautiful, once. It was a populated hub where people lived their whole lives, beginning to end. It's not a hotel or an apartment block or an office block or a futuristic resort. It's all of them, stacked one on top of the other. It's a city built upright."

"And something hollowed it out," the colonel said, eyes peering at every corner of the room. "Come on. We have a job to do."

The floor we were on seemed to be part of some hotel. Nothing too extravagant, but definitely somewhere a little fancy with its royal red carpet and peeling gold-filigree wallpaper. Some of the doors remained locked with funny looking card readers, others were smashed to pieces, revealing broken down interiors that were always similar but never quite identical. The soldiers looked everywhere for a sign of their friend, hoping to pick up on some kind of trail. I wasn't even sure we were technically in the same place, but I didn't want to say anything that might upset them. After all, my life was literally depending on them.

Instead, I chose to take notes of every little detail, and I quickly realised that the tower was a hell of a lot more real in person than it ever was in my dreams. I know that sounds stupid, but to stand there and see individual pieces of furniture with unique patterns of wear and tear, to actually *see* the broken chunks of wall and sagging ceilings and appreciate them as real physical things with weight... it was unsettling. In my nightmares it had felt like a threat to my sanity, but coming to grips with it as a place where you could breathe the air and open doors and push at ceiling tiles made it feel like something far, far more dangerous.

It felt like the kind of place that could swallow worlds.

We found odd scenes inside the rooms that had remained locked. A few had the windows broken outwards, as if the occupants had hurled themselves to their death rather than face whatever was outside. Others looked like they'd been the sites of some awful survivalist situation, with buckets in the corner, blankets and pillows in the bathtub, and sheets of plastic strewn along open windows to collect condensation. More than a few had been barricaded so heavily we simply couldn't break through without bringing heavy tools.

We did manage to find a few meaningful artifacts. There was a recruitment poster for what looked like a factory, and a pile of paperwork written in pure gibberish, but which had most of its lines redacted like a military document. One of the rooms even had a corpse. Well, more like a mummy, really. A paper-faced bundle of bones held together by brittle tissue and faded clothes that we found huddled in one of the shower surrounded by old food wrappers. The eyes were long gone, and their lips had receded so far they bore a ghoulish grin. In that same room was a balcony, and all of us were left aghast to finally get a glimpse at the building's exterior. It was huge, so large that we saw ourselves as only one tiny room in an infinite, vertical expanse of stone and glass. If I had to estimate, I would have said it was a column five miles in diameter, but I couldn't be sure.

There was also plenty of graffiti in the hallways, old messages scrawled haphazardly on mirrors and walls. But we simply couldn't read any of them, something I found very irritating. Still, it didn't take a genius to look at that desperate lettering and see a despair-filled plea for help.

After the initial bit of exploration, I became keenly aware of the ticking clock. And I made sure to mention to the colonel when we reached the half-way mark.

"We haven't even come close to where we need to be," he grumbled. "These stairs look nothing like the ones we first saw."

"I think that's closer to the apartments," I replied. "God knows where that is though."

"This isn't going to be easy," he said, more to himself than anyone else.

"Do you think there's a bottom?"

We were at the stairwell again and one of the soldiers had his light pointed straight down the centre of the spiral.

I had predicted that something like this might happen. We couldn't have gone more than a few floors up, but the act of going back down was something like a mental roadblock. It clearly bothered some of the younger men, and while the colonel looked as stoic as ever, I knew that was just a façade. It had already felt like I'd lived a thousand lifetimes in the tower and I knew with utmost certainty that going *down* just meant getting closer to whatever lived at the bottom of this place—something the human mind simply refused to do.

"Move up soldiers!" the colonel cried, giving us no time to dwell on our fears. He barged past us and quickly trotted down several steps like it was nothing at all, and then stood there staring at us, goading us to overcome our fear and join him. "Get your arses in gear!" he cried, turning back to us in red-faced anger. "We don't have time to fuck—"

Something pulled him through the railing.

And I mean *through*. As the men around me screamed, and a few even began to fire, I became faintly aware of something cold on my forehead, and wiped it off to find what looked a piece of skin still clinging to my fingertip. I turned to look at the man next to me, and saw that he had three ears. It took a few seconds of shock before I realised that one of them was plastered haphazardly to the top of his helmet and had likely come from the colonel. In fact, the air all around us was thick with an aerosol spray of fine misty blood, and bits of clothing and skin could be found everywhere—the floors, the walls, even the places above us. Using my own light, I took a look at the railing where the man had stood just seconds before and saw that the metal bars had been bent aside by a few inches, but not much else. The gap between them couldn't have been more than six inches. The pile of loose skin and clothing that remained bunched up around those bars made it pretty clear what had happened.

It was at this point I decided to leave. The soldiers were shouting and firing down the stairs, and some deep-seated instinct told me it was time to separate from the herd. This isn't a very noble thing to admit, of course. But then again, I'm not a very noble person. Otherwise, I might not have taken one of the duffle bags they'd dropped.

The very same one that I knew had all the rope.

You see, the longer I physically stayed in the tower, the longer I became aware of all those long-forgotten dreams. And a pattern had started to emerge in them. No one ever went down the stairs in the tower. It simply wasn't an option and oh boy, had the colonel proven why. For whatever reason, it woke something up that lived down there. I wasn't even sure if it was just one thing, or lots of things, but I knew it was bad the same way a rat knows to avoid the smell of cat piss.

But I did have memories of falling. Sometimes down elevator shafts. Sometimes out of windows. And as I hurried back into the corridor, searching frantically for that room with a balcony while trying to ignore the rapid increase in gun fire and ever-more-elaborate screams, I realised that I'd already unconsciously formed the first part of a plan. One that, I hoped, would let me make my way back down to that soon-to-disappear doorway.

I didn't give myself to think. I already had the bag open and the rope out before I found the room with the balcony. My heartbeat thundered in my ears so loud I was thankful since it blocked out the dwindling cries of the men I'd left behind.

Not to mention the sound of whatever had them.

I tied the rope around the balcony railing with the firmest knot I could. Then, wrapping the rope around my waist and clutching it with white-knuckled shivering hands, I awkwardly started to throw one leg over the ledge. It was around this point that my fear of heights kicked in and it damn near sent me back the way I came. It was a transcendent, almost-hallucinatory kind of terror. But then something from the hallway behind me moved, and I became acutely aware of the sound of dreadful feet padding closer towards the room.

It seemed best to just go for it, so that's what I did, swinging one leg over the other and letting inertia do the rest. For a few seconds, I hung against the balcony railing while my arms and legs refused to listen to any order coming from my brain. The sense of space around me was terrifying, not just the building that reached forever upwards to a baby-blue sky, but the continental-sized clouds and hurricane storms that raged what felt like miles below. It was the kind of cosmic insignificance I imagined astronauts felt on their very first spacewalk.

Slowly, I became aware of the fatigue in my arms and my legs. And a thought crystalised in my mind. If I didn't start going down now, hand-over-hand, foot-by-foot, then eventually exhaustion would win, and I would simply fall and all that fear I was holding on to would be realised in the most terrifying fashion. I took steps to control my breathing. And then, after a good five minutes of mental coaching, I managed to move one hand, and then one foot, and progress started to come my way.

Thank God I didn't have far to go. We'd only travelled up two floors. That was all. Easy going up. Not so easy going down. But I managed it after what felt like the worst ten minutes of my life and soon found myself staring at an open window two or three feet away. Unfortunately, my mind blanked and I couldn't even begin to think of how I might close the distance. I became convinced I would die the second I let go of that rope and there was nothing else to do except stay there or fall. It was during this panic that some stupid God-awful compulsion made me look down without meaning to, and all thoughts of life, or death, or anything else just melted away.

The clouds had thinned. Not a lot, but enough to reveal... *something*. It was huge, its arched back momentarily breaching the sea of hazy amber clouds to reveal a startling sense of scale.

That was all I needed to snap back to reality and focus on getting off that damned rope. I began to swing, awkwardly swaying my hips and feet in the hope of getting myself closer. Even the tiniest motion brought me into a near state of panic. With my whole body hanging helplessly over what looked like an infinite expanse of nothingness, it was hard not to think of just how long I'd spend falling before I finally found something to hit. But I had to get swinging. I just had to.

When it came time to finally let go at the apex of my lunge, I summoned all of my courage and hoped to God momentum would carry me. With my eyes closed, I flew through the air for a fraction of a second before landing in a nervous heap on the floor.

I was flooded with relief and finally opened my eyes to gauge the space around me. It was another hovel. Half the furniture had been piled up against one door, and the rest repurposed to become something new. In one corner was a planter made out of badly nailed planks of wood and filled with suspicious soil that stank of human waste. In another was an old mattress tossed half-upright against the wall.

Something moved in the darkness of the bathroom, and I froze, painfully aware that after everything I'd gone through, I'd probably die anyway. When the occupant finally emerged, a pale face in the shadow, I felt a confusing mixture of relief and horror. It was a man who looked like a literal apparition of death, like something taken straight out of the worst history books. He made me think of some nightmarish survivor of mankind's extinction, a half-starved creature that had spent its life hiding in the shadows for fear of being caught. His eyes and cheeks had become so sunken as to appear constantly hidden by shadow, even as his head emerged fully into the light. Arms so thin they were like hose pipes reached up to cover his face from the harsh glare of the window and for the first time I became aware that he was completely naked, his skin pocked and bubbling, ravaged by unknown diseases I couldn't begin to guess at. His limbs were grossly bowed and his stomach swollen from what must have been years of malnourishment.

"The dreamer stirs," he said, and although I could've sworn he wasn't speaking English, I managed to understand him all the same.

"Who?" I asked.

"The dreamer," he whispered. "This all belongs to him."

"Is that... is that what I saw down there?" I asked.

The old man paled, put a finger to his lips, and hushed me.

"Don't wake the dreamer," he hissed.

Suddenly his eyes went wide, and I turned on instinct, fixing the rope I'd come in on. It still hung there, floating in empty space, but it jiggled and swayed as if something was coming down it.

I ran to the barricade and began to pull the furniture away, only for the old man to leap out of the darkness and begin to attack me. Frightened as I was by the grotesque sight of his leprous body, he was too weak to do any real harm, and his cold, bony fingers gripped my collar in a futile effort to pull me away.

"Stop!" he screamed, but I ignored him, tearing at the objects in my path until I'd cleared enough room for the door to open. I had just managed to get the handle down when something wrenched me backwards and I turned to see the old man staring into my eyes with gut-wrenching fear written on his face. "Don't me go," he pleaded, and I saw the spidery fingers that gripped his head in a halo of writhing knuckles, the wrist winding across the floor and out the window where it coiled around the rope.

I grabbed his hand and squeezed so hard I probably broke a bone or two, prompting him to immediately scream and let go. He was still screaming when whatever had him ripped him out of the room and up to his death.

Wasting no time, I bolted back out into the hallway and ran in what I hoped was the right direction. From behind me there came the sound of hurricane-like destruction, a force of raging hunger that eagerly snapped at my heels. I knew with utter certainty that it was going to get me. I knew it the same way I knew what the old man had been saying, and in the same way that you always know how your worst nightmare will end.

I found myself hoping that's all it was.

A nightmare.

If there was any proof I needed that wasn't the case, it was the sight of a familiar hotel room, and the glowing doorway set ominously in open air. I don't know about you, but my nightmares don't end with me getting what I want. It was enough to actually confuse me, as if for a few seconds my brain had collapsed all notions of dreams and reality into a gruesome whole, and I had to remind myself to bolt through the broken doorway and straight into the portal onto the other side rather than just wait to wake up.

I emerged into the squalid flicker of fluorescent lights. Panting, almost-delirious at the sight of familiar old-tiled floors beneath my feet, I stumbled forward and wrenched the projector off the wall and smashed it against the floor. The last thing I remembered before collapsing was the sound of a dozen scientists crying out in confused alarm.

"As a rescue mission, it was a failure," I said, addressing the men and women who'd joined me in the observation room. "But as a fact-finding mission, it was a resounding success. We aren't necessarily in position to say anything with certainty, but we've been exposed to a few fascinating new ideas."

Nobody spoke. They all stared at me.

"I believe the locations we're seeing, the ones that appear again and again... I believe they are dreams, just not in the traditional sense. I believe that we are being exposed to the dreams of something that isn't human."

"What exactly?" asked one of the older men who sat closer to the front.

"I think it eats worlds," I said. "Or something like that. I think... I think we've been visiting these places all along. All of us. And I think this thing remembers everything that lives there, good and bad. I think we've already been exposed to some of these... entities. Not just during our excursion, but in our nightmares, all of us. We've read about them sitting on the chests of people trapped in sleep paralysis. We've seen them chasing us through dimly lit corridors. This thing... the dreamscape feels like a real place because it is, sort of. Its something's memories of real places, of the people who lived in them and the lives that they had. Maybe it's a literal absorption, something strange and metaphysical. Maybe it's just got a mind vast enough to remember every little detail. I don't know. All that I do know for sure is that I don't want to wake this thing up."

"You've always had a penchant for reaching," the old man said. "You can't seriously be suggesting we mothball this project based on your theory? I appreciate the veracity of your first-hand account. But having read your report in great detail, I'm not sure I make the same connections that you do."

"Oh God no," I said. "No one's saying we shut this down."

I reached out behind me and tore away a blank sheet to reveal an enormous whiteboard covered in a half-made map. We'd cobbled it together from over two decades of research notes taken by a very specific subset of our scientists. The tower sat squarely in the centre and even just looking at the words made my skin crawl, so I looked a few inches to the right and focused on a different set of words.

The Library.

"We're scientists," I said. "We collect data to prove our arguments. I say this thing swallows worlds. Well, let's take a look at some of the others. In hindsight, the tower was the worst possible starting location. Far, far too hostile.

"But there are other places in the dreamscape to explore," I added. "And hopefully some of them won't immediately spit us back out."

MORE CHILLS FROM VELOX BOOKS

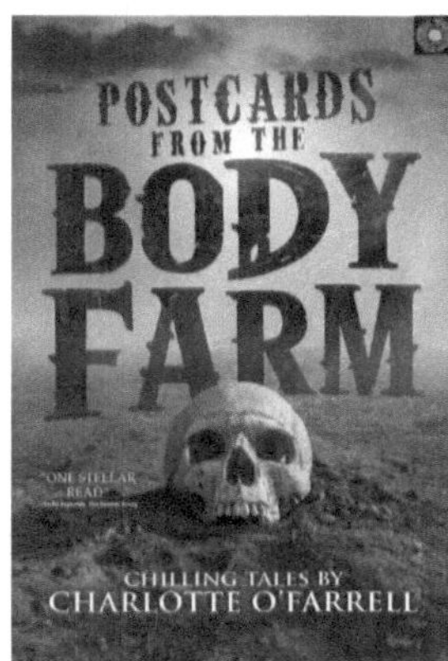

MORE CHILLS FROM VELOX BOOKS

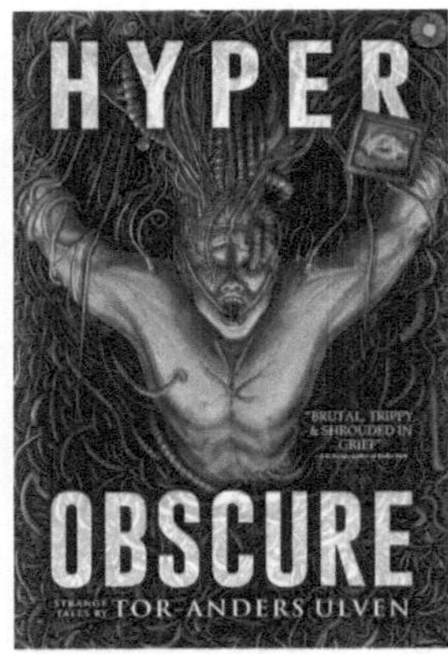

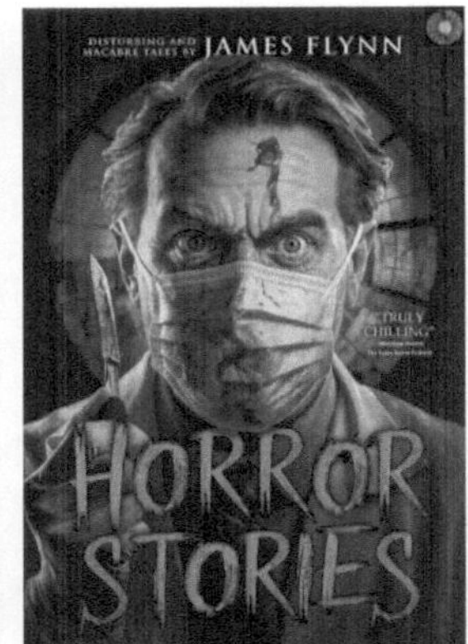

MORE CHILLS FROM VELOX BOOKS

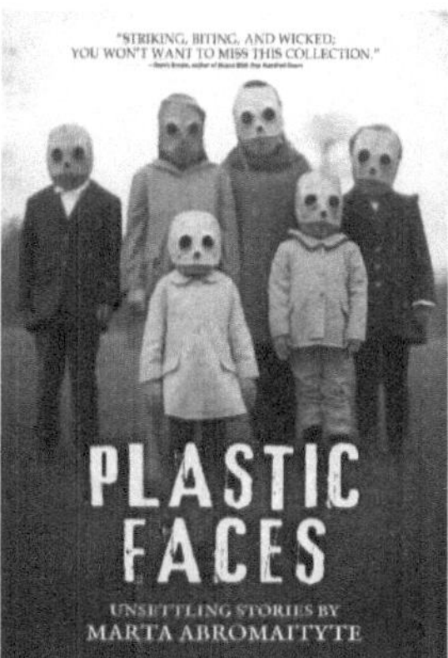